The muttered words gave Joy a scant second to brace herself before Charlie Comfort emerged from behind her "haunted house" carrying a basket filled with cardboard bats. He stopped abruptly when he saw her.

She felt the heat rise in her cheeks as she planned how to begin. "The kids have all gone..."

"Good," he said. "I came here tonight to explain why I can't—"

"I know why *you* think you came," she interrupted, hardly recognizing the calm, firm voice as her own. "But *I* think you came because you were meant to build this playground. My father knew it and I know it. I'm willing to double your usual fee."

"This isn't about money," he said.

"Then what is it about? What is so much more important than a dying man's final wish?"

His grip on the basket tightened and he answered gruffly, "Concern for the living, Ms. Porter."

ABOUT THE AUTHOR

Julie Meyers's interest in children's playgrounds developed before her daughter, Jessica, now five, was old enough to enjoy the neighborhood park. The author's curiosity was piqued by an article describing how schoolchildren and their parents had been consulted when new community playgrounds were being built. "Safety and the input of kids and parents are key elements in these playgrounds," says Julie.

Dream Builder is the author's second Superromance novel. She and Jessica live in Citrus Heights, California.

Books by Julie Meyers

HARLEQUIN SUPERROMANCE
396—IN THE CARDS

HARLEQUIN TEMPTATION
358—FACE TO FACE

Don't miss any of our special offers. Write to us at the following address for information on our newest releases.

Harlequin Reader Service
P.O. Box 1397, Buffalo, NY 14240
Canadian address: P.O. Box 603,
Fort Erie, Ont. L2A 5X3

Dream Builder

JULIE MEYERS

Harlequin Books

TORONTO • NEW YORK • LONDON
AMSTERDAM • PARIS • SYDNEY • HAMBURG
STOCKHOLM • ATHENS • TOKYO • MILAN
MADRID • WARSAW • BUDAPEST • AUCKLAND

Published February 1993

ISBN 0-373-70535-2

DREAM BUILDER

Printed in U.S.A.

This book owes a debt of deep admiration to two
'practical dreamers' who have made our world
a better place in which to live:
Bob Leathers, architect, playground designer, and all-
around inspiration, and
Dr. M.J. Willard, the founder and guiding light
of Helping Hands: Simian Aides For The Disabled.

It is also my privilege
to thank the following individuals:
The 'foster families' who offered up a wealth of
memories, snapshots, scrapbooks, journals
and letters about their wonderful monkeys:
Bette & Windy Hamm and 'Katie'
Melanie Hands and 'Sandy'
Anne Imperatore and 'Peppe'
Cathy McNeill and 'Jessica'
Helen Miner and 'Melanie'
Dorothy Wilmot and 'Friar Tuck'
Ellyn Hilliard and the rest of her amazing crew of
volunteers, who built Project Playpark
in Davis, California on April 11-15, 1991
And the 'family' who saw me through the tough times
and helped to guide Charlie and Joy
to their happy ending:
Janie Locke Begeman, Dorothy Blackwell, Georgia
Bockoven, Debbie Gordon, Jan McCarthy, and
Rosemary Vando

CHAPTER ONE

WHAT SHE WANTED to send was an anguished cry for help.

What she needed to send was a compelling business letter.

Joy Porter sat down at the computer and placed her trembling fingers on the keyboard.

Dear Mr. Comfort:
You don't know me but my father, Dr. Jacob Porter, was a great admirer of your work. As you may have read in the paper, he died last Tuesday, after a long illness that drained him of his health and his strength, leaving him with nothing to comfort him but a dream.

She hesitated, then deleted the last phrases, ending the sentence after "illness."

My father's last book, *The Playground Connection,* is scheduled for publication by Cross & Day sometime next summer, and the university here in Sacramento is planning to establish a scholarship in his honor. During his final illness, however, Dad talked about a more personal memorial—a playground designed and built by you, as his parting gift to the children of Sacramento.

Tears of grief and frustration stung Joy's eyes as she read the words she had typed. It all sounded impossibly stilted and clinical. How could she describe the enthusiasm and hope that the playground plan had given her father during the last harrowing stage of his illness? Just the mention of it had been enough to bring a smile to his lips, despite his pain and weakness. But how could she bring herself to reveal such intimate memories of those last days with her father to a total stranger? And even if she did, Mr. Comfort would probably think she was being manipulative. Once she'd made the initial contact and had a better idea of the sort of man she was dealing with, she would consider being more candid.

I'm sure your schedule is a busy one, but I'm hoping you can understand how anxious I am to set this project in motion at your earliest convenience. If you are interested, please contact me to discuss the details of scheduling and your fee.

Sincerely,
Joy Porter

The answer came a week later.

Dear Ms. Porter:
Thank you for your recent letter. Our firm is no longer undertaking commissions for playground projects. We hope, however, that you will con-

sider us when you are next in need of an architectural design firm.

                              Tinker & Comfort

Joy read the brief note with growing distress. It was
a form letter, a photocopy. Her name and address had
been inserted—but not quite aligned properly—in the
appropriate blanks; somehow that made Charles
Comfort's blunt refusal seem even worse.

The tiny monkey sitting on Joy's lap tugged at the
edge of the letter, refusing to be ignored any longer.

Joy responded automatically, "No, Jezebel." She
reached down to stroke the silky fur. "He could have
taken the time to write a real letter," she said around
the lump that was forming in her throat. "Or added a
P.S. to say he was sorry to hear about Dad. Or at least
have *signed* the damn thing! He didn't have to
just—"

Her voice failed her.

Lately, she thought in despair, tears seemed to be
her first response to everything. She had cried at the
funeral home. She had cried at the cemetery and at the
memorial service the university insisted on providing.
She had cried when the next day's mail brought letters addressed to her father that he would never read.
She had cried herself to sleep every night since his
death and eaten each morning's breakfast to an accompaniment of salty tears.

Today, for the first time in a week, she'd risen weary
but dry-eyed from her bed to face the day.

And now this.

Crumpling the letter, she threw it at the wastebasket.

When it missed the rim by a foot, Jezebel scurried to scoop up the paper wad and deposit it in the trash.

"Good girl," Joy praised. Pulling a fresh tissue from the box, she wiped her eyes, then blew her nose with noisy vigor as Jezebel clambered back into her lap.

"How can Mr. Comfort turn us down without even talking to me about it?" Joy demanded, looking down at her simian companion. "It isn't right. It isn't fair!"

The tiny monkey cocked her head, as if to say, *So what are you going to do about it?*

"There's nothing I *can* do about it," Joy said. "It's a free country. I can't make Charles Comfort take this job. I can't even make him tell me why he won't."

Or could she?

Torn between hope and fear, she retrieved Charles Comfort's letter from the wastebasket. Smoothing the crumpled paper, she set it beside the telephone on the kitchen counter and read the number beneath the address on the letterhead. Before her courage could fail her, she lifted the receiver and dialed.

Someone answered on the second ring. "Tinker and Comfort," said an assured female voice. "May I help you?"

"I need to speak to Charles Comfort," Joy said.

"Mr. Comfort is out of the office this morning, but I expect him back at one. If you'd like to leave a message, I'll have him return your call."

Joy groped for a reply as dismay welled up within her. She could give her name and number...but would he return her call? Or would he simply instruct his secretary that, for Joy Porter's calls, he was *always* "out of the office"?

"No, I—I'll call again later," she said, and hung up

hastily, her heart pounding as if she had just committed a criminal act.

It was almost eleven o'clock. The woman had said that Mr. Comfort would be back in his office by one. But by then....

Joy hung her head, wishing she didn't know herself so well. If she had been able to complete her call in the heat of the moment, her indignation might have overcome her natural reticence. But two more hours of running imaginary scenarios in her head would be enough to frighten her out of doing anything at all. She'd just have to write another letter to Charles Comfort. If she chose her words carefully enough, maybe he'd reconsider his decision.

And maybe pigs would fly.

Joy clenched her fists in frustration. If the playground had been just a passing fancy of her father's, she could have shrugged her shoulders in regret and considered the matter closed. But that wasn't the case. If she closed her eyes, she could almost hear his husky whisper as he described the wonderful "going-away present" he envisioned as his way of thanking the children he had spent his working life observing.

It would be a shame beyond words, she thought, if that thank you went unexpressed because Jacob Porter's daughter lacked backbone.

Joy looked up at the clock again.

In two hours, Mr. Comfort would be back in his office.

"Cage, Jezzie," she ordered, suddenly decisive, and followed the monkey out of the kitchen and down the hallway.

Jezebel entered the study willingly, but balked at the entrance to the six-foot enclosure that served as her sleeping quarters. Leaping onto the desk, she scrubbed nervously at her face, eyeing Joy as if to assess how seriously to take the request.

"Cage," Joy said again.

Slowly, the monkey crossed the room, clambered through the open metal door and pulled it shut.

"Good girl." Joy tried to harden her heart against the reproachful stare that Jezebel leveled at her through the half-inch mesh at the front of the cage. "It's not as if I'm looking forward to this, you know. For two cents, I'd curl up in that cage and let *you* drive to San Francisco to talk to Mr. Comfort."

The thought of Jezebel navigating the big white Oldsmobile along Highway 80 was ridiculous enough to bring a smile to Joy's lips, but the nervousness cramping her stomach quickly sobered her.

"Too bad, Jezzie," she said as she left the room in search of her car keys. "All things considered, you'd probably do a better job of changing his mind than I will."

"Wow, CATS AND DOGS!" Charlie Comfort called in greeting, as he completed a dash from the parking garage to the office building that housed Tinker & Comfort.

"This rain wasn't in the forecast," Matthew complained, scowling as he dried his glasses on his handkerchief.

Charlie was tempted to point out that rain in San Francisco at the end of October was hardly surprising, but there was no point. Until a few months ago, it would have been easy to kid his brother-in-law out of his black mood, but now, nothing he said was going to help. Matthew had chosen to take the storm as a personal affront, so Charlie simply made a non-committal sound and rang for the elevator.

His conscience twinged as he pushed the button. Just yesterday he'd vowed to start using the stairs in order to squeeze at least a little exercise into his schedule. Matthew's "all work and no play" regime was taking its toll. Six months ago, the sprint from the parking garage wouldn't have left him winded.

"Wimp," Charlie said witheringly to his own distorted reflection in the shiny metal doors.

Matthew replaced his glasses as the elevator arrived. "Pardon, Charles?"

"Nothing." He followed Matthew on. "So," he said to fill the silence as they ascended, "are you and Shelley going out to dinner to celebrate?"

Matthew looked at him blankly.

"Today's your anniversary, isn't it?"

"Is today the thirtieth?" Matthew looked surprised, then annoyed. "Damn it, Charles, don't give me that look. I can't be expected to remember everything. And I'm certainly not going to go out and get drenched again. She'll just have to settle for flowers. Besides, I have an appointment with the Bigelows at six. God knows what time I'll get home."

As much saddened as angered, Charlie bit his tongue, but he couldn't dismiss the exchange from his thoughts. He wondered if Shelley and Matthew had had a fight, or whether Matthew's testiness was just an offshoot of the strain they had all been under.

As he stepped out of the elevator on the fourth floor, he considered calling Shelley to make sure she wasn't knocking herself out, preparing some elaborate anniversary feast. Then again, he thought, maybe he should keep his nose out of it. After all, he was her

kid brother, not her father. However much he loved
her, he couldn't live her life for her.

Brooding, he followed Matthew down the hall and
through their office door.

The receptionist greeted them with a frazzled smile
and held out a sheaf of phone messages for Matthew.

"None for me?" Charlie asked as Matthew vanished into his office.

"No, but there's somebody here to see you."

Charlie turned to greet his unexpected visitor and
found her rising from one of the stylish but deep-
cushioned chairs Matthew had insisted on installing in
the reception area.

She was tall, slender and at least twenty years
younger than most of his clients. Optimistic that the
day was about to take a turn for the better, Charlie
approached her with a welcoming smile.

There was no answering smile on her face, just a
look of anxious inquiry. Beneath a luxurious mane of
chestnut hair, her face was as thin and pale as a Lladro
figurine. Seeing the dark smudges beneath her eyes, he
thought, *She looks as tired as I feel*.

He recalled that his first afternoon appointment was
scheduled for two o'clock, with new clients, a married couple named Walderman, from Marin County.
He offered his hand. "I'm Charlie Comfort. Are you
Mrs. Walderman?" he asked, hoping for a denial.

"I'm afraid not," the young woman replied softly.
Her fingers felt fragile in his grasp. Her skin was
smooth and cool. He strained to hear her words. "My
name is Porter," she said. "I sent you a letter about
my project, but then I found myself in San Francisco
unexpectedly, and so I...I took the chance you might
be in."

He made a show of looking at his watch, but he had already come to the decision that he'd make the time to learn more about Ms. Porter. "I've got an hour before my next client. We could at least talk about what you need done, okay?"

"Okay," she agreed, looking even more ill at ease than she had before.

Perplexed, Charlie kept up an easy line of small talk as he guided her through the sleek burgundy-and-gray reception area. Matthew had designed it to appeal to the upscale clientele he was so determined to attract, but there was something about the room that bothered Charlie every time he walked through it.

Joy Porter followed quietly at his elbow.

The plush carpeting and restrained color scheme stopped at the door to Charlie's office. Inside his domain, white walls caught and reflected every bit of available light, defying the dark drizzle beyond the window. The floor was planked oak, punctuated by bright scatter rugs. Given the long hours he worked, he'd designed the office with an eye to color and informality, a combination that rarely failed to energize him.

He tossed his trench coat across the broad back of an eight-foot-tall ceramic giraffe that took up one corner. Turning to his visitor, he gestured toward the trio of scarlet chairs that flanked his vast wooden worktable and said, "Please, make yourself comfortable. I'll take your coat."

Surrendering the coat, she perched herself on the edge of a chair.

"Can I get you a cup of coffee?" Charlie asked when he had hung her coat on the giraffe's left ear. "Tea? A soda?"

"No, thank you," she said, smoothing the material of her gray print dress across her lap in nervous little ripples of movement.

Charlie picked up a drafting pad and pencil and sat down in the chair closest to hers. "October 30th" he wrote at the top of the page, then said, "Okay, Ms. Porter, what is that you'd like Tinker & Comfort to design?" He looked up at her and broke off in surprise. Joy Porter's face flamed with color; even the skin of her slender neck was blotched with red. "Are you okay?" Charlie asked in alarm.

She raised her hand to touch one heated cheek. "It's nothing. Ignore it, please."

"But—"

"You already know what I'd like you to design," she said doggedly, overriding his concern. "I told you all about it in the letter I sent to you last week."

Charlie hooked his thumb toward the scramble of papers on the corner of his table. "I'm sure you did, but your letter's probably in there somewhere, still waiting to be read. I'm sorry. Things have been—"

"No. You sent a reply," she insisted, her eyes glittering suddenly with unshed tears. "A form letter."

"A form letter? Impossible. I don't use form letters. Look, I'm really sorry, but none of this rings a bell. What sort of project was it, Ms. Porter?"

The telephone rang.

Glancing toward his desk, Charlie saw the light blinking on his private line. He considered ignoring it...but another look at Joy Porter convinced him that she might benefit from a chance to pull herself together.

"Excuse me for just a second," he said as the phone rang again. He crossed the room to answer it, turning his back to give her at least the illusion of privacy. "Hello?"

"Charlie?"

Hearing his sister's voice, Charlie froze. It was a strange time of day for Shelley to be calling, and her voice sounded . . . odd. "Hi. What's up?"

"I'm calling to say goodbye."

The word brought him up short. "What do you mean, 'goodbye'?" he asked uneasily. "Where are you going?"

"I've left Matthew."

"Left . . . ? You mean you've moved out? That's crazy. I just had lunch with him. He didn't say anything about—"

"He doesn't know yet. I left him a note. He can read it when he gets home," she said, her voice tight. "Of course, with his schedule, that may not be for a week or two."

"Shelley, be serious! You can't just—"

"I already have."

"But it's your anniversary," he said, although he knew the words were inane in the face of all that she and Matthew had been through.

"Take care of yourself, Charlie. Matthew may be determined to run himself into the ground, but that doesn't mean you have to go along for the ride. Past a certain point, loyalty can be lethal." A harsh sound escaped her, part laughter, part pain. "Trust big sister on this one. There's no sense in both of us learning it the hard way."

Hearing the finality in her tone, Charlie shivered. "Don't hang up," he said anxiously, panic rising in his blood. "Where are you going to go?"

"I'm not sure yet. Somewhere. Away."

"Where are you now? At home?"

"Yes, but I'm leaving, as soon as we hang up."

"Don't. I'll come. We'll talk."

"No. I only called so you wouldn't worry."

"You think I'm not worried now?" Charlie demanded, sweat trickling down his spine. "Don't go. Not now. Not like this. I thought things were finally starting to get better. Give it some more time, Shell. We can't run away from what happened. It won't do any good to try."

"Damn it, Charlie, I'm not going to change my mind about this, and I don't have time to stand here arguing with you."

"You have all the time you want to take," he contradicted. "Let me come and help you make some plans, if you're sure this is what you have to do." Dimly, over the phone line, he heard a clock chime the quarter hour. "Do you have enough money?" he persisted.

"Plenty. More than plenty."

"I don't think you should be alone. Isn't there somebody you could go stay with?"

"You still don't get it. I *want* to be alone. The last thing I need right now is to take advantage of some friend who wouldn't feel she could say no to me even if she wanted to, since she knows..."

"About Penny," Charlie finished for her.

His sister began to cry.

"Shelley, please, Penny's gone. You and I have got to find a way to live with that...and so does Matthew. I know he's been impossible, but it's only because he's hurting, too. If he loses you now, it'll destroy him. That isn't what you want, is it?"

"I don't care!"

"Yes, you do, or it wouldn't be tearing you up like this."

"Oh, Charlie, I can't afford to care. Not anymore. Can't you see I'm fighting to stay alive? I need—" The sound of her choked sobbing filled his head. "I'm sorry, Charlie," she said at last. "Goodbye. God bless."

"Shelley! Michelle!"

The dial tone rang in his ear.

Adrenaline flooded his body; his mind was shouting for him to do something, to find her, to stop her...but how? San Francisco was a big city. If she didn't want to be found, there were a thousand places where she could lie low.

For a few precious minutes, he'd had her right there on the phone, his to console, his to persuade. But he'd blown it. Now Shelley was beyond his reach, alone and in distress, and he didn't have the vaguest idea where to look for her.

Unless she had been exaggerating when she said she was ready to go right then. If he got to her house fast enough, he might still be able to talk her out of leaving.

He was grasping at straws, but it was better than grasping at nothing at all. Jamming the receiver back into its cradle, Charlie whirled to leave...and saw Joy

Porter sitting in patient silence, her delicate face a portrait of confusion and concern.

He wished he could stop and explain, but there was no time. There wasn't even time to summon Matthew. Shelley could be latching her suitcase and walking out the door even as he hesitated.

"I'm sorry," Charlie said, grabbing his coat. "Family emergency. I've gotta go."

"Will you be back?" Joy asked, half rising from her chair.

"Maybe. I don't know. I'll try," he promised blindly, and bolted out into the hallway.

"Mr. Comfort?" the receptionist called as he hurried past.

"Later!" Shoving open the door, he raced along the corridor and through the fire exit, thundering down the four flights of stairs as if, by running fast enough, he could outstrip time itself.

JOY SAT STRANDED in her chair, bemused, wondering what she was supposed to do now—drive back to Sacramento with nothing at all accomplished or resolved? Her heart rebelled against such a defeat, but her only alternative seemed to be to sit where she was indefinitely, hoping against hope that Charles Comfort would return.

She raised her hand to her neck, fighting the temptation to scratch the itchy hives that the stress of the day had induced.

She didn't doubt the veracity of Charles Comfort's "family emergency"; his agitation on the phone had sounded all too real. The interruption had come at the worst possible time, though. Contrary to her expectations, she had found him intelligent and attentive, and he had acted as if her name meant nothing to him, as if he'd never seen her letter.

Maybe he hadn't, she mused. Maybe some secretary had read her letter and sent the photocopied reply. In that case, wasn't there a chance that Mr. Comfort would agree to her request once he knew the whole story? Maybe if she wrote out an explanation and left it on his desk . . .

"Excuse me," a voice said, and Joy jumped. Turning in her chair, she recognized the man who had been on the same elevator as Mr. Comfort. He looked around the room with an air of impatience, then returned his attention to Joy. "I was looking for Charles."

"He had to leave," she said.

"Leave?" His heavy eyebrows gathered into a single dark line as he frowned. "What do you mean?"

"He was . . . called away," Joy said uneasily, wondering how to defend her continued presence in the office. "An emergency."

"And he left you sitting here alone?"

Joy nodded, feeling her hives tingling.

"I am sorry," the man said, his thunderous scowl softening into a conciliatory smile as he came toward her. "Allow me to apologize for Charles, please. He's been under a lot of strain lately—not that that excuses him, but it certainly isn't our policy at Tinker & Comfort to run out on our clients in midappointment. This was your first meeting with Charles?"

"Yes."

"Then perhaps I can be of help in his absence. I'm Matthew Tinker."

Joy held out her hand. "Joy Porter."

"Porter?" His smile vanished. Taking the hand she offered, he pulled her to her feet, then released her as if the touch of her skin were unpleasant. "Didn't you get our letter?"

"The form letter?" Joy asked with a sense of sick foreboding.

"Yes. The form letter. If you received it, then you know perfectly well that we aren't in the playground business any longer, even as a sideline. Or was something about that letter unclear?"

"No, but—"

"Then you've wasted your time and ours in coming here, and I'll thank you not to waste any more of it."

"Please, I only want—"

Turning, he snatched her coat from the head of the fanciful giraffe and thrust it at her. "What *I* want is for you to go. Now." He towered over her, his face ruddy with anger. "Do I need to make myself any clearer, Ms. Porter?"

The raw animosity of the man was frightening. He looked wild, barely in control. Perhaps her father would have had the diplomacy and insight to handle him. She certainly didn't. "No," Joy breathed, thoroughly intimidated by his fury. "I'm leaving."

Clutching her coat to her breast, she slipped past him. As she made her way down the corridor, she could hear him behind her, keeping pace, herding her out of the office by the force of his disapproval. In the reception area, she ducked her head, avoiding the secretary's inquiring glance. She counted ten steps as she crossed the room and reached the outer door and the public hallway beyond. Only when she had left the offices of Tinker & Comfort, and was certain that Matthew Tinker was making no effort to pursue her farther, did Joy dare to slow her pace and take a shaky breath.

I'm sorry, Dad, she cried silently as she rang for the elevator. *I tried. I did the best I could.*

And she had failed.

CHAPTER TWO

IT WAS AFTER MIDNIGHT when the squeak of the front door woke Charlie from an uneasy doze on his sister's living-room couch.

"Shelley?" Getting quickly to his feet, he stumbled across the darkened room toward the bright foyer, hoping against hope that his long vigil was about to be rewarded by her return.

Instead, Matthew appeared in the archway, an angry silhouette. "Charles! What the hell are you still doing here?"

Charlie braced himself against his brother-in-law's attitude. Until recently, his respect for Matthew had been automatic. But now that respect, like so much else, was being called into question. "I told you I was staying when I called," he said firmly.

"That was ten hours ago!"

"So what? Somebody needed to be here, in case she came back, and you made it pretty clear that it wasn't going to be you."

Matthew stepped into the room, flicking on the lights. "Michelle's just angling for attention," he said. "She'll come home when she realizes it won't work. In the meantime, there's no point in turning our normal routines inside out."

At his tone of callous impatience, Charlie's control snapped. "You're a sorry excuse for a human being, Matthew Tinker."

"I beg your pardon?" Matthew could hardly have looked more surprised if the rug had risen up and bitten his ankle.

Charlie stood his ground. "Look, I know things are rough. You've been through hell. We all have. But that's no excuse for the way you've been treating my sister."

Matthew looked mildly amused. "Don't you think your ire is a little misplaced? As you may recall, your sister is the one who walked out on *me* today, not vice versa. I haven't done a thing."

"Exactly. You haven't done a damn thing for the past six months except bury yourself at the office. Shelley needed your time and your love, and you—you filed her away. You put her on hold," he said indignantly. "Just like you put me on hold this afternoon when I called to tell you she was gone."

"Charles, we've been through all this. It's late and I'm tired. I fail to see—"

"There's a lot you fail to see," Charlie said, shaking with frustration. "I couldn't believe it when Shelley said she hadn't told you she was leaving...but I'm beginning to see her point." He gestured at the bare wall to his left. "What happened to Penny's pictures?"

"I took them down."

Charlie's shoulder blades prickled. "When?"

"Yesterday."

And now, less than a day later, Shelley was gone. "Damn it, you shouldn't have done that."

Matthew's eyes narrowed. "I wasn't aware that I needed your permission to redecorate."

"It wasn't 'redecorating' and you know it. Did you tell Shelley what you were going to do?"

His question met with cold silence.

"For God's sake, why couldn't you have talked it over with her first?"

Matthew shrugged. "It was maudlin to leave the pictures up. I simply did what was best for both of us."

"Right. I can see what a resounding success that was." Charlie grimaced. "Want to hear something really dumb? When I called you this afternoon, I was afraid you'd fall apart. What a laugh! All you cared about was whether I was coming back to keep my appointment with Mr. and Mrs. Walderman."

"Which you should have done."

"The hell you say. I happen to think my sister's safety is a little more important than Ben Walderman's vacation home in Tahoe!"

"This is pointless," Matthew said.

"This is *exactly* the point."

"Whatever it is, it can wait for tomorrow, when you're calmer. I'm going to bed." At the foot of the stairs, he paused. "I suppose you ignored my advice and called the police?"

"I talked to them."

Matthew looked amused. "And did they send a carful of detectives over here, sirens wailing, to dust for fingerprints?"

"They said they can't do anything until she's been gone longer."

"Of course not. What did you expect? Michelle's a grown woman. She left of her own free will. You can hardly expect them to respond as if she'd been abducted at gunpoint. For that matter, I doubt if Michelle would thank you for your interference. Don't you suppose that's why she called you in the first place? To keep you from flying off the handle?"

The accusation stung. "No. I think she called me because she needed to talk to someone who loved her. She knew I'd worry if she just disappeared, which is more than she could be sure of with you." Charlie shoved his hands into his pockets. "I've called everybody I could think of, but nobody's heard from her. Not yet, anyway. Try to think, Matthew. Where would she go?"

"Go?" His brother-in-law reached for the banister. "Really, Charles, I have no idea."

Something in his tone and the careful tilt of his head snared Charlie's attention. "What's the matter with you? Are you drunk?"

"I'm exhausted," Matthew answered, climbing the stairs. "I've been at my desk all evening, completing the work you abandoned so blithely this afternoon. Really, Charles, unless you start applying yourself more conscientiously, I don't know what's going to become of the office."

One of us is crazy, Charlie thought, staring up at him.

He fought the temptation to push the confrontation to some sort of showdown, knowing that Matthew was right—both of them needed some sleep. Making one final effort to give him the benefit of the doubt, Charlie said, "She left you a letter."

Matthew continued to climb.

Incensed, Charlie raised his voice. "I said she left you a letter. It's on the dining-room table."

"I heard you the first time."

"Well? Aren't you even going to read it?"

"In the morning."

Six months ago, Charlie would have stated confidently that Matthew and Shelley were happy in their relationship. Regardless of the pressures and tragedies that had befallen them since then, he had trouble believing that a marriage could fall apart so completely in just half a year.

"Aren't you worried about her at all?" he asked in bewildered fury. "Don't you even care why she left?"

Matthew looked down on him, expressionless. "I've learned that it's futile to deny reality. Face facts, Charles. Michelle is gone. She chose to go—to leave us both behind. Maybe she'll come back, given time. Then again, maybe she won't. For now, I'm going to bed. I suggest you do the same. Oh, and Charles...?"

"Yes?"

"Be sure to turn the lights out when you leave," Matthew said from the upper landing, and disappeared into the master bedroom.

Charlie started up the stairs after him, then stopped. What was the point? As much as he hated to admit it, Shelley would have told him where she was going if she'd wanted him to know. And, although she'd sounded deeply distressed on the phone, she hadn't seemed irrational.

Maybe he was pushing too hard.

He told himself to give her a day or two. She'd call again, as soon as she got settled somewhere. And if she didn't...then he would take more drastic measures, whether Matthew liked it or not.

CONFRONTED BY HER MIRROR the next morning, Joy decided that the hollow-eyed creature reflected there looked as if she were suffering from a monumental hangover. This hangover wasn't from drinking alcohol, though, she thought dully, but from wallowing in her own shortcomings.

All through the long drive home, all through the evening and the restless night, her brain had spun thoughts of what she could have said, what she *should* have said to that frightening man. She'd made a fool of herself, allowing her shyness and timidity to defeat her, first with Charles Comfort and then with his partner, Mr. Tinker. The queen of hindsight, that's what she was. And what good did it do her? Faced with the same situation again, she'd probably still stand there, meek as a guilty schoolgirl, listening in silence to Mr. Tinker's angry words.

At three a.m., the memory of her cowardice had been crushing...but the morning sun had climbed over the horizon in spite of her. A new day had dawned, leaving her little choice but to rise and greet it.

After all, she asked herself, how important was one playground more or less in the overall scheme of things? Elsewhere in the world, children were homeless, or hungry, or dying. She could take the money set aside for the playground and donate it to charity instead. Or, if she still wanted to see the project through, she could hire someone else to build it. Ultimately, the children wouldn't care who designed the playground; they would simply enjoy it.

Besides, she had more immediate worries. In less than twelve hours she'd be faced with a houseful of young guests. Thanks to yesterday's wasted efforts, she still had cleaning to do, cupcakes to bake and a dozen errands to run.

Gazing into the mirror again, Joy attempted an energetic smile, and failed.

She turned away from the telltale reflection.

It was true that the kids wouldn't care about who built their new playground, but her father would have. Many times he'd spoken of the emphasis that Charles Comfort put on safety features in his playgrounds, and his practice of involving the children in formulating a design. It wasn't a question of buying a swing set and a slide; Charles Comfort's playgrounds were unique.

Joy, too, had cared. She'd set out to fulfill her father's last request and had been shot down in San Francisco yesterday. Her self-esteem had taken a beating. Somehow, accomplishing this goal—realizing her father's final project—had become a testing ground for the stronger, more independent person she wanted to become.

So find a way to try again, she told herself, wondering if she could. If she dared.

She thought of Charles Comfort and remembered the intelligence of his blue-eyed gaze, the casual cut of his light brown hair, the laugh lines that bracketed the corners of his mouth. This man wasn't an intimidating automaton. He had listened to her attentively, even when she stumbled over her own tongue. Looking back, she almost believed that things would have worked out if only the telephone hadn't interrupted them.

She reminded herself that that was wishful thinking. Tinker & Comfort didn't build playgrounds anymore; Mr. Tinker had made that painfully clear. In fact, he'd looked sorely tempted to pick her up bodily and throw her out of the office. If she showed up there again, he'd probably have her arrested!

Stop it, Joy's inner voice commanded. If she was really serious, she told herself, she'd take all this energy she was wasting on worry and use it to find a way to try again. A new way. A way that would work. *You can do it,* the voice urged. *At the very least, you can try.*

She turned to the closet and chose her outfit for the day ahead, thinking that after yesterday's fiasco, the odds against her were worse than ever. She couldn't kid herself about that. But maybe inspiration would strike and she would come up with a way to win Charles Comfort over. What she needed was a plan.

At the very least, it would give her something constructive to think about while she was stringing crepe paper and painting herself green.

By EVENING, Charlie's sister and her problems had been temporarily shoved to second place on his worry list.

Driving his car through a maze of tree-lined, residential streets, he peered alternately at the map of Sacramento on the seat beside him and the return address on the letter in his hand. The words typed so neatly beneath it jumped out at him: *Dear Mr. Comfort, You don't know me but my father, Dr. Jacob Porter, was a great admirer of your work....*

"Damn!" he said harshly.

After his run-in with Matthew, he had lain awake for hours, unable to short-circuit the worries buzzing in his brain. At dawn, admitting defeat, he'd show-

ered and dressed and driven to work, wondering
whether Shelley had slept at all, and if so, where.

Unlocking the entrance to Tinker & Comfort and
turning on the lights, he'd forced himself to put aside
his worries about Shelley long enough to unravel the
smaller task of tracking down Joy Porter. He wanted
to make amends for abandoning her in his office, but
there was nothing in his notes except the date and her
name. No address. No telephone number.

He remembered her insistence that she'd written a
letter to him a week ago and received a form letter in
return. He also recalled his glib dismissal of that possibility. In the end, he'd decided to set his mind at ease
by consulting the chronological file of correspondence. Claudia, the secretary he and Matthew shared,
maintained the "chron file," and he'd retrieved it
from her desk. Expecting the effort to prove futile,
he'd started going through the papers.

Finding the photocopied form letter there was an
awful shock. To Charlie, the worst part was that
Matthew, in defiance of their partnership, had made
and implemented such a high-handed change of policy without even mentioning it to him.

With growing horror, he'd flipped back through the
chron file and discovered that dozens of form letters
had been mailed out over the past months.

He had let himself into Matthew's office then, feeling both guilty and vindicated as he searched through
the desk drawers. He was looking for the file his com-
pulsively organized brother-in-law would have kept.
The slender file marked "Playground Correspondence" contained Joy Porter's letter, politely worded
and yet so anguished and urgent. It hurt him to imagine her distress at the reply she had received.

He'd been tempted to pick up the phone and call her right then, but realized it was still too early. Besides, that would have been the easy way out; pride demanded that he offer his apologies to her in person. And pride demanded that he be there, facing her, when he explained why he still couldn't grant her father's last request.

So it was, at the end of the long day, that he came to be driving through the dusk in search of her. As darkness approached, the sidewalks were becoming populated by an increasing number of costumed children, carrying bags to hold the treats and candies they hoped to gather on their Halloween rounds.

Their presence at each corner and intersection slowed Charlie's pace still further. "Three four six nine Arelyn Drive," he said at last when he found the address he sought. The street bordered the university campus, he noted, pulling over to the curb. He cut the engine, climbed out of the car and made his way to the front walk.

The tall, graceful, tile-roofed house that stood before him was Spanish in style, and surrounded by flowering shrubs and towering trees. In the fading light its whitewashed walls glowed softly, projecting a promise of serenity and welcome. *Come in,* it seemed to say. *Dinner's nearly ready. Put your feet up and relax.* Except Charlie knew that the hospitality of this house and its owner was meant for others, not for him. Straightening his tired shoulders, he rapped on the front door.

It was opened promptly by a ghost, a dragon and a half-peeled banana.

The sight of his welcoming party brought a bittersweet smile to Charlie's lips. It was impossible to tell whether these children were boys or girls, costumed as they were, but they looked about six years old. *Penny's age,* he thought, accepting the coincidence and the painful awareness that, unlike them, the Penny of his thoughts would be six forever.

They were looking up at him, their cheeks rosy, their eyes bright with expectation. Kneeling to bring himself down to their level, he said, "Trick or treat!"

The dragon giggled.

"Whose dad are you?" the banana asked. "You're too early. The party isn't over. Nobody wants to go home yet."

Looking over their heads, Charlie saw a dozen children and a smattering of adults milling around in the hallway, vanishing into the brightly lit rooms beyond, their voices blending in a happy buzz.

"You can't come in without a mask," the ghost announced, holding out a wicker basket. "Miss Porter says everybody's gotta wear a mask or a costume. Even Jezebel."

Jezebel? Charlie thought. What sort of children's party *was* this? But the dragon and the banana were nodding in agreement. Outnumbered, Charlie looked at the colorful disguises that filled the basket: paper half masks of Cleopatra and Henry VIII, wax mustaches, black cloth dominoes, plastic spectacles with giant eyebrows and noses attached and an array of lifelike rubber beaks and snouts.

Stepping further inside, Charlie closed the outer door and glanced into the nearest room. Amid the throng of children, three adults were in sight: a green-skinned, black-garbed witch serving drinks from a punch bowl, a pirate wearing a gold earring and an eye patch, and a roaring twenties' flapper. All of the kids around them were wearing costumes, some sketchy, some elaborate. No one was unadorned.

Charlie donned a rabbit's nose. Nibbling an imaginary carrot, he drawled, "Eh, what's up, Doc?"

His small audience looked at him blankly.

Realizing he'd run head-on into a generation gap, Charlie exchanged the rabbit nose for a long yellow beak and said in a nasal voice, "Hey, Snuffy, have you seen Kermit around?"

"Big Bird!" the banana exclaimed. The dragon giggled.

"*Now* can I come in?"

"Sure," said the ghost, stepping aside. "But you gotta keep your beak on. Wanna go through the haunted house with me? Chad and Joey are afraid to go again, 'cause it's really gross!"

"With a recommendation like that, how could I resist?" Charlie asked, allowing the little ghost to take his hand and pull him forward. "I haven't seen anything really gross all day."

"We aren't either scared to go again!" protested the dragon, tagging along on Charlie's left.

"Well, I am," the banana whimpered. "There were *eye*balls."

"They weren't real eyeballs," the ghost insisted as the dragon slowed, dragging uncertainly at Charlie's hand.

"Oh, yeah? Then what were they?" the banana demanded. "They felt like eyeballs to me. And that bucket of brains...what was *that?*"

"Cold spaghetti," an adult voice replied. It was a voice he recognized, although its current tone of good-natured vigor was at odds with the soft hesitance he remembered from their first meeting.

He had found Joy Porter.

Charlie looked up from his small escorts to greet her, and found that she was the slender witch from the punch bowl.

"Spaghetti?" the dragon echoed.

"Just spaghetti," Joy confirmed. "And the eyeballs were peeled grapes."

"Promise?"

"Cross my heart," she said. Charlie watched as she drew an *X* across her chest with a wrinkled green finger. "I peeled them myself."

"Told you so, told you so," the ghost chanted in gleeful triumph. "Let's go! And then can we come back and see Jezebel?"

Joy nodded. "Of course. I'll be bringing her out in just a little while."

"Come on, you guys. Last one there's a pumpkin head!" All three children pelted off down the hallway.

Joy watched them go, then turned to look at Charlie, her gray eyes merry beneath the brim of her pointed black hat.

It was the stuff of farce, or so it seemed to Charlie. He'd spent the drive up from San Francisco worrying about this moment, recalling every detail of their brief, interrupted interview, practicing the heartfelt apology he'd come to offer her, wondering whether she would slam her door in his face...and it had all come down to this: Big Bird meets the Wicked Witch of the West.

"Are you the father of the dragon, the ghost or the banana?" she asked pleasantly.

He felt absurdly hurt, for a moment, that she didn't recognize him, but reason returned. He had come here expressly to seek her out, so it had taken little for him to see through her disguise. She, on the other hand, had no cause to expect to find him in her house.

"None of the above," Charlie replied, looking down his yellow beak, charmed by this version of her. Despite the black costume and green skin, she looked vibrant, a far cry from the strained and anxious young woman who had come to his office. "In fact," he admitted with a smile, "I'm not a father at all."

"Oh?" She peered at him.

Quickly, before the uneasiness in her eyes could sharpen into alarm, Charlie pulled off the rubber mask. "Hi."

"Mr. Comfort!" she said, looking as if Dracula himself had suddenly risen up before her, unfurling his cape.

"Yep, it's me again." Chagrined by her reaction, Charlie spread his hands. "Look, I'm sorry to show up unannounced, but we need to talk." Another pair of raucous children careened past. Taking a step closer to Joy, Charlie lowered his voice and said, "When you came yesterday, I didn't know about your father. I mean, I'd seen in the papers that he . . . passed away. But I didn't know you were his daughter, and I didn't know anything about the playground you wanted me to build."

"Is that why you're here?" she asked. "You've changed your mind?"

The sudden expression of hope on her face tore at Charlie's conscience. He didn't have to answer; his hesitation was enough to extinguish the light in her eyes. "I came to offer my condolences," he said uncomfortably, "and to explain why I can't help you."

"Can't we at least talk it over?" she entreated. "I know what Mr. Tinker said, but—"

"You talked to Matthew about this? When? What did he—"

"*There* you are," a stout, white-haired woman said peremptorily, stepping up to join them. Dressed in a blue hooded robe, she looked like Cinderella's fairy godmother, and she exuded the same air of brisk efficiency. "Excuse me for interrupting, Joy, but Jezebel is screaming for you."

Joy looked stricken. "I'd better go see what's wrong. Eleanor, could you keep an ear out for the doorbell, in case we get more trick-or-treaters?"

"Wait!" Charlie protested. "We need to—"

"She'll be back," the plump woman assured him as they watched Joy thread her way swiftly through the crowd of brightly dressed children. "But I can't guarantee you won't be interrupted again. It isn't easy, playing hostess to a mob of six-and seven-year-olds." She held out her hand. "I'm Eleanor Anderson."

"Charlie Comfort," he said, accepting the warm clasp of her hand with a sigh of resignation. He would simply have to wait his turn.

Mrs. Anderson smiled apologetically. "I'm sorry I had to intrude, but Jezebel didn't sound at all happy. And, quite frankly," she added, fixing him with a look of undisguised appraisal, "judging by the look on Joy's face when I walked up, whatever the two of you were discussing wasn't making her very happy, either." She glanced down as a pint-sized tiger scurried past them. "Alison, dear, pick up your tail before someone steps on it," she advised as the child hurried on.

"Excuse me," Charlie said, "but who *are* all these kids?"

"First graders from Dunnett Elementary School, of course. You must be new around here. This party is a thirty-year tradition." She looked him up and down. "Are you a friend of Joy's?"

He was less than a friend...and he wished it wasn't so. "We met yesterday. We had some unfinished business to clear up, so I dropped in unannounced. I guess I should have called first. I didn't expect to find her quite so...occupied."

"You find it peculiar that Joy chose to throw a party so soon after Dr. Porter's death?" she asked defensively.

"Surprising, maybe, but not peculiar," Charlie protested. Now that he thought about it, he supposed Matthew would have been appalled, seeing only the apparent disrespect, but Charlie understood—understood and approved. "People die," he said, choosing his words carefully, "but the world goes on spinning. At least, it should."

"Absolutely. Still, some people seem to enjoy leaping to unfair conclusions. I've known Joy since she was a little girl, and I've never met anyone with a kinder heart. After the funeral, she and I discussed cancelling this year's party, but she didn't want to disappoint the children."

Charlie's gaze strayed back to the happy young party-goers. "Yeah, Halloween's pretty heady stuff when you're six," he said. A tiny ballerina was pirouetting nearby, resplendent in a pink tutu, her curly dark ponytail bouncing.

Last year, Penny had been a ballerina.

Feeling as if he were caught in an undertow, Charlie forced his attention back to the woman beside him. "Are you one of the teachers?" he asked, struggling to regain his composure.

"I'm the principal at Dunnett Elementary," Mrs. Anderson replied. "I've had the privilege of making one of our first-grade classes available to Jacob Porter for his research for each of the past twenty years. I'll miss him very much. Did you know him, Mr. Comfort?"

The little ballerina melted into the crowd, out of his line of sight. Charlie took a deep breath. "Know him? No, not personally. I've heard of him, of course. My sister has all of his books. I guess you could say I know him by reputation."

"Reputations are cold, formal things, Mr. Comfort. I'm not denying that Jacob had a distinguished academic career, one that earned him a national reputation, but his real genius lay in his ability to communicate with children. First graders were his particular favorites, but he wrote about all of the elementary grades with an insight and accessibility unmatched by any other educator I've studied. When I give one of his books to parents who come to me for advice, I know they won't feel intimidated or confused by what he's written. If I had my way, he'd be canonized, along with Brazelton and Spock."

"That's quite an epitaph."

"He was quite a man. He'll be sorely missed. And now," she said with a self-deprecating smile, "if you'll excuse me, I'll climb down off my soapbox. Thank you for indulging me. To the children, this is just another Halloween party, but to the rest of us I'm afraid it's also serving as a wake." She squared her shoulders. "Come to the dining room and I'll introduce you to our chaperons. The parents are due to arrive soon, so it won't be long before you can have Joy's undivided attention."

Her undivided attention? Great, Charlie thought as he followed Eleanor Anderson into the next room. *All I have to do now is figure out what to say once I have it.*

CHAPTER THREE

HE FOLLOWED Eleanor Anderson down the hallway, swept along by the crush of tiny bodies. "Where are they all going?"

"Into the dining room to wait for Jezebel," Eleanor replied, as if that explained everything, and guided him to a halt beside the tall man in the pirate costume and the petite blonde dressed as a flapper. "Mr. Comfort, I'd like you to meet our first-grade teacher, Lisa Stone, and her husband, Nathaniel. Lisa, Nathaniel, this is Charles Comfort, a friend of Joy's."

Charlie shook hands with them, noticing the way Nathaniel Stone kept one arm around the waist of his pretty wife while the introductions were completed. *A happy couple,* he thought, and felt a pang as he remembered Shelley's bitterness on the telephone when she'd spoken of Matthew: *Past a certain point, loyalty can be lethal.*

He roused himself from his thoughts as the children around him began pointing toward the door and shushing one another, their sibilant demands for silence creating almost as much noise as their talk and laughter. Turning to find out what had attracted their attention, Charlie saw that Joy had returned.

Even in her outlandish costume, she looked beautiful. He admired her guiltily as she stood in the doorway, cradling some sort of doll in the crook of her arm and smiling as she watched the children. He wished she would smile that way at him, but he knew what it would take to make that wish come true. . . .

Joy stepped into the room, and the "doll" in her arms let out an ear-piercing screech. Startled, Charlie took a closer look at it. "I'll be damned. It's alive!"

Lisa Stone looked at him in surprise. "I thought Eleanor said you were a friend of Joy's."

"A business acquaintance," he clarified unhappily.

"Well, anybody who's known Joy for long knows Jezebel. She's a capuchin—an organ-grinder monkey."

Charlie took another incredulous look. "It's wearing a costume!"

"Of course," Lisa said. "She always does on Halloween. Last year Joy was Grandma, Dr. Porter was the Big Bad Wolf, and Jezebel came as Little Red Riding Hood. The year before that, when Jezzie was just tiny, they were Mama, Papa and Baby Bear, and Mrs. Anderson dressed up as Goldilocks. The children loved it."

"I'll bet," Charlie said, tickled by the notion. "But what's the monkey supposed to be this time?"

Lisa looked at him as if he were being intentionally obtuse. "Dorothy, of course. And Joy is the Wicked Witch of the West. Originally, Dr. Porter was going to be the Wizard of Oz and Joy was going to be Glinda, the Good Witch of the North, but . . ." Her voice trailed off unhappily.

Disconcerted by the sorrow in her gaze, Charlie broke eye contact, giving her a moment to compose herself. Not far away, he could see Eleanor Anderson smiling at Joy with open approval, and the chaperons looked as pleased as the kids. Still, he wouldn't have pegged Joy Porter as the kind who'd have had a monkey. Wasn't there some law against keeping exotic animals as pets?

"You'll all get a chance to say hello to Jezebel," Joy was saying to the youngsters crowding around her, "but she isn't used to seeing so many friends all at once. It's a little scary for her. If you sit down, Jezzie will show you what she's been learning lately. Then we'll come around so everybody can get a good look at her."

The children dropped obediently to the floor.

Placing a chair in front of the dining-room table, Joy seated herself and lengthened the amount of slack in Jezebel's leash. The monkey scurried down Joy's long, black witch's dress to the floor, hiding from the excited audience.

"Now be very quiet and we'll see if she'll come back up."

Again the children shushed each other.

When the noise level had dropped as far as could be expected, Joy looked down at Jezebel. "Sit," she said, prolonging the *s* sound. "Come on, Jezzie. Sit."

To the children's delight, the monkey clambered into her lap.

"Good girl," Joy said, and produced something from the pocket of her skirt, which the monkey promptly snatched and ate. "We'll do an easy one next." Producing a white handkerchief from her pocket, Joy wadded it up, tossed it to the floor and said, "Fetch, Jezzie. Fetch."

In a flash, the monkey leaped to the floor, grabbed the handkerchief and returned to Joy's lap to place it on her outstretched palm.

"*Good* girl." The praise was followed by another tidbit. As soon as the monkey had chewed and swallowed, Joy lengthened the leash to allow Jezebel to climb up onto her shoulder. Then, giving the monkey's long tail a gentle tug, she said, "Down."

Reluctantly, Jezebel dropped back into her lap.

"Good girl!" Joy produced a third treat from her pocket and said to the children, "Well, that's what she's been learning, just like you've been learning to read and add. Didn't she do a good job?"

Taking their cue, the children applauded enthusiastically.

"That's it?" Charlie asked rhetorically, as Joy and Jezebel began their slow progress through the crowd.

Nathaniel Stone looked at him in surprise. "What were you expecting—flaming hoops and a trapeze?"

"Well, no, but I guess I thought it would be more like somebody's performing dog. You know—shake hands, roll over, play dead...."

"But none of that would be very useful."

Charlie shrugged. "Who's talking useful? It's a pet monkey."

"Not 'it,'" Lisa corrected. "She. And Jezebel isn't just a pet. When she's old enough, she's going to be trained at Monkeys Do."

"Monkeys Do?" The name rang a vague bell with Charlie. Had he seen it in the paper or heard it on television....? That was it. The evening news. He remembered watching in amazement as a monkey flicked a light switch up and down, then slotted a cassette into a tape recorder for a woman in a wheelchair. "This is one of those monkeys that's going to help people who are paralyzed?"

Behind him, something made a noise like the twittering of a bird.

Turning his head, Charlie saw Joy walking past with the monkey perched on her arm. Her attention was focused on the children, but her monkey looked up at him with apparent interest and made the soft twittering sound again.

Disconcerted by how human the tiny face appeared, he remembered Lisa's words: *Not it. She.*

Charlie exchanged glances with Jezebel. Was it his imagination, or was there something innately feminine in the way the little monkey held his gaze, as if she sensed his interest and was reveling in it? Her fur was thick and lustrous, her eyes cinnamon gold. Like a practiced coquette, she batted her eyelashes at him.

Entranced, Charlie reached out, wondering if Jezebel's fur could possibly feel as plush as it looked.

Joy stepped back hastily. ''Don't!'' she said, her gaze rising to lock with his.

He was getting almost used to her green skin. ''I wasn't going to hurt it,'' he protested.

''I'm sure you weren't. But monkeys see a reaching hand as a threat, and Jezzie has teeth a shark might envy. If you want to be friendly, crook your elbow and hold it out like mine, instead.''

Cautiously, he did as she instructed. Instantly, Jezebel grabbed his sleeve with one long-fingered hand, wriggling in protest as Joy's hold on the leash prevented her from climbing onto Charlie's arm.

Lisa laughed. ''Well, Mr. Comfort! You seem to have made a conquest. Better be careful, Joy. Jezzie's going to get herself into trouble some day, latching onto every handsome stranger she meets.''

Looking flustered, Joy opened her mouth as if to reply, but the chiming of the doorbell sounded first. To Charlie's disappointment, she disengaged Jezebel's grip from his coat sleeve with quick efficiency. "Excuse me. I'd better go answer that."

Left behind with the Stones, Charlie forced a chuckle and said, "An unlikely pair."

"They're inseparable," Nathaniel asserted. "A real mutual admiration society. Joy's a natural with Jezzie, just like she is with the kids. Put her in a roomful of adults and she freezes, but she's the original earth mother with anything under four feet tall."

Lisa nodded her agreement. "It's a shame she isn't in the classroom anymore."

"She teaches?" Charlie asked.

"She did, before Dr. Porter got so sick. First grade, like me."

Nathaniel gave his wife a gentle squeeze. "Joy and Lisa grew up together," he explained to Charlie. "Best friends since the fourth grade. We've done what we could to help Joy out these past few years while her dad was sick, but—"

Across the room, Eleanor Anderson was clapping her hands for attention. "All right, boys and girls," she announced in carrying tones, "the car pools are arriving. Find your partners and line up behind your leader. When everyone in your group has been checked off the list and your driver is here, you may get your coats and jackets from the living room. Remember, no pushing or shoving. Ms. Porter and Jezebel will be at the front door to say good night. As you go out, be sure to thank them for the nice party."

Charlie expected it to be an exercise in chaos, but there was at least some method to the madness as the

three-dozen children divided themselves among their
teacher and the room mothers like chicks returning to
the proper mother hen. Lists were consulted, names
were called off and soon the room was nearly empty.

"I'm impressed," he admitted to Eleanor Anderson. "Does it always go that smoothly?"

"Of course not. More often than not, someone
strays off or a parent has car trouble at the last minute. But we do our best." She surveyed the room. "If
you'll excuse me, Mr. Comfort, I'd like to get started
on cleanup."

The sooner the mess was cleared away, Charlie reasoned, the sooner the others would leave and allow
him the private moment he needed with Joy Porter.
"Can I help?"

"If you like." Eleanor handed him a large plastic
garbage bag. "Perhaps you wouldn't mind dismantling the haunted house. It's at the end of the hall, the
last door on the left. Don't bother trying to salvage the
crepe paper, but we would like to save the bats."

"By all means," Charlie assured her with a crooked
grin. "We wouldn't want to waste the bats."

DROPPING COINS INTO the pay phone, Michelle Comfort Tinker dialed her brother's number and waited,
tight jawed, through one ring, two rings...

Come on, Charlie. Answer it.

...three rings...

Where was he? Still at the office, slaving away with
Matthew?

...four rings...

She was ready to jam the receiver down in frustration by the time the sharp click of a connection inter-
vened. "Hello," Charlie said conversationally.

She drew breath to reply.

"This is Charlie Comfort," his voice continued before she could speak. "Please don't hang up."

It was his answering machine, she realized, but it wasn't the gag recording with the drawling John Wayne imitation that he usually used. This was his own voice, sounding strained and oddly intent.

"Sorry I'm not home right now," it elaborated, "but if you leave your name and number I promise I'll get back to you right away. Just tell me what's on your mind. You have no idea how much I've been looking forward to your call."

Maybe it was her loneliness that made his words seem so apt . . . or maybe Charlie really had fashioned them with her in mind, dictating a message innocuous enough to pass unremarked by casual callers while trying to ensure that, if she did call, she wouldn't simply hang up. God knew, it was the sort of clever, two-edged thing he might do.

Giving him the benefit of the doubt, she said quietly, "Hi, it's me. I'm fine. I've found a place to stay. I'll call again, once I've had time to get my head screwed on straight. Tell Matthew . . ."

She closed her eyes, appalled. Where had that come from? She had nothing left to say to Matthew, nothing that could be said now, anyway . . . and maybe never. But the words had been spoken and recorded, and the tape was spinning on, relentlessly recording her moments of stricken hesitation.

"Damn it, Charlie," she said at last, "that's what I hate about answering machines. Once you say something, there's no way to take it back. I'll call again in a couple of days. Be there, huh?" Her head had begun to ache again. "I miss you," she admitted, and hung up before she could say anything else she might regret.

By THE TIME Joy had waved goodbye to the final carload of children, her impatience and anxiety were at a fever pitch. What if Charles Comfort got tired of waiting for her and slipped out the back door before she had a chance to talk to him? He'd already made it clear that he had come to make a final, formal refusal on the playground project . . . which meant that it was up to her, somehow, to change his mind.

All evening his presence had tugged at her, distracting her from her responsibilities as hostess of the children's party. In San Francisco, she had been struck primarily by his gentle manner and intelligence. But tonight, watching him within the framework of her own home, she had seen his willingness to look silly wearing Big Bird's beak and his comfortable rapport with the children as well as the adults. It all appeared genuine, the acts of a relaxed and confident man, a man whose actions were as attractive as his looks.

Charles Comfort was kind and smart and handsome. So of *course* she was cast in the thankless role of having to harass him to do something for her he didn't want to do. Was fate never kind?

Closing the front door, she went in search of him.

Instead, she found the Stones and Eleanor Anderson, busily engaged in their cleanup efforts. "Oh, that isn't fair," Joy said when she saw the progress they had made. "I didn't mean for you to do so much. Just leave the rest, please. I'll finish up tomorrow."

"Nonsense," Eleanor said over the noise of the vacuum cleaner. "You don't want to have to face this in the morning."

"Then I'll do it now."

"I doubt that," Lisa Stone said with kindly severity. "You look like a candidate for total collapse. You want my advice? Take advantage of the help that's offered and save your strength for scrubbing that green goo off your skin before it becomes permanent."

"Why don't you go and settle Jezzie for the night?" Nathaniel suggested. "It won't take us long to finish, with everybody gone."

"Everybody?" Joy echoed unhappily.

"Well, everyone but Mr. Comfort," Eleanor said.

Joy's spirits rose. "He's still here? Where?"

"I sent him down to dismantle the haunted house. Why don't you tuck Jezebel in for the night? I doubt if Mr. Comfort will be leaving anytime soon."

"Go on," Lisa urged. "Jezzie needs her beauty sleep."

In the face of their united front, Joy surrendered with weary gratitude. "You're saints, all of you."

"I don't think they canonize pirates," Nathaniel said with a laugh, and went back to bagging leftover pumpkin cookies.

"By the way," Eleanor said, smiling in a way that promised mischief, "we thoroughly enjoyed meeting your friend. He's a personable young man."

Joy nodded noncommittally. At the moment, she knew it shouldn't matter to her whether Charles Comfort had purple hair and the manners of Attila the Hun. It was his talent she needed, and his cooperation. "I'll be back in just a few minutes," she promised, and hurried down the hallway to the sanctuary of her father's study, closing the door behind herself with more haste than grace.

Dropping into the Morris chair beside her father's desk, she unfastened the Velcro tabs at the back of Jezebel's costume and drew the tiny dress over the monkey's head, then untied the diaper and removed it. "You were great tonight," Joy assured her, unfastening the waist leash. "The kids loved you."

Jezebel wriggled with approval as the restraint fell away, then launched herself on a manic tour of the room.

"Lord, I wish I had a tenth of your energy. Go ahead, you deserve it." The nimble monkey leaped from bookcase to desktop to couch, then scrambled back into Joy's lap. "Well, it's been a long day," Joy said, tickling her gently under the chin. "And it isn't over yet, at least for me. Wish me luck?"

Jezebel reached up to touch Joy's face.

"Tomorrow we'll rehang your swing, but right now it's time for you to call it a night. Cage, Jezzie."

With a show of reluctance, Jezebel obeyed.

"Good girl." Rousing herself from her chair, Joy turned out the light. "Sleep tight," she said, walking to the door. "I'll see you in the morning."

A subdued cheep was the only answer.

Slipping out, Joy closed the study door. Cheerful voices and the muted clatter of crockery floated from the direction of the kitchen; the only other sign of life was the glow of light spilling out through the open doorway of the haunted house.

Ready or not, the moment for confronting Charles Comfort was upon her.

Reaching the den doorway, she saw that most of the dismantling had already been achieved. The movable dividers provided by the school to form the maze were still scattered around the room, but a heap of black crepe paper lay crumpled in the middle of the floor and the peeled grapes and other displays had been gathered together on one of the small card tables.

By the glare of the overhead light, it was a fairly pathetic-looking collection, but in the dark, with a sound-effects tape moaning in the background and tendrils of black crepe paper hanging down to brush the faces of the unwary, the dimly lit "horrors" had been more than enough to spook a willing group of youngsters. She just hoped she wouldn't be receiving any angry phone calls from parents, blaming her for some child's nightmares.

"Blasted bats."

The muttered words gave Joy a scant second to brace herself before the "personable young man" emerged from behind a divider, carrying a basket filled with cardboard bats. He stopped abruptly when he saw her. "There you are," Charlie said, his face unreadable. "Are the kids all gone?"

She nodded, feeling the heat rise in her cheeks as she tried to plan how to begin.

"Good," he said, coming toward her slowly. "Look, I drove up here tonight because I needed to explain to you why I—"

"I know why you think you came here tonight," she interrupted, hardly recognizing the calm, firm voice as her own. "But *I* think you came because you were meant to build this playground. My father knew it. I know it. And you know it too, if you'll just admit it."

"Ms. Porter—"

Marshaling her arguments, she plunged on. "My father loved children. He spent his career observing them. Learning from them. Teaching other people about them. This playground will be his final gift to them.''

"It's a wonderful idea," Charles Comfort agreed soberly, "and I wish you all the luck in the world with it. But I still can't—"

"It isn't just the way your playgrounds look that made my father admire your work," she said, overriding him again. "It's the way you use the kids' input when you develop the design. Most people who make things for children totally ignore what they have to offer. Their ideas. Their energy and enthusiasm. Their originality. It drove my father crazy. But when he saw pictures of your first playground, he knew what you'd done. 'It looks like a kid's drawing,' he said to me, and he meant it as the highest possible compliment. And when he read the article and learned about the safety research you incorporate—"

"I *know* all this," Charles Comfort said explosively, his face as red as hers felt. "Your father was a great man. He left behind an impressive body of work. I'm sure he deserves some kind of monument—"

"Then why won't you design one for him? Just because Mr. Tinker doesn't want you to? I know playgrounds aren't prestigious, and probably not very lucrative, either, but I'm willing to double your usual fee, if you think that would soften your boss's objections."

"Matthew isn't my boss, he's my partner…and my brother-in-law. This isn't about money."

"Then what *is* it about? What is so much more important than a dying man's final wish?"

"Concern for the living."

It wasn't the answer she'd expected. "I don't understand," she said, feeling the tide of righteous indignation that had carried her so far begin to falter and ebb.

"You don't need to," he said gruffly.

"Yes, I *do*. Explain it to me, please."

"In a nutshell? You aren't the only one who's had to deal with a death in the family." His grip on the basket tightened. "Let's leave it at that, okay?"

But she couldn't. The stark expression of pain and loss on his face wouldn't let her. "Who?" she asked. "Who died?"

"My niece," he answered softly. "Penny Tinker."

"Tinker? Your partner's—"

"Shelley and Matthew's daughter. Their only child." He took a careful breath. "She was six. That isn't long enough to produce a "body of work"—it's barely long enough to learn to read—but she was no less a person for that."

Joy's mouth went dry. Nearly half the children at the party had been six. Full of enthusiasm and intelligence, they were tiny bundles of potential, poised on the brink of life. To think of one of them dying was a sacrilege. "What happened?"

"She died in a playground accident."

She flinched. There were no words she could say, no solace she could offer in the face of that horrific irony. She thought about the past week and how dangerously easy it had been to lose herself in her grief, filled with the morbid certainty that no one's pain could be as deep as her own, no one's loss as great.

Six years old. Dear God.

"The kitchen's done," Lisa announced from the hallway, her words shattering the silence. "You two need a hand?"

Hush, Joy wanted to admonish. *Show the proper respect.* But that was unfair; Lisa had no way of knowing what had just been said.

Charles Comfort cleared his throat. "No, thanks, we're through. Just tell me where to leave these bats and I'll be on my way."

"They came from the school. Come on. We'll put them with Eleanor's things."

"All right." He turned his face toward Joy, looking through her with ghostly eyes. "Goodbye, Ms. Porter. I really am sorry things didn't work out."

He was leaving. He was leaving, and in all decency there wasn't a thing she could do about it. "Goodbye, Mr. Comfort," she said mechanically as he walked past her. "Thank you for coming. Thank you for...explaining."

He nodded, without looking back.

And then he was gone.

CHAPTER FOUR

As a rule, Charlie enjoyed driving. His little red Miata was nimble and responsive, and the unbroken ribbon of road that stretched from Sacramento to San Francisco was just the sort that best encouraged his thoughts to flow freely.

In the wake of Joy Porter's party, however, he found that mental freedom a curse, not a blessing. New memories and old were equally unsettling, and his foot pressed heavily on the gas pedal as though he sought to outdistance his troubled conscience.

His eyes were gritty with fatigue by the time he reached home. When he opened the door to his unwelcoming apartment, the darkness was broken only by the flashing signal light on his answering machine.

Fighting a numbing lethargy, Charlie came inside, ordering his body to undertake the necessary motions. *Turn on the light. Close the door. Hit Playback—*

"Hi, it's me," Michelle said, her voice slightly distorted by the answering machine's tiny speaker. "I'm fine...."

The tape played on. Charlie stood frozen, cursing the fate that had sent him out on this night of all nights. Had she called hours ago or had he missed her by mere minutes? If he hadn't gone, if he'd driven just a little faster—

Abruptly, the message ended. Bending over the machine, he pressed Rewind and then Playback. Anxiously, he listened again, and then again, studying her words, tracking her silences and hesitations, trying to project himself into her thoughts. Where had she been calling from? Was she really all right? *I'll call again in a couple of days. Be there, huh?* she said near the end. So she intended to stay in touch. But what could he say to her?

Charlie paced the room. He supposed he ought to call Matthew and let him listen to the tape...but he felt a strange reluctance. If Michelle wanted to talk to her husband, she certainly knew how to reach him. *He probably wouldn't care, even if you told him,* Charlie thought unhappily. *Go to bed. Go to sleep. You're going to be a zombie in the morning.*

But sleep refused to come. Shortly before dawn, as he turned from his back to his stomach for the hundredth time, a new question occurred to him. What would Michelle make of Joy Porter's request and Matthew's embargo? In light of Penny's death, would she condone her husband's high-handed cancellation of any further playground work? Or possibly, just possibly, might she share his own renewed urge to tackle the problem head-on....

Slowly, his thoughts became less focused until, at last, he stumbled upon the wellspring of sleep that had evaded him for so long. When he woke hours later, he found that his ambivalence had vanished.

Wisely or not, he knew what he was going to do.

And why.

And for whom, regardless of the consequences.

JOY WOKE WITH THE SUN in her eyes.

Giving a drowsy groan, she freed her arm from the tangle of blankets and squinted at her watch, first idly, then in horror. Half-past nine? Why hadn't her alarm gone off? She'd slept right through her father's eight o'clock medication....

Fighting panic, she reached for the intercom that kept her in communication with his room.

Her palm struck the cool, bare surface of the bedside table.

Only then, with a shock, did memory come clear. The intercom was in the closet, packed away, no longer required. And her alarm hadn't rung because she hadn't bothered to set it. There had been no need. The long, punishing battle of attrition was finally over, and Jacob Porter was at peace, beyond the need of her protective vigilance.

Acknowledging that reality, Joy waited for the familiar fog of grief and depression to settle over her. Instead, to her astonishment, what she felt was a faint stirring of relief—hesitant and guilt-tinged, but relief, nevertheless.

Before she could begin to explore the feeling, a series of high-pitched screeches shattered the morning silence. Jezebel, caged downstairs, was demanding her morning ration of food and attention with ever-increasing volume and indignation.

Joy pushed back the covers hastily and groped for her robe, but the sight of the sunlight on her pale green hands stopped her in midmotion. Rising more slowly, she crossed to the bureau and eyed herself cautiously in the mirror.

As she'd feared, her face was the same delicate shade of pistachio green as her hands. "Water soluble, eh?" Joy said scathingly to her reflection. Last night she had taken a hot shower to remove the garish face paint, and her skin had appeared normal enough afterward, but she suspected now that lamplight and the vigorous toweling she had given herself had conspired to create a falsely rosy glow. Clearly, another round of soap and elbow grease was called for.

Downstairs, Jezebel began to shriek again.

Joy started for the stairs . . . then turned back with a decisive shake of her head. True, Jezebel was unhappy, but she was perfectly safe in her cage.

Heading for the bathroom with an air of grim determination, Joy muttered, "For once, sweetheart, you're going to have to wait your turn."

FOR THE SECOND TIME in twenty-four hours, Charlie Comfort parked his car at the curb in front of Joy Porter's house and made his way up the walk to knock at her front door.

Last night, the welcoming committee had been a ghost, a dragon and a half-peeled banana. He wondered what it would be today.

He had plenty of time to speculate. His first knock was followed by a second; he waited; he pressed the doorbell. *Maybe she isn't home. You should have called first.* Ruefully, he took a business card out of his wallet and turned it over. He could leave her a note, at least, and check back again in an hour or two. . . .

As he began to write, the door opened a crack and then swung wide. "Mr. Comfort!" Joy said in artless astonishment.

"In the flesh," Charlie confirmed, trying to mask his own surprise as he faced her in her latest incarnation. This was not the tongue-tied wraith who had come to his office two days ago, nor was it the black-

garbed witch of last night's party. This morning, her
face looked ruddy and fresh-scrubbed, and her chestnut hair hung loose, cascading over the shoulders of
a scarlet blouse. She had traded her air of fragility for
an aura of high-strung energy, and he was finding it a
potent aphrodisiac.

Aware that he was staring, he said, "May I come in?
I need—" He broke off as a series of ear-piercing
screeches split the air. "Is that your monkey? What's
wrong with her?"

"Nothing serious."

"Are you sure? It *sounds* serious."

Joy shook her head. "She was about to have a bath.
When the doorbell rang, I put her back into her cage
instead. Believe me, nothing's hurt but her feelings."
She brushed a strand of hair back from her face. "I
didn't think I'd be seeing you again, Mr. Comfort. Did
you forget something here last night?"

"No, I..." Charlie groped for the clear, logical explanation he had rehearsed during the drive, but it was
hard to think above the din of Jezebel's lamenta-
tions. "Maybe we'd better go in and check on her," he
said. "We could talk while she's having her bath."

"That would be giving in to her," Joy said, standing her ground.

Charlie glanced around uneasily. "Aren't you afraid
one of your neighbors will call the SPCA?"

"They know Jezzie too well for that."

The frantic keening was making Charlie's molars
ache. During Penny's infancy, he had never been able
to harden his heart to her cries, even when Michelle
teased him about being a soft-hearted pushover....
"Look," he said a little desperately, "if you won't do
it for Jezebel and you won't do it for your neighbors,

then do it for me, okay? Please? As an act of Christian charity? If I promise to tell you everything?"

"But she's perfectly all right."

"Well, *I'm* not." The short night had left him feeling raw and vulnerable. Intellectually, he knew that the sounds of distress came from a petulant monkey, not a human baby. Nevertheless, he wanted—needed—to know that those cries would be soothed. Human or simian, pain was pain. Unhappiness was unhappiness. With more passion than he'd intended, he asked, "Would it really be such a crime to give her what she wants?"

He could see that the vehemence of his words had startled her.

"No, of course not," Joy soothed, stepping aside for him to precede her through the doorway. "Come on in."

Despite the ruckus Jezebel was creating, there was an air of stillness about the house, a sense of privacy and isolation that made Charlie feel as if he were trespassing. It was a mannered house, conservative in both its architecture and its furnishings. When he and Joy entered the handsome, book-lined study, Charlie gaped at the incongruous sight of the big cage that stood against the far wall. It was as tall as he was, an arm span wide and several feet deep. Within it, Jezebel swung from a long pole. At the sight of them, she stopped keening and chittered in happy welcome.

"Don't give me that gleeful look," Joy chided as she opened the cage. "Tail, Jezzie."

Jezebel swiveled to drape her thick tail across Joy's outstretched palm. As Charlie watched in surprise, Joy used it to swing Jezebel out of the cage, allowing the monkey to straddle her forearm.

"I never heard such a shameful commotion," Joy scolded. "You'd better say thank you to Mr. Comfort."

As if in obedience to Joy's prompting, Jezebel reached for Charlie. Remembering the lessons of the previous night, he resisted the temptation to hold out his hand, offering his bent arm instead.

This time, with no leash to restrain her, Jezebel crossed over to him and clung to his sleeve. "I think she likes me," Charlie said, gratified.

"No offense, but she likes most men. Women are another matter altogether. She and I understand each other, and she tolerates Eleanor, but her preference is definitely for men."

"So I shouldn't mistake this for love at first sight?"

"I'm afraid not," she said with a twinkle in her eyes. "I hope you aren't too disillusioned."

"I think I can bear up under the strain." Moving with slow care, he stroked Jezebel's back. "Take your time," he told the tiny creature. "Get to know me. I don't believe a lady's affections should be rushed."

At the sound of his voice, Jezebel nestled against his body and peered up at him, her miniature face disconcertingly expressive.

Charlie had to laugh. "She really *is* a flirt. You'd better rescue me, before I lose my heart."

"Of course. I'm sorry. Come on, Jezzie. Bath time." He felt the gentle pressure of Joy's fingers as she insinuated them between his chest and Jezebel's warm fur in an effort to dislodge the monkey.

For a moment, it seemed she would succeed. Then, with a shrill screech, Jezebel redoubled her grip, sandwiching Joy's hand against the rough yarn of Charlie's sweater.

Trapped, Joy looked up at him in amused apology.

She smelled faintly of apples. Gazing down at her, Charlie saw that her eyes were the soft gleaming gray of water-washed stones or dense velvet.

His body quickened in response to her nearness.

It was as if, until this moment, he had been forced to view her through a series of distorting lenses: first as a stranger and potential client, then as a troubling mystery to be solved and finally as a potential pawn in his upcoming power struggle with Matthew. But now, finally, he felt as if he had shed those external definitions, leaving him free to consider her simply as Joy, the individual. The woman.

Too intense, he would have said of her on that first day. *Too thin. Not my type.* But he felt now as if she had managed to redefine his "type," perhaps for all time.

He wondered whether she recognized his sudden acute awareness of her. Perhaps. Perhaps she had somehow invited it, or even shared it....

"Oh, dear," Joy said in a small voice as his scrutiny persisted. "Am I still green?"

Green? For a minute, he balked at the word, then he remembered her costume and chuckled. "No," he assured her, as amused by the memory of her appearance as by his own swiftly punctured fantasy of mutual attraction. "No, I don't see any green on you. Not a speck."

"Thank goodness. I've scrubbed until my face feels raw. I hated to think ... Well, never mind that. Right now, we need to get you two untangled."

She suited her actions to her words, but again Jezebel offered frantic resistance, clenching her tiny fingers in the wool of Charlie's sweater and letting out a shrill stream of what Charlie had to assume were monkey curses.

"I'm sorry," Joy said, raising her voice to be heard. "She isn't usually this difficult. She's annoyed with me for abandoning her while I answered the door, and she's still a little overexcited from the party."

"It's okay," Charlie said, wondering if Joy could feel the thumping of his heart against her fingers. "Don't force her."

"But—"

"Couldn't Jezebel and I just follow you to the bathtub?"

"You know, that might be a good idea. When she sees the water, she'll probably let go. She really does love baths. You wouldn't mind holding her a little longer?"

"I'd be flattered. It isn't every day that a female throws her arms around me and refuses to let go."

It was a silly thing to say but it seemed to amuse Joy. "Right this way then." She led him out of the room and down the hallway.

He followed willingly in her footsteps, savoring the sight of her leggy stride and the swing of her long hair. Charlie cradled Jezebel against his chest, unexpectedly content with the present moment, entranced by both the monkey and her mistress.

It turned out that their destination was not a bathroom but the kitchen. "I hope this doesn't mean you've decided to turn her into capuchin cold cuts," Charlie quipped as Joy knelt and opened the storage cupboard beneath the sink.

"No," she said over her shoulder, "although there are times when I've been tempted. Don't worry. We're in here because the kitchen sink makes a perfect monkey bathtub. Not too big, not too small, right at waist level—it really couldn't be better.'' She rose and turned, holding a plastic dishpan, a bottle of baby shampoo and a faded yellow rubber duck.

At the sight of the duck, Jezebel chirped brightly.

With a knowing smile, Joy turned the water on, adjusting the taps before she slid the dishpan into the sink. ''You can bring her over now. I think our problem is about to solve itself.''

It was true. As Charlie neared the kitchen counter, Jezebel released her grip and launched herself into the ''tub,'' liberally splashing Joy in the process.

Peace descended. Joy gently lathered the monkey's fur while Jezebel occupied herself by pushing the rubber duck beneath the surface of the water and releasing it, reacting with theatrical delight each time it bobbed to the surface.

Charlie folded his arms and watched, charmed by the wacky domesticity of the scene. When several minutes had passed in relative silence, he said, ''I've done a lot of thinking since last night.''

''Oh?'' Joy said mildly, not looking up from her work on Jezebel.

Charlie realized that, for whatever reason—pride, fear, perversity or a misplaced sense of politeness—she had decided not to question him about his unannounced arrival. If he wanted to thrash the matter out with her, he would have to take the initiative.

''Yeah.'' He cleared his throat. ''And if you still want me to, I'll build your father's playground.''

This time she looked at him. In fact, she stared wide-eyed and open-mouthed, turning toward him so suddenly that it startled Jezebel. The monkey re-

sponded by leaping out of the sink and clambering up
to hide her face against Joy's throat.

"Jezzie, no!" Water streamed from the monkey's
fur, soaking the front of Joy's scarlet blouse.
"Down," she commanded, her gaze still locked with
Charlie's as she gripped Jezebel's soggy tail. "Down!"

He felt a rush of appreciative arousal at the sight of
Joy's wet blouse clinging to the curves of her breasts,
but his pleasure died abruptly when he saw that her
face had gone chalk white. He'd expected his announcement to elicit surprise, yes, but her look of
bone-deep shock made him feel a surge of guilt and
regret. Gone was her air of self-assurance, replaced by
the look of stressed apprehension she had worn at
their first meeting.

The transformation tore at him.

Joy lowered Jezebel into the sink again. "Why?"
she asked unsteadily. "After what you told me last
night, why would you even consider changing your
mind?"

On the drive up, he had warned himself to expect
exactly that question, but he had brushed the worry
aside, telling himself that she would be too pleased by
the turn of events to look a gift horse in the mouth.
Certainly, it was what he wanted to believe. His reasons were painfully personal, hopelessly intercon-
nected with his family's frailties and foibles.

Nevertheless, the look on Joy's face made it clear
that she couldn't trust what she didn't understand. If
she thought his change of heart was simply arbitrary,
how could she be sure he wouldn't alter his decision
again tomorrow, or next week, or a month into the
project?

He owed her some peace of mind. He owed her an explanation.

"Dry Jezebel off," he suggested, "and I'll tell you all about it on our way."

"On our way where?"

"To see the playground site your father chose," he replied, and was gratified to see a faint stain of color return to her cheeks.

"YOUR SISTER DIDN'T tell you where she was calling from?" Joy asked, carefully navigating her car along the tree-lined street.

"No, but she might next time, if I'm there to take the call."

"And she isn't coming home?"

"Not yet," Charlie admitted. "But she called. That's a start."

Joy ached for him, touched by the stubborn hope that underscored his words. It was clear to her that Charlie and his sister were close; surely Shelley would come to see that she could trust Charlie with the secret of her location or, better yet, find the courage to return home.

Joy had always regretted her only-child status. How wonderful it would be to have a brother who was your staunchest ally, ready to stand with you against the world. How wonderful it would be to have anyone, anyone at all. . . .

She jerked her thoughts out of the downward spiral of self-pity and focused on Charlie's words. "I should have known something screwy was going on," he was saying. "I mean, *months* went by, after Penny died, and there wasn't so much as a phone call about any new playground work, not even a casual inquiry. At first, I was mostly relieved. It would have been hard to face. And it isn't like we were sitting around, staring at the walls. There was more than enough other work. But I missed the playgrounds.'' He shook his head as if to clear it. "I told myself I ought to go easy, to spare Matthew. But that was before I realized that I was taking too narrow a view of the problem . . . and before I found out that he'd already tried to take the decision out of my hands.''

She wished there was something she could say to ease the burden of blame he was claiming, but she didn't know where to begin.

"Given what happened to Penny," he continued, "I guess he has a right to feel the way he does . . . but I think he's wrong. Penny's death is exactly why we have to go on.''

"What do you mean?''

"She fell off of a jungle gym and hit her head. Fractured her skull on the concrete. But there shouldn't have *been* any concrete. It's a proven statistic—more than half of the playground accidents that happen in a year are caused by the surface *under* the equipment, not the equipment itself. If she'd fallen on tire chips or wood fibers or even pea gravel, she'd be alive today. But nobody made it their business to make that old playground safe. And, at this rate, nobody ever will.'' Falling silent, he rolled his window down and leaned back against the head rest.

Joy inhaled the sweet cold air greedily, as if it could cleanse her of the sad burden of Charlie's tale. He had her sympathy, but her heart was already heavy with sorrows of her own. What possible solace could she offer him?

They were nearly to the site before he spoke again. "It wasn't a fluke," he said, his voice low and dreary. "There are thousands of old playgrounds scattered around the country, like time bombs waiting to explode. And new ones are being built every year that are just as bad, out of ignorance or laziness or..." He lifted his head, his words coming more strongly. "Damn it, it's a crime. Somebody needs to make a crusade out of this... and I'm starting to think that somebody should be me, whether Matthew likes it or not."

She believed him. She believed *in* him. He had the talent and, unhappily for him, the motivation. It was a dream that would have stirred her to approval even if she had been a disinterested observer. His commitment made sense to her, and she could see how her own dream of a playground in her father's memory might be caught up within Charlie's more ambitious goals, to everyone's advantage.

All they had to do now was cement the deal.

"Here we are," she said as she pulled up to the curb of the vacant lot her father had purchased.

Charlie looked at the lot in silence for several minutes, then turned to her. "This is going to sound crazy... but didn't there used to be some sort of store here, with a cow painted on the side of it?"

"Holstein's Books," Joy replied, astonished. "Mr. Holstein had a mural of a cow painted on the side of the building. But he went out of business years ago, and the store was eventually torn down. How on earth did you know?"

Charlie smiled. "Well, I'm not psychic, if that's what you're asking. My family moved to Sacramento when I was seven. I went to elementary school not far from here. Then my dad got transferred, the year I started college, and there didn't seem to be much point in coming back. When I crashed your Halloween party the other night, it was the first time in fifteen years that I'd set foot in this town." He turned to look at the vacant lot again. "So. No more cow, huh?"

"You could always design one for the playground," she said, and was gratified when he laughed in unguarded delight at the suggestion. "Would you like to get out and take a closer look?"

Charlie was already opening his car door.

By the time she had killed the engine and unfastened her seat belt, he was halfway across the lot, turning in place as he surveyed the area. Joy crossed the open space between them, trying to see it through his eyes. There were a few trees clustered near the back boundary, and a small knoll off to the left, but most of the quarter-acre parcel was flat and bare. She hoped it would meet whatever mysterious criteria Charlie set for his playgrounds-to-be.

"Well," he called to her as he came full circle, "when do you want to get started?"

"Whenever you like," she assured him, giddy with relief. "What's the first step? Shall I write you a check for your retainer?"

He waved the suggestion away. "That can wait. The important thing will be getting our signals straight with the city—permits, insurance, a ton of red tape. And this job is going to have to be invisible at Tinker & Comfort, at least temporarily."

"Invisible?"

"Yeah. I'll keep the paperwork at my apartment, where there's no chance of Matthew stumbling across it. For now, I can give it evenings and weekends. That ought to be enough to keep it moving, in the preliminary stages. By the time things heat up, I'll have found a way to explain it to Matthew. In the short run, though, you'll have to be my local surrogate."

"Surrogate?"

Charlie smiled. "The one who makes the initial contacts."

Her relief eroded into confusion. "I don't understand. Wouldn't you rather hire the crew yourself?"

"Crew? To do what?"

She stared at him. "To build the playground, of course."

Charlie shook his head in brisk denial. "No. That isn't how I work. This will be a group project. The kids will help me brainstorm the design, and they and their families and anybody else we can recruit will go out into the community to solicit money and materials. When the plans are done and we're ready to build, those same kids and their families and friends will be my crew."

Her disbelief must have been apparent, because Charlie stopped and smiled at her, a disconcertingly personal smile that made the distance between them seem like inches rather than feet.

"This works," he said. "You'll see. Once people get involved, once they *invest* in what we're going to do here, it makes all the difference in the world. They'll become proud and protective about this playground, and that will be what *really* makes it theirs. They'll own it in the very best sense of the word." He came closer and took her hand in his. "Trust me. Help me make this happen."

Overwhelmed, she tried to step back, but he retained his gentle hold on her hand. "How?" she asked, afraid to hear the answer.

"By going out and talking to them, kid by kid, grown-up by grown-up, family by family, business by business, block by block."

If she had felt confusion before, it was now threatening to escalate into panic. "You want me to recruit volunteers? To ask strangers for money?"

"Exactly," he said with warm approval.

"But I'm the worst possible choice for a job like that," she protested. "I'm no good with people."

"You were great with the kids at the party last night."

"I'm no good with strangers," she amended in agitation. "Please, don't make the mistake of thinking I'm some reincarnation of my father. I'm not. Ask Eleanor. She'll tell you."

"Eleanor and I had quite a talk last night, and nothing she said made this sound so impossible."

"Then she was being polite, or trying to impress you with something I'm not. All my life, people have expected me to be some great analyzer of strangers, to be glib and sociable, to be...to be Jacob Porter's daughter, according to *their* definition of what that meant. But I'm not. I never have been. I'm just me."

"And is that such a bad thing to be?"

"It's a very *ordinary* thing to be, but nobody wants to believe that. You know what comment showed up most often on my report cards? 'Doesn't work up to her potential.' But it wasn't a question of *my* potential. It was a question of other people's inflated expectations. All my life, people have been disappointed in me. And now you want to start the whole cycle in motion again." But this time it was worse, much worse, because she wanted so badly to succeed . . . and because she wanted so badly for Charlie to think well of her.

"I just want you to help."

"But I'd be a hindrance to you, not a help. If I tried to promote your project—"

"Our project," Charlie corrected.

"Whoever's project it is, can't you see that no one would listen to me? The playground would never get built!"

He shrugged and his smile deepened. "You sound pretty convincing right now. If you'll just bottle all that passionate rhetoric and put it to use for something positive, you can't miss. Don't worry, I'll provide you with a detailed battle plan. And you can enlist some helpers of your own. Maybe Eleanor, for starters. I don't think anybody gets away with telling *that* lady no."

"Charlie, I just don't think it would work."

"It'll work. It has to."

"But—"

"Hold on. There's something I want you to see." He released her hand and pulled his wallet out of his back pocket, opening it to the first see-through flap. "Here. This was taken last December."

The full-color studio portrait had caught the Tinker family at their best. Matthew looked benignly distinguished; Michelle was resplendent in holiday scarlet; and Penny, perched on her father's lap, wore a smile bright enough to have served as the star atop the family Christmas tree.

Heavy-hearted, Joy studied their faces for a long, silent minute.

Closing his wallet, Charlie said, ''You and I are going to get this playground built, Joy. For your dad and for Penny. People will help. You'll see. But first you have to help me. And you have to let me help you.'' He reclaimed her hand. ''Deal?''

What he was asking was impossible . . . but, impossible or not, how could she live with herself if she didn't at least try?

''Well?'' he prompted anxiously.

Taking a deep breath, Joy nodded. ''Deal.''

CHAPTER FIVE

November 1

Dear Joy:
Here are the work plans and information sheets I promised you, along with the names and phone numbers of past clients who can act as resource people for you if you have a general question and can't reach me. Yeah, I know, I can hear you right now: "I couldn't possibly phone a total stranger!" But you can, and these folks are willing to give you the benefit of their experience.

I'll plan on coming to Sacramento for stage two at the end of the month. In the meantime, you can start contacting the local businesses closest to the playground site. I've enclosed a list of them.

Whatever you decide to tackle first, relax and take it step by step. Rome wasn't built in a day, and this playground won't be, either. Trust me, you'll be great and so will it.

All my best to you and Jezebel,
Charlie

November 4

Dear Charlie:
Thanks for following up so quickly. I spent yesterday reading through the material you sent. The

project looks awfully intimidating, but I'm trying to follow your advice and focus on one thing at a time.

I met with Eleanor this morning and showed her your letter. Typically, she agreed to help us in any way she can. She also asked me to pass along an invitation to have Thanksgiving dinner at her house if you're back in town over that long weekend. I'm going, and so are Lisa and Nathaniel Stone. You probably have other plans, but Eleanor made me promise I'd ask.

I'd better finish this off since I have a two o'clock appointment at that health club next to the playground site. I'll keep you posted on how it goes.

Sincerely,
Joy

Closing the document, Joy instructed the computer to print the text of her letter before she could succumb to the temptations of revision one more time. She'd already spent half an hour rewriting it, and she wasn't the least bit sure that the first version hadn't been the best. *It's just a business letter, not brain surgery,* she reasoned, but she couldn't shake the superstitious sense that she needed to impress Charlie with her industry and attitude, now that he was officially committed to the project.

The printer's mechanical clatter woke Jezebel from a warm doze on Joy's lap. Fleeing to the top of the bookcase, the monkey huddled at the edge like a gargoyle, scolding.

"What a performance!" Joy scoffed. "You've heard me run this printer a thousand times. It can't hurt you. You just got caught off guard, and now you're too embarrassed to admit it.''

Scowling at the offending machine, Jezebel held her ground.

''Suit yourself,'' Joy said as the platen released her letter. ''Sulk up there all afternoon if it makes you happy.''

Jezebel shinnied down and scampered across the desktop, passing within inches of the silent printer as if daring it to show its true colors.

''See? Safe and sound.'' Joy crooked her elbow in invitation. ''Ready to kiss and make up?''

Still grumbling, the little capuchin turned her back and settled herself on the far edge of the desk.

Joy laughed, but the sight of the finished letter sobered her again. Suppressing a sigh, she signed it and slipped it into an envelope, wondering why people persisted in believing that great and capable people automatically produced great and capable children. What would Charlie think if he knew she'd hung up three times before she found the nerve to talk to the receptionist at the health club?

''Maybe it wouldn't surprise him at all,'' she said aloud to Jezebel, reaching out to lift the small monkey into her arms. ''Come on, let's get you weighed, then I can drop this letter off while I'm out.''

Jezebel complied grumpily, huddling on the weigh plate of the baby scale with ill grace.

The weighing was a monthly ritual, part of the routine of care and observation that Joy undertook on behalf of Monkeys Do. Given the small size of the monkeys, a gain or loss of ounces could give an early warning of illness, and Joy was scrupulous in her observation of the routine.

As she wrote down Jezebel's weight, however, her thoughts strayed back to Charlie Comfort. The project Charlie's documents described was intimidatingly complex, and yet he had apparently accomplished plenty of others like it, with great success and equally great enjoyment. She found the blend of competence and enthusiasm he displayed seductive; when she was with him, it effectively overrode her natural caution. If Charlie said something could be done, it could be done.

But when he was gone, the doubts returned.

During their visit to the site, he had spent nearly an hour exploring the immediate neighborhood on foot, jotting down notes to himself as he walked. Those notes were before her now in the form of index cards covered in his neat printing, keyed to a diagram of numbered squares. The box at the western boundary of the site was labelled *#1*. On the matching card, Charlie had written: *Good Sports gym/health club. Money? Manpower?*

Maybe Charlie was right, and the people there would be receptive to her speech and would offer their enthusiastic support. Or perhaps they would listen with expressions of polite disinterest and send her, empty handed, on her way.

There was only one way to find out.

WHEN HIS private line rang, Charlie jumped, as he had jumped each of the half dozen other times that it had rung over the past four days. Intellectually, he knew that Shelley was most likely to phone him at home, as she had done before; nevertheless, he lifted the receiver gingerly, as if it might break. "Hello?"

"Hello, Charlie."

His pulse doubled at the sound of his sister's voice. "Are you okay?" he demanded.

"I'm fine. Didn't you get my message?"

"Yes, but..." *Take a breath*, he counseled himself. *Slow down. Don't scare her off.* Down the hall, he could hear Matthew's voice. "Shell, can you hang on for two seconds while I close my door?"

"Sure."

He started to set the receiver down, but a new fear blossomed in his mind. "You won't hang up, will you?"

"I won't hang up," she assured him with elaborate patience. "Go close the door."

When he had done what he could to insure their privacy, he lifted the receiver again. "Thank God you called. Where are you?"

"No, Charlie. Don't even start. If you want to talk to me, talk. But if all you want to do is interrogate me, I'll hang up right now. I'm where I want to be, and I'm safe and well. Beyond that, it's nobody's business but my own."

"Hey!" he protested. "It's my business, too. I love you."

"I know. That's why I'm calling. But this is something I have to work out for myself, little brother."

"What about Matthew?"

"What about him? Do you think he's lost any sleep over my being gone? Has he cried on your shoulder? Said he's worried? Made one move to try and find me?"

"I'm sure he's been—"

"Don't bother trying to make excuses for him, Charlie. The fact is, Matthew abandoned me months ago. My moving out just put a public face on it, that's all. Except for the legalities, our marriage is over.''

Chilled, Charlie asked, ''Do you really think you two are in any shape to be making such a major decision? Can't you give it a little more time? Get some counseling, maybe?''

''You think I didn't suggest it to him? You think I didn't beg? Damn it, Charlie, I'm not a quitter. I don't walk away just because things get a little rough. I never have. But this has been...'' She broke off abruptly, her breathing audible.

''I know,'' he said to fill the painful gap. ''I know. I just hate to see it happen.''

''Staying would have been worse,'' she insisted, and sighed. ''Look, I know this is going to put you on the spot, professionally. I'm sorry about that.''

''Don't be ridiculous. I'm a big boy. I'll manage. It may even be a blessing in disguise. Matthew and I aren't a match made in heaven, you know. It's never been an easy partnership, and lately I've been wondering if the smart move wouldn't be for *us* to split up.''

''That's pretty drastic.''

''Excuse me, but haven't we just switched scripts here?''

''Maybe we have, but that doesn't make it any less valid. What you're talking about is a divorce, too. Just a different kind.''

''If so, Matthew's already made a move in that direction,'' he told her, experiencing a fresh wave of anger as he remembered the playground file he had found and the cool, officious language of the form letter. ''He's being as high-handed and closemouthed in the office as he was with you at home. You pretty well summed things up—if I decide to split off from him, I'll just be putting a public face on what Matthew has already set in motion.''

''What do you mean? What has he done?''

There was no foolproof way to predict what her reaction would be to the bittersweet tale of Joy and Jacob Porter, but it was a risk Charlie felt he had to take. Hoping for the best, he leaned back in his chair and proceeded to lay it out for her, chapter and verse.

When he was done, she said, ''Food for thought.''

''Yeah.''

''I'm glad you're making your own decisions. And I'm glad you've decided to go ahead with this new project. Jacob Porter's daughter, eh? Pretty fast company.''

Charlie allowed himself a private smile. ''I don't think anyone has ever described Joy Porter as 'fast company.' She's about as low profile a person as you're apt to find.''

''I was talking about her father's reputation and— Oh, forget it. You know exactly what I was talking about. So, it's happening in Sacramento, eh? The old stomping ground.''

''Yeah, right where Holstein's Books used to be. I got kind of a kick out of being up there again.'' He suspected that he ought to leave well enough alone, but he asked, ''You understand why I'm doing this, don't you, Shell? The playground, I mean.''

''I understand. I approve. In fact, I may...'' Her voice trailed off.

''May what?''

''Send them a donation,'' she said, and then changed the subject. Charlie was left with the unsettling conviction that it wasn't what she'd started out to say at all.

JOY LINGERED on the sidewalk in front of Good Sports for a few nervous minutes, watching the comings and goings of the club's clientele—a mixture of men and women, business suits and sweat suits, legitimate athletes and weekend warriors. If there was a single unifying factor, it was the apparent energy level of the people she saw, a vibrancy that made her feel sluggish and old.

I'm only twenty-eight, she reminded herself, but a nasty suspicion lingered that life had already somehow passed her by.

In earlier days, she would have been branded an old maid, as much for her lack of life experience as for her age. For the past four years, she had turned her back on the outside world while she cared for her father. During those four years of limbo, she had watched as old friends like Lisa mated and married. Now, when the time had come to pick up the threads of her life, she no longer knew where to begin.

Just take it one step at a time, she counseled herself, and followed a trio of boisterous young men inside.

The reception area was bright and spacious, ending at a clear barrier of Plexiglas that doubled as the back wall of a handball court. There was a game in progress, and a few spectators had gathered to watch two sweaty giants fling themselves about in pursuit of the speeding ball.

Though she was early, Joy found herself eager to put the ordeal behind her now that she was inside. Steeling herself, she walked up to the registration desk.

"Hi," said the girl seated there. "I'm Alison. Can I help you?"

"Yes, please. I'm Joy Porter. I'm here to see Mr. Blade."

"Garrett or Austin?"

Joy swallowed at the unexpected question. "Whichever one is the owner. Nobody mentioned his first name when I made the appointment."

"They're co-owners. Brothers." Alison gestured over her shoulder at the handball players. "The man in the red shorts is Garrett. He manages the club and acts as our resident pro. As you can see, he's in the middle of a lesson right now. Austin keeps the books and handles the business end of things."

"Then my appointment must be with Austin."

"Okay. I'll buzz him and let him know you're here." She pressed a series of buttons on the telephone console in front of her and said, "Austin? I've got a lady named Joy Porter out here to see you."

"Joy Porter?" a cheerful tenor voice repeated blankly.

Joy's neck began to itch.

"It might be Garrett she's here to see," Alison elaborated. "She says she has an appointment—"

"Oh, right, the playground lady! Send her in."

"Right away," Alison assured him, and smiled up at Joy. "Well, that's one mystery solved. Austin's office is the first door on the left. Just let yourself in, okay?"

"All right, thanks," Joy said, and dried her damp palms on her handkerchief as she walked away. *It was just an innocent mix-up,* she told herself. *Don't let it rattle you. Everything's okay now.*

Her hives remained unconvinced.

Reaching the door Alison had indicated, Joy tapped on it tentatively.

"Come on in."

Moment of truth, Joy thought in panic, and opened the door.

"Good morning!" Austin Blade caroled as she stepped inside. "There's coffee in the pot. I hope you aren't one of those liberated women who's going to feel insulted if I ask you to pour a cup for me."

"I don't—" she began, but the rest of the sentence seeped out of her mind as she took in the sight of him. The brazen grin. The mop of wheat-colored hair and neat wheat-colored beard. The blue eyes, bright as mosaic tiles.

The wheelchair.

"You don't...what?" he was prompting. "Care for any? Have time?"

"Mind at all," Joy said, walking to the counter where the old-fashioned percolator stood. "I used to bring coffee to my dad, when he was all wrapped up in a project."

"The blue mug's mine," Austin instructed, his fine-boned hands quiet in his lap. He had turned his head to track her as she walked to the counter, but otherwise he was unnaturally still. A quadriplegic, she guessed, without the use of his arms or legs; the kind of person Jezebel would soon be trained to assist.

His request for coffee, she supposed, was a ploy to give her something to do while she recovered from the shock of facing his condition. She was grateful for the reprieve, but only because she was nervous about promoting the playground, not because Austin's paralysis disconcerted her to any significant degree.

Fragrant wisps of steam rose to tickle her nose as she filled his blue mug and a yellow one for herself. "Cream? Sugar?"

"Black. My mug fits into the holder," he explained, gesturing with his chin. "Yeah, like that. And the straw. Right. Thanks. Pull up a chair, okay?"

She sat down and took a cautious sip of coffee, feeling the heat on her tongue and down her throat as she swallowed. In a minute, she would do her best to describe Charlie's playground to this young man and enlist his aid. In just a minute. But first...

"Tell me," she said, meeting his smile with a genuine one of her own, "have you ever heard of Monkeys Do?"

CHAPTER SIX

November 22

Dear Charlie:

Okay, you were right. Talking to people about the playground project has gotten easier (not easy, but at least easier) with practice. I've visited every business within a four-block radius of the site and about half of them have agreed to get involved. So far, Austin Blade is my star recruit. He claims that handling the project's financial records on his computer is duck soup compared to keeping the books for the health club. I can hardly wait for you to meet him.

We've printed up a flier, which has attracted a new crop of volunteers, and I'm having lunch on Wednesday with one of them. Believe me, at this point I don't say no to anybody.

Eleanor is delighted that you're joining us on Thanksgiving Day, and she's arranged for us to use the school's multipurpose room on Wednesday evening for your presentation. With any luck, the turnout will be respectable. I'll have a lot to show you, and even more to tell.

Until next week,
Joy

STRETCHED OUT on the couch in his den, Charlie re-read the letter, glad that the short work week was behind him. In the morning, free of the demands of the office, he would drive to Sacramento to confer with Joy before the evening's public meeting.

He rotated his head slowly in an effort to ease the knots of tension in his neck as he considered her closing words. *I'll have a lot to show you,* she had written, *and even more to tell.* He had no doubt that her progress on the project had been substantial, but that was only a part of the story. Her letter showed that she, herself, was progressing, as the passage of time and her involvement with the playground combined to distance her from the shock of her father's death.

Charlie smiled pensively, remembering his last visit to Sacramento. Joy had been showing signs of recovery even then—faint stirrings of confidence and vitality, like the first green shoots of spring after a harsh winter. He'd been able to read it in the tilt of her head, the lilt in her voice, the way she walked.

Yes, indeed, the way she walked. How many fruit-less minutes of reverie had he spent since that last visit, reliving the sight of her long-limbed stride? It reminded him of an old line about Katharine Hepburn: Not much meat on her bones, but what there was was choice.

There would be plenty of business matters vying for his attention when he reached Sacramento. Nevertheless, he looked forward most of all to assessing the changes he might find in Joy. Sooner or later she would lift her nose from the grindstone long enough to notice who was working so closely beside her. And when she did...

The telephone rang.

Charlie jumped for it eagerly, then caught himself. What was he hoping for? The odds of it being Joy so soon after her letter were slim, and a call from Shelley was almost as unlikely. Although their last talk had been a good one, she'd told him not to expect to hear from her again until Monday night, after the holiday weekend. Anything sooner would probably be a sign of trouble.

Schooling his expectations, Charlie lifted the receiver. "Hello?"

"Clear your calendar for tomorrow afternoon," a harsh voice said without preamble.

"Matthew?" It took a conscious effort for Charlie to switch mental gears. "Is that you? What's wrong?"

"Alan Winston's ready to give us a green light on that new office complex he's been planning. I want you to sit in on the meeting."

"Why? You don't need me." Charlie squinted at his watch: eleven forty-five. "It's late. Where are you calling from?"

"Where do you suppose? The office."

"The office? But you weren't there when I left, and that was three hours ago. I thought you'd gone home."

"I was at dinner with Winston. I came back here afterward to finish up some correspondence."

"At this hour? Don't you think you should call it a night?"

"It isn't as though I have anything to go home to."

"And whose fault is that?" Charlie asked, goaded by the petulance in Matthew's voice.

"Apparently you think it's mine," came the frosty reply. "Well, believe whatever you need to believe, as long as you don't let it interfere with getting down to business. I've organized a two o'clock meeting with Alan Winston for tomorrow so that we can go over his requirements for—"

The conversation was getting out of hand. "Didn't you read my memo?" Charlie interrupted. "I won't be in the office tomorrow. I have another commitment."

"With a client?"

Charlie hesitated. If he said yes, Matthew was bound to ask *which* client, and to expect the time to show up on the week's billing ledger. Feeling trapped in the web of lies he had begun to spin, Charlie said, "No. Personal."

"Then cancel. You're already taking Thursday off."

"For God's sake, Matthew, it's Thanksgiving."

"Even so, you don't need tomorrow off as well. This meeting is important."

"So are my plans."

"Perhaps I haven't made myself sufficiently clear," Matthew said, his words insultingly slow and measured. "Alan Winston expects to sit down tomorrow to talk with the full partnership of this office. One way or the other, Charles, that's precisely what is going to happen."

Don't do this, Matthew, Charlie thought bleakly. *You've got no right. Don't turn this into a showdown. . . .*

"The number of chairs at the conference table is up to you. But be warned, Charles—if you decide not to attend, I will take that as a clear statement of intent."

"Take it however you like," Charlie said flatly. "I won't be there. And frankly, I've about had it with your holier-than-thou attitude. I'm not yours to order around. A little common courtesy would be appreciated."

"Then you should make more of an effort to earn it. I'm tired of making allowances for you on the basis of our family relationship."

"Allowances?" Charlie felt fury rising in his veins like lava. "Since when haven't I pulled my own weight?"

"This is a business," Matthew said, avoiding a direct answer. "I intend to run it as a business. If you aren't prepared to be a productive part of the organization, then it's hard to imagine what legitimate place there could be for you here."

"Then let's call it quits. Right now."

"Don't be reactionary, Charles."

"Why not? Are you afraid redesigning the letter-head will be too expensive?"

"I need your help, not your flippancy."

"I didn't think you needed anything, least of all from me."

"I need you at that meeting!"

Charlie opened his mouth to repeat his refusal.

"Please," Matthew said unsteadily. "This is important to me."

It was his tone as much as the words that brought Charlie up short. The pompous belligerence seemed to have drained away between one moment and the next, leaving a fragile husk behind.

Reluctantly, Charlie reconsidered.

The playground meeting in Sacramento wasn't scheduled to begin until seven in the evening. He supposed the earth would go on spinning if he put in the morning at the office. He could feasibly sit in on the meeting with Matthew after lunch, and still reach the elementary school with time to spare.

He could do it. He just didn't want to.

It was sobering to realize how much he had counted on spending the afternoon with Joy Porter, but he would still see her at the meeting, and the next day at Eleanor's for Thanksgiving dinner. He knew that eventually—soon—he and Matthew were destined to clash, but he wasn't sure if this was really the right time and place.

"This is damned short notice," Charlie said, struggling to subdue his anger and achieve a civil tone. "But if you really think Winston's ready to get off the dime and you want me at the meeting, I'll do my best to be there. Just do me a favor in return—set aside at least an hour on Friday morning for the two of us to sit down and talk. You and I need to get some things settled, once and for all."

"The Winston meeting will start at two o'clock sharp," Matthew said, and broke the connection.

Not sure whether to laugh or curse, Charlie hung up.

What did you expect? he asked himself as he rose wearily from the couch. *A gracious thank you?* Not from Matthew, he thought. Not these days. If it was gratitude he wanted, he'd just have to wait until he got to Sacramento.

He was honest enough to admit, as he turned out the lights and headed for bed, that gratitude was the least of what he had begun to want from Joy.

ENTERING THE RESTAURANT on Wednesday morning at precisely eleven o'clock, Joy closed her wet umbrella and scanned the sparse prelunch crowd.

"Just look for a bright blue coat," Sheila Taylor had instructed during their phone conversation. It hadn't sounded like much to go on, but Joy's gaze was caught almost immediately by a vinyl raincoat of vibrant turquoise, worn by a tall blond woman. Approaching the woman, Joy cleared her throat. "Excuse me . . . Ms. Taylor? I'm Joy Porter."

The fair-haired stranger turned to face her, a nervous smile tugging at her mouth. "Please, call me Sheila. You're right on time. I think they have a table ready. Shall we sit down so we can talk?"

"Sure," Joy said. "That would be fine." Following her to a booth by the front window, she was tantalized by the sensation that there was something familiar about Sheila Taylor. They had never met before, Joy was almost certain of it. And yet . . .

"So," she said to Sheila when the waitress had taken their orders, "where did you hear about our project?"

"From . . . a friend of mine. The project sounded interesting, so I gave you a call." Her busy fingers reduced a paper napkin to confetti. "My days are free and I thought it might be fun to get involved."

"You don't work nine to five?"

"To tell you the truth, I've never had any outside job, but I've been thinking about getting one lately. The trouble is, nobody wants to hire you if you don't have an employment record. I thought maybe if I do volunteer work for you for a while and you like my work, you could give me a letter of reference."

"I'm not sure that a letter of reference from me would do you much good."

"It would be better than a blank résumé. Look, I'm not asking for charity. I can handle phones and I know how to type and file—I used to help out in my husband's office, years ago, when he was first getting started. What do you think?"

"Honestly?" Joy asked in surprise, embarrassed at being asked to pass judgment on this woman's acceptability as a volunteer.

"Honestly," Sheila said, her voice heavy with apprehension.

Joy smiled. "I think you sound like a gift from heaven. What's the catch?"

"No catch, except for wanting a reference if I do okay."

"When would you be free to start?"

"This afternoon, if you have something that needs doing."

"Well, sure, but..." She hesitated as the waitress returned, bearing a pot of hot tea. "How involved do you want to get?"

"Very," Sheila said intensely.

Joy shifted in her chair. "Great, but could we pin it down a little? How many days a week did you have in mind? How many hours a day? Don't get me wrong— I'll be grateful for whatever time you can spare. Even an hour helps. But I don't want to set you to work on some long-term project if—"

"I could come on weekday mornings, say from nine until lunchtime. How would that be? Would you have enough work for an arrangement like that? I'd be happy to do whatever needs doing."

"But what about..." Joy began, then hesitated with the words "your family" burning on her tongue. The sense of déjà vu had suddenly intensified and her memory jolted into focus.

She *had* seen Sheila's face before...or, rather, a picture of it. The pretty face had been smiling then, not as thin, less strained, framed by artful blond curls above the neckline of a beautiful dress in holiday red.

Now, in her gauntness, the curve of her jawline and cheekbone was uncannily like that of another face Joy had recently studied with guilty pleasure.

"Tinker, tailor, soldier, sailor," ran the old counting rhyme.

Shelley Tinker. "Sheila Taylor."

She wore her hair straight and more closely-cropped than it had been in the photograph, but there was no doubt in Joy's mind that the woman sitting across the table from her was Charlie's Shelley. The sister who had run away. The mother of the little girl who had died.

You and I are going to get this playground built, Charlie had insisted. *For Penny and your dad. People will help, you'll see.*

Not even Charlie could have foreseen assistance from this unexpected source.

Across the table, Sheila was saying earnestly, "What you're planning to do is important to me. I want to be a part of it. I can help— I know I can. Give me a week and I'll show you."

Joy groped for a response. Where did her loyalties properly lie? Charlie was worried to distraction about his sister's well-being; Joy knew that as surely as she knew her own name. How, then, could she justify letting the deception continue? Wasn't it her duty to call him up and inform him of his sister's whereabouts?

But Charlie said he had grown up in Sacramento, and the same was probably true of his sister. That meant that she had chosen to hide out in familiar territory, even if she had isolated herself from the support of her family and friends. If Joy told Charlie where his sister was and he sought her out, she might feel compelled to flee again, this time to some less-familiar sanctuary.

Joy was convinced that Shelley's well-being was at the root of Charlie's concern. That certainty was the key Joy needed to make her decision. If she could maintain contact with Shelley, she would be able to see from day to day how Shelley was faring. The price Joy would pay was shouldering the burden of responsibility that came from making decisions about other people's lives, and she was not, by nature, a presumptuous person. Was she willing to intentionally deceive both Shelley and Charlie in the name of the greater good she perceived?

"Well?" her companion asked, in a voice stretched thin by tension. "Do I get a chance to show you what I can do?"

I'll take good care of her, Charlie, Joy thought, and said aloud, "Yes. I'd like that very much. Welcome to the team."

CHARLIE SHIFTED in his chair, trying not to fidget. The afternoon meeting had dragged into early evening and still Alan Winston and Matthew were dickering. Nothing had been decided, nothing resolved. If he didn't head out soon, he'd be late arriving in Sacramento to start the playground meeting. . . .

"That's a fine idea," Matthew said, and tidied the papers on the conference table into a folder. "Any suggestions, Charles?"

Like a schoolboy caught daydreaming in class, Charlie gathered his straying thoughts. "Not off the top of my head," he equivocated guiltily, wondering what crucial turn in the negotiations he had missed. "How about you, Matthew?"

"Well, that would depend. What do you have a taste for, Alan? Japanese? Italian? Or, if you prefer, I know a place that serves a steak you won't soon forget."

Charlie barely managed to suppress a groan. Dinner. After three hours of guarded debate, all they could agree on was taking a break for dinner. With sudden clarity, he realized that Alan Winston was no more ready to cut a deal than he had ever been. The Alan Winstons of the world lived for power, thriving as much on a deal withheld as on a deal struck.

Charlie suspected that, on some instinctive level, Matthew understood Alan Winston perfectly well. He simply wasn't prepared to admit it, to himself or anybody else.

But why? It didn't make any sense. Why would Matthew put himself in the path of such aggravation when they already had more work than they could handle? Why would he insist on Charlie's presence if he suspected that no agreement would be reached?

Maybe for the same reasons that motivated Alan Winston—power and the ability to control the actions of others.

Or maybe, perversely, Matthew was looking for a way to fail.

Give it up, Freud. You don't understand what makes Matthew tick. Maybe you never did.

The others had risen to their feet and were watching him. Alan Winston's expression was impatient, Matthew's annoyed.

"Don't let me hold you up," Charlie said, pushing back his own chair on the thick carpeting. "I won't be joining you. I have a meeting to get to."

Matthew's face darkened with unhealthy color. "Could you excuse us for a moment, Alan? We'll catch up with you in the lobby."

"All right," Alan Winston agreed, making an elaborate show of consulting his watch. "But don't be long."

As the door closed behind him, Matthew turned on Charlie. "Don't you *ever* embarrass me in front of a client like that again."

"Like what? I just stated a fact. I won't be joining the two of you for dinner."

Matthew shook his head in angry dismissal of the words. "Get your raincoat," he ordered. "And for God's sake, pay better attention at dinner than you have so far. A man like Winston notices every time your mind wanders, don't kid yourself that he doesn't."

"If I've been such a liability, then you should be relieved that I'm not coming along."

"Oh, you're coming," Matthew said with infuriating assurance. "If you want to go on working here, you're coming."

There were limits to what he could tolerate, for Shelley's sake or Matthew's or anyone else's. Choking on cold fury, Charlie said, "Forget it. I'm your partner, not the hired help."

"That, like everything else in life, is subject to change."

"Then consider it changed." As he spoke the words, his anger changed to relief, as if he had finally earned a reprieve from some long-endured punishment. "Consider it changed," he repeated firmly, "because I'm out of here."

He expected to see anger on Matthew's face, or perhaps smug satisfaction. What he saw instead was a flash of panic.

But then his brother-in-law's face hardened at his words. "Fine. I'll inform the attorney and the accountant."

There didn't seem to be anything left to say. In silence, Charlie left the conference room and walked down the hallway to his office. His trench coat lay slung across the colorful back of the giraffe that doubled as his coat rack. Drained, Charlie rested his cheek against the sleek ceramic neck, using its coolness to ease the hectic flush heating his skin.

He was free. Whatever unpleasantness had gone before, surely that was the important thing to remember. He was free to leave tonight for the meeting in Sacramento. Free, in the weeks and months ahead, to oversee the building of the playground there and as many others, elsewhere, as he might choose to undertake. Free at last to make his own decisions and fashion his own future, free of the dragging anchor of Matthew's foul moods and unfair treatment.

He should be elated. Why, then, did he have the feeling that he had just been manipulated into doing something terribly, dangerously wrong?

WHEN ELEANOR first suggested holding the playground's public meeting in the school's multipurpose room, Joy had hesitated before accepting, afraid that the big room would prove an embarrassment if the turnout was sparse. But now, standing beside Austin Blade while his brother Garrett and Nathaniel Stone set up additional rows of folding chairs to accommodate the overflow crowd, it was an embarrassment she would have welcomed.

"Who *are* all these people?" she asked in stricken astonishment."

"Friends," Austin answered promptly, and smiled up at her. "Friends of the project. Isn't it great?"

"Wonderful," she said. But it didn't feel wonderful; it felt appalling to be faced by such a mob of new faces.

She turned nervously to watch the door, searching for Charlie. What would she do if he was late? Dear heaven, what would she do if he didn't come at all?

"Are you okay?" Austin asked solicitously.

"I'm fine," she said, refusing to admit to the flutters in her stomach. At least, knowing how tense the evening might become, she had had the good sense to skip dinner. "But I'll be a lot finer when Mr. Comfort gets here."

Lisa arrived at their side, smoothing her rain-damp hair. "No sign of a red Miata," she said apologetically. "I checked the front curb and the parking lot. But things are filling up fast. He might have decided to park down the street."

Austin craned his head to peer up at the big clock mounted on the wall. "Just about seven. Gee, Joy, maybe he changed his mind about coming," he said with apparent concern, then grinned. "Gotcha. You should have seen the look on your face."

"It isn't funny," Joy scolded. "He *has* to come. Tonight is my emancipation, the night the project gets transferred to more capable hands. Before I leave here tonight, I intend to be blissfully unemployed."

"Except for monkey-sitting, you mean."

"That doesn't count."

"And checking the galleys of your dad's book," Lisa added. "And acting as executrix for his estate."

"Well, yes, but—"

Austin laughed. "Just your basic unemployed, overworked jack-of-all-trades. Sure. No sweat. I get it now."

"Stop it, you two. The point is, I know how to do those other things. But I don't have the first notion about how to get this playground built."

"Oh, really? All these people just wandered in to get out of the rain?"

"Austin!"

"Okay, relax. He's coming, I guarantee it. But the storm probably slowed traffic down, and we don't want to make a bad first impression. Maybe you should introduce yourself and welcome everybody. By then, he's bound to be here."

Joy felt suddenly hollow, as if she'd driven too fast over a bump in the road. "And what if he isn't?"

Austin grinned. "Well, they're a captive audience," he said as Garrett returned to take up his usual protective stance behind his brother's wheelchair. "Want me to try out my new routine on them?"

Joy eyed him uncertainly. "Routine?"

"Jokes. I'm a pretty fair comedian. Really."

Garrett rolled his eyes. "Don't encourage him, Joy. He's a natural-born ham."

"That's one man's opinion," Austin said archly. "I prefer to think of myself as a silver-tongued raconteur of irrepressible wit."

"Like I said, a natural-born ham."

They continued their teasing with the easy camaraderie of brother against brother, but Joy scarcely heard them. She was too uncomfortably aware that

Austin was right; it was her responsibility to start the meeting, in Charlie's continued absence.

These people are all on your side, she told herself with as much conviction as she could muster. *They've come here on a wet, windy night when they could just as well have stayed home. You've already met some of them, or at least talked to them on the telephone. They're here because you invited them. You can't just leave them hanging. At least tell them how glad you are that they came. Explain that Charlie's been delayed. It's only fair. It's only polite.*

She might just as well have tried to convince the sun not to set. Her feet refused to budge. The air she breathed seemed to wedge in her throat. She was stiflingly hot in the overcrowded room, and yet her fingertips, when she scratched her itching neck, were icy. All logical arguments aside, she could no more walk to the front of the room and address the several hundred people sitting there than she could sprout feathers and fly. Austin's jokes, however bad they might be, would accomplish more than—

"Seven on the nose," Charlie said from behind her. "You didn't think I'd miss the party, did you?"

She whirled to face him. "Oh, Charlie, you're here! I've never been so happy to see anybody in my whole life!"

"That's quite a welcome." He closed his hand around hers, widening his eyes in a show of surprise when he felt her chilly flesh. But he made no comment, saying instead, "I remember Lisa, of course...and these must be the infamous Blade brothers. I've been looking forward to meeting you two."

Something was wrong with him. Even through her overwhelming relief, Joy could see the tension revealed in his overbright eyes and overwide smile. Like a generator building toward overload, there was an almost discernible hum about Charlie, an aura of manic energy that disturbed her.

If the others sensed it, they gave no sign. Charlie released his hold on her long enough to shake Garrett's hand and then retwined his fingers through hers. "Well, if you gentlemen will excuse us," he said, "it's time to get the ball rolling." Raising his voice to a genial shout, he called out to the room at large, "Good evening! I'm glad you all could come."

The crowd fell gradually silent as more and more heads turned toward him.

It was like standing under the merciless beam of a searchlight. "What are you doing?" Joy demanded, trying in vain to withdraw her hand from his. "Let go. I'll wait for you back here. I promised that I'd sit with—"

Ignoring her, Charlie again addressed the crowd. "We have a lot to do tonight! Are you ready to start?"

A ragged chorus of voices replied.

"Come on," he challenged them, "you can do better than that. Are you ready to start?"

"Yes!" the crowd replied with astonishing volume.

"Great!" Charlie said, and started up the central aisle between the rows of folding chairs, with Joy trailing helplessly in his wake, convinced that she had stumbled into a nightmare.

STANDING THERE, with a roomful of eager eyes focused on him, Charlie felt a familiar thrill shoot through him. He really loved beginnings.

"Hi. Welcome. I'm Charlie Comfort, and I hope you folks are as impressed as I am by the size of tonight's turnout. We're off to a flying start!"

A spate of self-congratulatory applause rippled through the crowd.

"Some of you," Charlie continued, "came here tonight because you've heard a rumor about the playground we're going to build, and you want to hear more. Some of you came because you've already heard more and you're ready to help. Most of you don't know each other yet, and almost none of you know me. But I can tell you two things, right now, about each and every person in this room: you care about the needs of kids, and you know that involvement keeps a community strong."

As he spoke, he savored the feeling of Joy's fingers slowly warming in his. Seated beside him on the shallow platform that served as their stage, she was like his talisman. Touching her helped him hold at bay the distracting knowledge that Tinker & Comfort no longer existed, and the dark memory of Matthew's bitter words.

"Everybody here has at least one skill we'll need if we're going to get this playground built. And this is going to be a great opportunity for learning new skills. Think big and dream wild. We're going to break a lot of stereotypes in the next few months."

The speech he was delivering was one he could have given in his sleep. Through trial and error, he had long since worked out the blend of information and cheerleading needed to fuel the enthusiasm of an opening-night crowd. For now, he was equal parts entertainer and instructor, intent on convincing as many volunteers as possible to formalize their commitment to the project. Later, the work would generate its own enthusiasm as they came to share his vision, turning them into solid converts who would, in turn, recruit others. But someone had to dream the dream, first. For now, the dream—and the duty and pleasure of communicating it—was his.

"Some of what we'll need is glamorous stuff. You may see yourself on television or in the newspaper, shaking hands with the mayor. On the other hand, most of what we'll be doing is a lot less visible. Somebody's going to be asked to organize the care and feeding of two thousand ravenous volunteers during construction weekend. Somebody else is going to figure out where to store six-dozen old tires until we're ready to use them. It's all going to be part of the puzzle."

The group was a good one. He could feel the tight focus of their attention and the growing intensity of their interest as he moved beyond generalities and described the ways in which each of them could play a part in stage two of the project. When he asked for volunteers to head up the various groups, he had at least one volunteer for each vacancy. In cases where more than one hand went up, he divided the duties between them or, if that wasn't possible, appointed assistants.

It was exhilarating, as if the energy of the crowd were his to tap into at will. This was one of his favorite moments, when mildly interested bystanders were transformed into the backbone of a new project. The men and women in the audience were looking up at him as if he were the font of all wisdom and information, little realizing that he was just a technician; they were the playground-to-be's lifeblood.

The moment was so heady that it seemed mean not to share it. As soon as he had distributed the assignments and announced a rough timetable for stage two, he said, "In a minute, I'm going to have you split into the groups we've discussed so that everybody has a chance to sign up for something that interests them. But first I want you to hear a little about what prompted this project in the first place, and introduce you to the woman responsible for it. Ladies and gentlemen, may I present your stage two project coordinator, Joy Porter."

"No, Charlie," she whispered urgently. "I can't!"

The crowd was applauding warmly. He gave her hand an encouraging tug, but she made no move to rise, continuing her muted protests.

It wasn't fair for him to hog all the glory when she had done so much of the work. She deserved some recognition. "Don't be modest," he insisted, pulling her to her feet. "Just say a few words to them."

She stood motionless, staring out at the crowd.

"Go ahead," Charlie encouraged.

Her lips moved soundlessly, and Charlie realized that her hand had grown icy to the touch again.

"Joy?" he queried with dawning concern.

In response, her knees began to buckle and she took a staggering step to the side.

He'd never actually seen anyone faint, but this had all the earmarks. Heart pounding, Charlie threw his arms around Joy, steadying her protectively against his chest. "Easy does it. Let's get you flat."

"No!" Her hands fisted in his shirtfront. "Just help me sit down."

She seemed to weigh nothing as she leaned on him. Supporting her every inch of the way, he guided Joy into her seat. The room was buzzing, and people were surging toward the platform. Ignoring them, Charlie pressed Joy's head toward her lap.

"I'm all right now." She resisted his touch. "I just got overheated and overexcited."

Eleanor appeared, kneeling beside Joy with surprising agility. "And when did you last eat?" she demanded.

"Lunch," came the muffled reply. "Charlie, let me *up.*"

Undecided, he looked down at Eleanor, who nodded and said, "As long as she's sitting, she'll probably do well enough."

Reluctantly, Charlie lifted his hand from the smooth skin at Joy's nape.

As soon as he allowed her to straighten, she entreated, "Please, can't we go on with the meeting?" He saw the haunted glance she cast at the milling groups of concerned volunteers hovering just beyond the edge of the platform. "You said you were going to break them into groups. Please..."

In her place, he guessed he wouldn't have wanted a bunch of strangers staring at him, either. But it wasn't easy to put his anxiety aside and agree to forge ahead with the evening's work, not while he could still remember so clearly how insubstantial she had felt in his arms.

The real work of the evening was still waiting to be accomplished, however. And it was what Joy wanted. Any attempt to reschedule the remainder of the meeting would be a nightmare task.

"Okay, so be it," Charlie said, and turned away from Joy's look of gratitude to try redirecting the attention of a roomful of agitated people.

CHAPTER SEVEN

CHARLIE SLEPT THAT NIGHT in a large motel on the edge of town, grateful for the seclusion it provided. Was this the sort of lonely peace that Shelley had found, he wondered, wherever her travels had ended? For better or worse, in this generic room there was no one to answer to but himself: no troubled sister, no embittered brother-in-law, no trusting client....

Joy Porter is a lot more to you than just a client.

Charlie sighed. Yes, Joy was more than a client to him, but she was still far less than a lover, despite the strong attraction he felt toward her. He didn't know whether she would be flattered or appalled if she knew how seriously he had begun to think about her.

The evening's debacle had been painful proof of how little he understood her wants and needs. He'd been absolutely sure he knew best, sharing the limelight with her "for her own good." Some good. He'd made her so upset she nearly passed out. *What do you do for an encore, Comfort? Shoot her out of a cannon?*

The carping inner voice followed him into sleep, coloring his dreams with dark distortions of the evening's events. Twice he woke sweating in the unfamiliar room and had to force himself to close his eyes again.

When he woke a third time, he decided to shave and shower and dress, thinking that, by then, he might be ready to buy a morning paper and face breakfast at the all-night coffee shop next to the motel. Once he'd eaten, he could return to pack and check out. From there, if it was still unreasonably early, he would content himself with parking across the street from 3469 Arelyn Drive.

"You're turning into a pretty pitiful case," he told himself as he put his plan in motion. But he knew of no other way to set his worries to rest and satisfy the growing need he felt to be near her.

TO CHARLIE'S SURPRISE, lights were already burning at Joy's house when he drove up a little before six a.m. Worried that it might be a sign of trouble, he parked at the curb and sprinted up the front walk.

Joy opened the door with the security chain still fastened. "Charlie? What on earth are you doing here so early?"

It was, he thought, a very good question. "I wanted to be sure you were feeling okay this morning," he said simply, unwilling to admit to the dreams that had driven him from his bed. "You're up pretty early yourself, aren't you?"

"I have pies to bake, to take to Eleanor's."

"Oh. Well, in that case, I guess I'd better let you get to it." He retreated a step, reluctantly.

"Do you have to go?"

Charlie hesitated in the narrow slice of light that spilled through the open doorway. "Well, no, but..."

She smiled. "I could use the company. And the help. How are you at paring apples?"

"Probably lousy, but I'm willing to give it a shot if you're willing to risk employing an amateur apple cutter."

"Believe me, the job isn't that complicated. You'll do fine. Hold on a second...." She closed the door and unfastened the chain. "Come in and make yourself comfortable."

He started forward, then hesitated at the threshold when he saw that she was still in her robe. It had the look of a long-time favorite—yards of smoky blue chenille, belted at the waist and falling in warm folds to the floor. Looking at it, he knew how soft its aged nap would feel beneath his fingertips, just as he knew how soft the triangle of skin exposed at the base of Joy's throat would be....

"There's coffee in the kitchen," she was saying. "If you don't mind helping yourself, I'll go upstairs and get dressed."

Charlie fumbled for words. "I could wait out here until—"

"No need," she said with guileless trust, holding the door open wide. "Come on in. I'll only be a minute."

And so he entered, in the bittersweet knowledge that her innocence was all the protection she required against the guilty hunger within him.

BY SIX-FIFTEEN, Charlie had a cup of coffee in his hand and a large blue apron tied around his waist. By seven, the apple pie was in the oven, the kitchen had begun to smell warmly of cinnamon and spices, and Charlie was becoming thoroughly frustrated by the difficulties of flirting with a woman who was preoccupied with culinary pursuits.

While the first pie baked, Joy assembled fillings of pumpkin and mincemeat, giving him small bits of busywork to perform as she progressed. "I haven't seen Jezebel yet this morning," he commented as he watched her set up a food processor on the counter. "Is she still asleep?"

"Hardly. Jezzie's the original early riser. You haven't seen her because she's in her cage, which is exactly where I intend to leave her until these pies are an accomplished fact."

Her stern tone was so uncharacteristic that Charlie had to smile. "Do I detect an anecdote?"

"You certainly do. Last August, I fixed a chocolate cream pie for Dad's birthday and made the mistake of leaving it on the counter while I took a piece in to him. By the time I got back...well, let's just say Jezzie had disgraced herself."

"She ate it?"

"Ate it. Wallowed in it. Painted the walls, the counters, the refrigerator door and a good part of the ceiling with it, not to mention the curtains."

Charlie eyed the crisp white curtains that adorned the kitchen windows and tried to imagine them covered with chocolate paw prints.

"Go ahead and laugh," Joy invited indignantly. "You aren't the one who had to clean it all up."

"What did you do to her?"

"What *could* I do, except tell her she was a bad girl and give her a bath? It was as much my fault as hers. She knew she was doing something she shouldn't, but it never would have happened if I hadn't left the pie uncovered on the counter. I made the mistake of thinking she'd outgrown that kind of deviltry. But I've learned my lesson. When I get ready to bake these days, the first essential step is preheating the oven, and the second essential step is making sure that a certain inquisitive little monkey is securely under wraps."

"I don't think it was really deviltry. I suspect she just wanted a little of your attention," Charlie observed. When Joy didn't reply, he prodded, "I can certainly sympathize. Maybe I should start throwing ingredients around. Or would you lock me in a cage, too?"

"Have I been ignoring you?" Joy asked, looking troubled.

"Shamefully," he replied, and smiled. "But you could make it up to me."

Her eyes widened warily. "Somehow I get the feeling that I'd better not ask how."

He took a step closer. "Really, Ms. Porter? Whatever gave you that idea?"

"Just a hunch."

"And do you always follow your hunches?" he asked softly.

"Hardly ever," she confessed, and fled to the cupboard. "We have a lot to do if we're going to have these pies ready in time. I'd really appreciate it if you wouldn't distract me."

"Is that what I'm doing? Distracting you?"

She nodded.

"And you'd like me to stop?"

"Yes. Please." She lowered her eyes, and a blush stained her cheeks as she added, "For now."

"Coward," he accused, but he took pity on her and returned his attention, grudgingly, to measuring raisins.

"What did you think of Austin and Garrett Blade?" Joy asked, as if determined to steer their conversation back onto safer ground.

"I was surprised," he admitted. "Did you know he's a celebrity of sorts?"

"Austin?"

"Garrett. The name rang a vague sort of bell when I read your last letter, but I didn't put two and two together until I saw the size of him last night. He used to play pro football for the Rams . . . or maybe it was the Raiders. Made quite a big splash his first year or two, and then just sort of disappeared between one season and the next. An injury, I think. I don't remember, exactly. Anyway, that's him."

She shrugged and smiled. "I've never paid much attention to football. But I suppose it would make sense, his running a club like Good Sports. I've never heard Garrett or Austin mention anything about Garrett having a pro career, but maybe they just assume that everybody knows. Or that it really doesn't matter anymore, if he's retired."

Charlie handed her the raisins and said, with studied nonchalance, "In a sense, you could say that *I'm* retired now. Or at least redefining my career."

"What do you mean?"

"Matthew and I dissolved the partnership. It'll take a while to wade through the paperwork, but Tinker & Comfort no longer exists."

"Oh, Charlie, I'm sorry. Was it because of the playground?" she asked, sounding horrified by the possibility.

"No," he assured her. "It might have been, eventually, but we never got that far. Matthew and I have been on a collision course for a long time, and we met head-on yesterday. In a way, it's lucky timing, because I'll be free to pick up more of the slack for stage two. If necessary, I can spend part of each week up here, now that I won't have any regular office hours to keep.''

Joy's gaze was solemn. "I don't know what to say. I guess I should be relieved—and I am, really—but it must have been hard, breaking things off like that with your brother-in-law.''

"I don't suppose it would ever have been easy. Except for Shelley, Matthew and I didn't have anything but the office in common, anyway,'' he said, and felt a pang of conscience at his glib dismissal of more than a decade of involvement. In his role as brother-in-law and partner, Matthew had been a major force in Charlie's life. It was odd, trying to imagine what the future would be like without him.

It was a relief to share the bleak news with someone. No, not just with someone, he corrected himself, with Joy. He wanted to confide in her. He wanted her to get to know him, so that she could see him not just as a hired architect but as an individual. As a man.

"Could you look in that drawer for me?" Joy asked, indicating the one in question with a nod. "I forgot the mace.''

"Mace?" Charlie repeated, jolted out of his reverie. Determined not to darken the morning with his sorrowful memories, he cowered theatrically behind his hands and said, "What do you want with Mace? Have I been that offensive?''

The sound that escaped from Joy was very nearly a giggle. "Not the kind you spray in someone's face,'' she corrected. "Or the kind you use for hitting someone over the head. Mace is also a spice.''

"I see. Well, I've learned something new this morning. And to think I was still recovering from finding out that mincemeat pies don't necessarily have meat in them."

"Well, proper ones *do* have meat, or at least suet. But this kind is quicker, and it still tastes wonderful. And," she said pointedly, "it will taste even more wonderful if you can find the mace for me."

To Charlie's relief, the easy banter continued between them all morning, as if the events of the night before had never happened. Instead of the wounded reproach he had braced himself to withstand, there was a new openness in Joy's manner. It was as if now that he'd seen her at her worst, she was free to relax.

If he had felt attracted to her before, he was all the more tantalized by the glimpses this morning had provided of the woman beneath a camouflage of stress and unhappiness. By the time the two of them were due to leave for Eleanor's, Charlie found the thought of sharing Joy with a roomful of people daunting. However pleasant those other people might be, they weren't the reason he had come to Sacramento. He wanted to spend the time alone with Joy.

He wanted a lot of things he couldn't have.

Shortly before eleven, she excused herself and vanished upstairs for a second time, returning shortly in a dress the same tawny shade of brown as the apple pie she had baked. Her dark hair was twisted into a complicated swirl on the back of her head, and she wore a long gold chain around her neck.

"You look...elegant," Charlie said, stunned.

Joy shrugged the compliment aside with a self-conscious smile. "Eleanor calls this my grown-up dress."

"She's absolutely right."

"No, she means I wear it when I'm playing grown-up. She claims I drag it out for every state occasion." Under the force of his continued scrutiny, Joy fingered the neckline as if it had suddenly grown too tight. "I'll probably get teased for wearing it today."

"Not by me. Why is it so hard for you to accept a compliment?"

"It's not."

"Okay, it's not." He took a step closer. "You're beautiful."

Joy grimaced. "You just aren't used to seeing me without a wet monkey wrapped around my neck."

"See?"

"Oh, come on, Charlie, it isn't a fair test when the compliment is a ridiculous overstatement. You weren't serious."

"I was. I am." He knew the dangers of rushing her, and he hadn't meant to let things go so far, but her persistence in selling herself short goaded him on. For any serious relationship to develop between them, they would have to be able to communicate honestly and openly with one another. How could he accomplish that when she undercut everything he said?

Even now, she was shaking her head. "I may clean up well enough, but I'm not beautiful. Never have been. Never will be."

Charlie walked toward her, finally stopping with his nose three inches from hers, giving her nowhere to look but into his eyes. "To me," he said, pronouncing each word with care, "you are beautiful. I'm not asking you to believe that you are. But I am asking you to believe me when I say that *I* believe you're beautiful. No jokes. No qualifiers. Beautiful. Got it?"

Wide-eyed, Joy nodded. Surprise had parted her lips and painted a flush across her cheekbones. Instinct and inclination clamored for him to cap his argument with a kiss, but intellect argued that he had already made one impetuous error during his visit. Was he really so sure that kissing her now wouldn't prove to be another of his "for her own good" mistakes?

Charlie turned aside, allowing the intensity of the moment to seep away. "Well then," he said, as conversationally as he could manage, "let's load up these pies and take them to Eleanor before she decides to start the meal without us."

CHAPTER EIGHT

BEAUTIFUL? He couldn't have been serious. And yet...

On the drive to Eleanor's, those incredulous thoughts circled through Joy's mind again and again, rocketing her from caution to elation and back again as she tried to make sense of what Charlie had said and why.

She supposed that he might not be above a well-intentioned effort to bolster her self-confidence. But he had sounded so calm, so sure of himself! *To me, you are beautiful. No jokes. No qualifiers. Beautiful. Got it?*

And she had nodded, despite the fact that she didn't get it at all.

She thought about what it might mean if he had actually been speaking the truth, at least as he perceived it. Would it complicate everything? Or might it be the start of something almost too wonderful to contemplate?

It was impossible to know... and yet she trusted Charlie. She believed in him. How, then, could she doubt his word, no matter how irrational it sounded?

"Got it all worked out now?" he asked genially as she pulled into Eleanor's driveway.

Joy cut the engine. "What do you mean?"

"Well, it's obvious you've been thinking hard, so I wondered—what's the verdict? Am I some sort of liar with an ulterior motive or are you going to deliver me to the nearest mental health clinic for observation?"

He was too clever. "Are those the only possible explanations?"

"No, but I was afraid they might be the only two you'd consider." He unfastened his seat belt. "Don't try to make it more mysterious than it is, Joy. I meant exactly what I said."

Before she could respond, Eleanor's front door opened and Nathaniel emerged. "Need a hand?" he called from the porch.

"No," Joy said, climbing out, "I think we've got everything under control."

But it wasn't true. It wasn't even close.

"SO YOU'LL BE COMING BACK next month to meet with the kids?" Lisa asked, holding out a gleaming bowl of cranberry relish.

Charlie took it from her, scanning his plate vainly in search of a square inch of vacant china on which to place a helping. "Yeah, that's where the real fun begins. I'll meet with kids from all the grades and decide on a theme to work from. Then we'll make a wish list of things to include." He settled for spooning the cranberries onto the edge of a slice of turkey, and set the bowl down beside Eleanor, who was deep in conversation with Joy. "After that, it'll be up to me to fit in as many of the kids' ideas as possible."

"It sounds like a tall order."

"No, it's a riot. The kids are a fountain of ideas. And as long as the playground's fun to use, with lots of variety, they're pretty forgiving about any suggestions that fall by the wayside.''

"You sound like the voice of experience," Nathaniel observed. "How many of these things have you masterminded?"

"Only seven, but I hope to boost that number soon." He nodded toward the cranberries. "Would you like me to pass those across to you? We seem to have hit a slight bottleneck."

Deep dimples appeared in Lisa's cheeks. "Eleanor must be giving Joy the good news."

"What news?"

Before Lisa could answer, Joy gave a happy cry and rose from her chair to throw her arms around Eleanor's plump shoulders.

"No need for such effusive thanks," Eleanor laughed, patting Joy's back. "I can't guarantee when you'll be needed, or how often, but I'm confident that you'll be a real addition to the staff. We've missed you."

"What staff?" Charlie asked Lisa in a stage whisper, disconcerted to find himself the only person in the room with no notion of what was being discussed.

"Joy applied to the school board as a substitute teacher, and Eleanor just told her that Dunnett Elementary has put in a request for her. From now on, whenever we need a substitute at Dunnett, Joy's name will be the first one called. She did a lot of subbing at Dunnett a couple of years ago when she first came back to help her dad, before he got so bad that he needed her right there at the house all of the time."

Shooting a look at Joy, who was talking excitedly with Eleanor, he asked quietly, "What exactly was wrong with Dr. Porter?"

Lisa looked unhappy. "No one thing," she murmured. "That's what made it hard. He had congestive heart failure, which got steadily worse over time, and rheumatoid arthritis. About a year ago he had a stroke, and then another one last month, much worse than the first one. He died a few days later."

"And she nursed him through all that herself?"

"Well, when she first moved back to Sacramento, it was more to help her dad with his book than to take care of him physically. It was really only during this past year that he needed a lot of—" Lisa broke off, smiling past him at Joy. "I was just telling Charlie how you helped with your dad's book. Have the publishers sent you the galleys yet?"

"I'm expecting them any day now."

"Have they given you a publication date?" Nathaniel asked.

"Early summer, the editor said. In June."

Charlie straightened in his chair, feeling like a hound who has just caught the first elusive scent of fresh game. "A book of your father's is coming out in June? A new book?"

Joy nodded.

"What's it called?"

"Well, Dad's title was *Play As Work: A Child's Perspective,* but the editor preferred *The Playground Connection.* It's a collection of essays on the whole learning-through-play school of thought."

Charlie tried to control the Cheshire-cat smile he could feel spreading across his face. "We could have the playground finished by the beginning of June, if we hustled," he observed.

"That's good," Joy said, but he could see that she hadn't gotten the point. Not yet.

Nathaniel Stone, however, caught the gist. "A tie-in?"

Charlie nodded. "Why not? It's a natural."

"But what would be the point?" Nathaniel asked. "No offense, but the interest in the book will already be high and the publisher wouldn't get much of a national push from linking it to this playground project, since it's just a local thing. And, really, the playground won't need—"

"*This* playground won't need," Charlie interrupted. "But what if we used it as the launch point for a national campaign?"

"Oh! That *would* make a difference. Of course, something like that might be a pretty good deal for you, too. No offense."

"None taken. I admit, I'd stand to gain a lot from a promotion like that, but it isn't a question of giving my own career a boost. You'd need a hundred playground designers, if you really tried to get the problem solved."

"Excuse my ignorance," Eleanor said, "but what problem?"

"Playground safety...but don't get me started. It isn't what my mother would have called 'dinnertime conversation.' Suffice it to say that a lot of kids are needlessly hurt or killed, every year, and I intend to do something about it."

"Laudable. And some high-profile publicity would certainly help your effort."

"Absolutely." He turned his attention eagerly back to Joy. "Do you think you could put me in touch with your father's publisher? If you mentioned me to the editor..."

"Of course. I'd be glad to. But I can't guarantee that they'll want to get involved."

"I'm not looking for guarantees, just opportunities, and this one sounds too good to pass up. Do you have a copy of the manuscript at home? I could read through it and try to find any natural overlaps between what your father had to say and the message I'll be working to put across. I'd like to do my homework before I approach the publishers. That is, if you don't feel it would compromise your position to let me see the manuscript."

"Not at all," Joy said. "I just don't want you to pin too many hopes on it. Like Nathaniel said, the publishers might not be interested. And even if they are, nobody can guarantee that the book will be a success."

Eleanor hooted derisively. "Not a success? What nonsense. Every last one of your father's books is still in print, some of them after thirty years or more. They're de rigueur reading for any self-respecting educator and for a great many parents, as well. Only Spock and Brazelton have enjoyed a bigger following. I hardly think you need concern yourself about the book's success, Joy."

Across the table, Nathaniel Stone was lifting his wineglass. "A toast," he proposed, "to successes in the year to come. To the new book, to Charlie's playground, to Joy's return to teaching...and to Lisa's do-it-yourself project."

Not understanding, Charlie looked at Lisa, who was blushing and looking pleased.

"Or do-it-ourselves project, I guess I should say," Nathaniel corrected with a self-satisfied grin.

"A baby? Really?!" Joy went to Lisa and enveloped her in a hug. "That's absolutely fantastic," she said, her voice choked with emotion. "I'm so happy for you. When?"

"The end of May. Believe me, the flapper costume I wore at your Halloween party was no random choice. I was absolutely sure you and Eleanor would catch on before we could make the big announcement today."

"Congratulations to both of you," Charlie said. "It looks like we're all going to have a busy winter."

"The very best kind," Eleanor concurred. "However, all of that work will take energy—especially Lisa's—so I suggest we settle down and finish eating."

With wholehearted enthusiasm, Charlie turned his attention to doing exactly that.

As AFTERNOON FADED into early evening, Nathaniel and Charlie claimed kitchen duty, leaving "the ladies" to recover from dessert in front of the fireplace. Feeling drained by the sustained conviviality of the day, Joy relaxed gratefully against the cushions of Eleanor's overstuffed sofa. "Thank you for having us all today. Dinner was delicious."

"My pleasure, dear. A holiday alone is no holiday at all. And your Mr. Comfort seemed to fit in very easily, all things considered."

"I think he enjoyed himself," Joy agreed, resisting the urge to stress that he wasn't "her" Mr. Comfort. Her putative relationship with Charlie wasn't something she felt ready to discuss.

After a relaxed silence, Eleanor said, "You know, I think I'd brush up on first-grade curriculum if I were you." She gestured toward Lisa, who was nodding drowsily in her chair. "Even under the best of circumstances, she may not be able to finish out the school year, and it's possible that she'll need to claim maternity leave earlier than she expects. As I see it, that could translate to a permanent sub position for you to finish out the school year with Lisa's class...assuming that you want it."

"Want it? Absolutely. Why wouldn't I?"

"Well, it would tie you down for a month or two, maybe more. And I wondered whether you might be wanting to move back to Boston, once the estate is settled."

Joy shook her head. "No. I'll admit, Boston was a good temporary solution when I moved there after graduation. I needed to put some distance between Dad and me, and it gave me a chance to explore who I was, on my own. Still, I stepped out of that life four years ago, and a lot of the people I knew there have moved on, too. Even if I did go back, it wouldn't be the same."

"I'm glad you realize it. But I remember how unhappy you were when you first came back here to take care of Jacob, and I was afraid we might be about to lose you again, now that you're free to make fresh choices."

"No," Joy said, "I don't intend to make any major decisions for a while. I'll just drift along." She laughed ruefully. "It isn't as though I won't have enough to keep me busy! Next summer, after the school year is over, will be plenty soon enough for any changes I decide to make. As things stand, I should have enough to tide me over comfortably for at least that long."

Eleanor smiled. "Then I'll definitely count on you to fill in for Lisa, when the time comes. And we'll see how many other assignments we can send your way in the meantime." Her smile deepened as Lisa began to snore delicately, nestled in the angle of the wing chair. "Poor dear, she really should be home in bed." A sympathetic yawn escaped her. "Oh, my. I think the day is catching up with me, too. Why don't you tell Nathaniel and Mr. Comfort to abandon their efforts? I'll do the rest in the morning."

"Nonsense. Charlie and I can finish." She stood up, ignoring Eleanor's protests. "I seem to remember you manning the cleanup crew at my house, after the Halloween party. The least you can do is let me return the favor."

"All right, but be sure to tell Nathaniel to keep out some turkey for everyone to take home, or I'll be eating it for a month."

In the kitchen, Joy found Charlie loading plates and bowls into the dishwasher, while Nathaniel worked at storing the leftovers.

"Hi, guys. Nathaniel, you'd better go take pity on Lisa. She's sound asleep out there."

"Yeah, she's been doing that a lot lately. Goes with the territory, or so I'm told. I'm about done here, anyway."

"Ah, perfect timing. Anyway, Eleanor says you're under strict orders to take a few pounds of that turkey off her hands."

"Absolutely. It'll save us from having to cook tomorrow night."

Charlie groaned. "Tomorrow night? Philistine! I don't think I'll be able to eat again for a week."

"Don't kid yourself," Nathaniel said, washing his hands at the sink. "We ate early. By midnight you'll be looking around for a drumstick to gnaw on. But you won't find one," he added, grinning wickedly. "I took them both."

"Fine by me. I'm a white-meat man myself." Charlie measured detergent into the dishwasher, closed it and dusted his palms together. "There. All done. Nathaniel and I make a pretty good team, don't you think?"

"Magnificent," Joy agreed. "From now on, you two can handle all the KP duty."

Nathaniel rolled his eyes. "Thanks, Comfort. Thanks a ton." He bent to kiss Joy's cheek. "Good night, kiddo. Lisa and I were relieved to see you looking so good today."

"Do me a favor—forget last night happened, okay? I'm fine. Save your worry for Lisa."

"Will do. Good night, Charlie. I'm glad you could come. Give us a call the next time you're in town."

"Oh, you'll be hearing from me. We have a lot of work to do between now and next June. When it comes to volunteers, I never forget a face. And thanks for the tip."

"My pleasure. Bye, all."

"What tip was that?" Joy asked Charlie as Nathaniel left.

"Funny you should ask." He fiddled with the dial on the dishwasher door until the machine began to roar obediently. "There. Great invention, dishwashers. Come on, let's thank our hostess and reclaim our coats. We don't have much time."

"Why? Where are we going?"

"It's a surprise. I thought it was a shame to let the evening end so early, so I asked Nathaniel for some suggestions on Sacramento nightlife and he came up with a good one. Are you game?"

It was tempting, but Joy felt a pang of conscience. "I really ought to go home to Jezzie...."

"Come with me for a while first. Then we'll *both* go back to your place and play with Jezebel. Please?"

Why do you want me to? she wanted to ask, but she lacked the nerve to do it. And the thought of spending the rest of the evening with Charlie was undeniably appealing. "All right," she said at last, "but not for long. My day started pretty early. So did yours, for that matter!"

"Fair enough. We'll go for a little while, and you can give me the high sign as soon as you want to go home. Let's go tell Eleanor good night."

Admitting defeat, Joy followed him out of the kitchen, unsure of what she had agreed to, but willing to follow Charlie's lead long enough to find out.

FOLLOWING NATHANIEL'S directions to the letter, Charlie soon found his way to the heart of Old Sacramento. When their destination was in sight, he pulled over and helped Joy out of the car. "Right this way," he invited.

She looked at the brightly lit storefronts and tourist attractions with surprise, but she asked no questions as he guided her down the boardwalk. Only when he stopped at the door to pay their admission did she say, "The Komedy Klub? *That's* where we're going?"

"Don't you want to?" Charlie asked in surprise. "Nathaniel spoke pretty highly of it. I thought it sounded like fun, but we don't have to go in, if you'd rather—"

"No, I'd like to. I've never been here before." She smiled. "Let's give it a try."

Inside, the house lights were low in deference to a stand-up comedian who was in midset. Blinking to adjust to the dimness, Charlie hesitated at the back of the room, looking for a vacant table.

"Over here," someone hissed. "Joy! Charlie!"

Startled, he turned and spotted Garrett and Austin Blade seated against the back wall of the club, with their table angled to allow room for Austin's wheelchair.

Compared to San Francisco, Sacramento was a small town, but the coincidence of running into the Blades was amazing enough for Charlie. Joy, however, seemed to take it in stride, immediately joining them at their table. Settling beside her, Charlie resigned himself to spending what was left of the evening as a foursome.

It turned out to be no hardship at all. The comedians were varied in style but consistently witty, and Austin Blade displayed an uncanny ability for topping their best lines, just loudly enough for his tablemates to hear. By the time an hour had passed, Joy's laughter was unrestrained, and Charlie's sides hurt. Only when a short intermission was announced did Joy look down at her watch and say, with every evidence of reluctance, "It's almost ten o'clock. I guess we'd better go."

Resisting temptation, he didn't try to talk her out of it. They said good-night to the Blades, who were staying for the final set of the evening, and made their way back to Charlie's car.

"That was fun," Joy admitted as they walked side by side. "It's been a wonderful day."

"That it has," Charlie agreed, wondering how she would react if he took her hand in his. He considered finding out. "I almost forgot to ask," he said, to cover his nervousness, "how did your new volunteer work out?"

Joy stopped short. "New volunteer?"

Charlie stopped, too, turning to face her. "The lady in your letter, remember? The one you were going to have lunch with yesterday."

"Oh." She began to walk again. "You mean Sheila. She worked out fine, actually." Her new pace was a quicker one. Charlie had to lengthen his stride to keep up with her.

"Did I meet her last night?"

"No, she wasn't there, but I think she's going to be a big help. Of course, I won't need her so badly, now that you're going to be more involved in the day-to-day details."

"May as well keep her on board. On these projects there's always plenty of work to go around."

"Oh, I'll be sure to keep in touch with her," Joy said as they reached the car.

It seemed to Charlie that he heard an undertone of tension in her voice. Unlocking her door, he held it open. "Are you worried about stage two? There's no reason to be. You've already done the hardest part of the groundwork. From here on out, you'll be working with people you know, just helping to direct what they do." When she was safely inside, he closed her door and went around to climb into the driver's seat.

"And it'll be even more fun, once I meet with the kids next month and the design starts to take shape."

She nodded and smiled, though she still seemed subdued. On the drive back to her house she was quiet, and Charlie wondered if he had said something to upset her. She'd been in high enough spirits when they left the Komedy Klub, he reasoned, and they'd engaged in nothing but idle chatter since then. Perhaps the long day was simply catching up with her. He could understand that; he, too, was tired, and the long drive back to San Francisco was looking less appealing by the minute.

When he pulled up in front of Joy's house, she said hastily, "You don't have to see me to the door."

"It's no trouble," he said, turning off the engine.

"No, don't bother, please. I mean, it isn't as if we'd been out on a date."

"No?"

"No!"

Charlie unfastened his seat belt, fighting laughter at the vehemence of her answer. "Would it have been so awful if we were?"

She froze. "Oh. No, of course not. I didn't mean to make it sound like that. I just—"

"We can decide in a minute whether it was a real date." Moving closer, he touched her cheek lightly. "Do you know what I'd like to do first?"

She shook her head, her eyes wide as she peered at him in the car's dim interior.

"I'd like to kiss you." He threaded his fingertips gently through the loose tendrils of hair at her left temple. "Okay?"

She nodded, and the jerky motion made her hair move beneath his fingers like silk. Slowly, giving her every chance to recoil, he lowered his mouth to hers in a slow, soft kiss.

He lingered with his lips pressed gently against hers for a long moment, maintaining the kiss without deepening it. Then, straightening, he unfastened her seat belt and said, "Would you like to try it again, now that you're free to flee?"

To his relief, she smiled. "Yes, please."

This time, reassured, he allowed the kiss to develop at its own pace. "In my book," Charlie said when they finally parted, "that makes this an official date. Do you have a problem with that?"

"No, Charlie."

"Good. And now I'm going to walk you to your door. Are you going to give me an argument about it?"

"No, Charlie."

"Even better."

When they reached the house, he waited while she unlocked her front door. Eyeing the soft glow of the porch light, he asked, "Will the 'decency league' rise up in force if I kiss you again here, where the neighbors can see?"

"No," Joy said, with a shy smile, "but you'll probably give old Mrs. Langston a thrill."

"Well, then, let's dedicate this one to Mrs. Langston."

It was the best yet, a kiss that carried them from warm affection to the first fiery boundaries of passion. Breaking from it, Charlie made a show of fanning his face. "Lady, you're dangerous. If I make it

back here next week, will you let me take you out
again, or are you going to try to pretend that none of
this happened?''

"None of what?" Joy asked ingenuously, then re-
lented. "I'd like it very much if you could come back
next week."

"Then count on it," Charlie said. "Under the circumstances, though, maybe I'd better take a rain
check on my promise to come inside tonight and play
with Jezebel, hmm?"

"Maybe so," Joy conceded.

"In that case, why don't you go inside and lock
your door, before Mrs. Langston calls the police?" He
kissed the end of her nose. "Sweet dreams."

"Sweet dreams," she echoed and, to Charlie's
mixed relief and rue, slipped inside before his gentle-
manly instincts could weaken.

The drive back to San Francisco passed in a cheerful haze, with reality intruding only as he neared the
freeway exit nearest to the offices of Tinker & Comfort. It struck him suddenly that the most valuable
thing he needed from the office wasn't in his desk at
all, but in Matthew's: the file containing more than a
dozen letters addressed to him by people interested in
having playgrounds built—more than a dozen potential clients for his fledgling solo career. A gold mine,
if only he could claim it.

Within minutes, he stood in the dark reception area,
flipping the light switch that would illuminate the
hallway. Filled with purpose, he strode down the corridor and turned the knob of Matthew's door.

The door opened a foot and stopped. Charlie gave
it another shove, but it stayed stubbornly immobile.

Reaching inside, he flipped the switch for the overhead light and poked his head through the gap to see what was obstructing the door.

What he found was Matthew, sprawled facedown on the floor, with one arm trapped beneath him and the other outflung.

CHAPTER NINE

THE FIRST THING Charlie noticed was the blood. The second was the almost overpowering smell of alcohol. The third, as he forced the door open far enough for him to slide inside, was the glitter of glass . . . from the broken globe of the desk lamp, from a shattered bottle of Johnnie Walker Red, from a splintered picture half-hidden beneath Matthew's body.

Holding hard against panic, Charlie knelt and pressed his fingers against his brother-in-law's neck, praying for a pulse. After an anxious minute, he found one, thin and thready beneath his touch. Bending low, he cupped his palm over Matthew's mouth and was relieved to feel a warm flutter of breath issuing from between the slack lips.

He didn't dare ignore the bleeding wrist a moment longer. Pushing back the scarlet-stained cuff of Matthew's shirt, he saw that the blood was welling from a pair of cuts, long and roughly parallel.

So. Not an accident.

Sick at heart, moving quickly, Charlie carefully tugged at Matthew's right arm, pulling it from beneath him, and found that wrist sliced open by a single, shallow cut.

Charlie draped his folded handkerchief over the double cuts on the left wrist and closed his hand around it, applying pressure. Then, with his free hand, he snagged the telephone from Matthew's desk and pulled it to the floor.

His finger shook as he punched out 911. "Hello? My name is Charlie Comfort. I need an ambulance at 903 Baxter, Suite 301. My brother-in-law is bleeding and unconscious...." His eyes focused suddenly on the photograph in the broken frame that lay beneath Matthew's limp form; it was an enlargement of the holiday portrait of Matthew, Penny and Michelle that Charlie carried in his wallet.

"Hurry," Charlie said, and swallowed against the knot of tears forming in his throat. "Please."

"YES, JEZZIE, I KNOW. You've been neglected disgracefully and you aren't going to let me forget it for an instant," Joy said through a yawn as she fumbled with a package of filters. "But I'm warning you right up front that I tossed and turned all night, so don't expect much from me until I've got a cup or two of coffee under my belt. If there was ever a morning when I needed a jump start—"

She was interrupted by the doorbell.

"Not *that* kind of a jump start," Joy groaned. "What did you do, Jezzie, hang out a sign that said Early Morning Visitors Welcome?" Still grumbling, she shut Jezebel into the kitchen and shuffled down the hallway toward the front door, pushing her hair out of her eyes as she went.

As far as she could recall, her night had been free of dreams, but she had still awakened half a dozen times before morning. Each time she woke, her brain had begun to buzz with memories and speculations. Charlie's kisses were still vividly imprinted on her mind, if not her lips, and the sweet gentleness of those kisses made it difficult to dismiss his actions as an empty, wolfish pass....

The doorbell rang again.

Have a heart, Joy thought. *It's barely six o'clock.* Flipping the switch on the porch light and making sure the security chain was on, she opened the door and peered out.

Charlie Comfort stood on her front porch, looking so lost and disheveled that her heart went out to him. *Déjà vu.*

"Can I come in?" he asked, looking not at all certain of her answer.

"Of course. Just a second." Closing the door, she fumbled quickly with the security chain, wondering what on earth could have befallen him in the few hours since he had last stood there, joking about Mrs. Langston. "What happened?" she asked as she let him in. "I thought you were going back to San Francisco."

"I was. I did. But—"

He was shivering convulsively, whether from reaction or the predawn chill, she couldn't begin to guess. "Come sit down in the kitchen," she urged. "I'll make us both a cup of coffee."

He followed her without a word, his steps slow and heavy. In the brighter light of the kitchen, Joy saw that he was unshaven, and that his heavy-lidded eyes bore dark smudges of weariness beneath them.

"Have you been to bed at all?" she asked.

"Bed? No. I was..." His voice trailed off.

"Never mind. You can tell me in a minute, when you're settled." When he started to shrug out of his jacket, she put a hand on his arm to stop him. "Why don't you leave it on until you warm up? I'll have coffee ready in a minute. Would you like some toast with it? Or a piece of pie?''

He shook his head mutely, standing with his hands at his sides.

''Sit down, Charlie.'' Cutting a wedge of apple pie, she placed it on a plate and popped it into the microwave, then turned her attention back to preparing the coffee. The sight of Charlie at her kitchen table, silent and wan, was an unsettling one, but he didn't seem to be injured and she could see no sense in hurrying him. Whatever had happened, he'd driven all the way from San Francisco to tell her about it. Whether he did the telling now or in five minutes wasn't apt to matter much, in the overall scheme of things. Something had shaken him badly, and she was familiar enough with inner turmoil to grant him the time to find his own way of broaching whatever he had come to say.

Jezebel looked down from her perch on top of the refrigerator and chirped a greeting. When Charlie failed to respond, the monkey leaped to the counter, and from there to the floor, where she scurried over to play with the cuff of his left trouser leg.

Joy watched with some misgiving, but Charlie roused himself from his black study and bent to look under the table. ''Hi, sweetheart. How are you doing?''

Jezebel raced away, shrieking.

''I seem to be having that effect on a lot of people lately,'' Charlie said dryly, but his self-deprecating smile wobbled out of control and he turned away abruptly.

Biting her lip, Joy opened the cupboard and reached for a pair of mugs.

It wasn't until Charlie had finished his coffee and eaten half a piece of pie that he met her concerned gaze again. "I know I shouldn't have shown up like this, but . . . something happened."

"What, Charlie?"

He wrapped both hands around his empty mug. "There's no pretty way to say it, I guess. My brother-in-law's in the hospital. He tried to kill himself. I drove by the office on my way home last night, and . . . there he was."

Joy felt her stomach knot. "How is he now?"

"Stabilized, but so far he's refusing to see me. They said I could try again this afternoon."

He lapsed into silence, nodding his thanks when Joy refilled his mug. Watching him, she felt her own misgivings increase. In the face of this new complication, how could she justify keeping Charlie in the dark about his sister? Surely Michelle Tinker had a right to know what had happened to her husband, and she and Charlie could at least provide each other with moral support.

"To be honest," Charlie said, breaking into her thoughts, "I didn't even make a conscious decision to come here this morning. When I couldn't face going home, I just started to drive." He toyed with his fork, flaking bits of piecrust into crumbs. "And this is where I ended up."

"Good. At least your instincts are still in working order. Now we need to work on the rest of you. When do you have to be back in San Francisco?"

He sighed. "Two o'clock, they said."

"Do you want to call now and tell the hospital where you can be reached?"

"I guess I'd better," he said, but he looked daunted by the prospect.

"Which hospital is it?"

"The Med Center in San Francisco."

"I'll call them."

"You wouldn't mind?"

Of course she would mind; phone calls to faceless institutions still rated low on her list of favored activities. But she could handle it, and for Charlie she would. "Consider it done," she said, and the abject look of gratitude he turned on her reawakened her guilty conscience. "Charlie," she said, determined to level with him, "your sister—"

"Oh, God," he groaned, "don't even mention Shelley. That's all that made last night bearable— knowing that she wasn't having to go through the same nightmare. By the time she calls on Monday night, I should know enough to be able to put her in the picture, but right now it's a blessing not to have to break the news to her. It isn't like she could do anything, and I honestly don't think I could deal with one more—" His voice broke, and he buried his face in his hands.

Heavy-hearted, Joy went to him and rested her hands on his shoulders. "What you need right now is some sleep, especially if you plan to turn around in a few hours and drive back to San Francisco. Not that two mugs of Java City Colombian is a prescription for sound sleep, but—"

"No problem," Charlie assured her dully. "I could fall asleep right here at the table, but I'll settle for the motel, instead."

"Forget it," Joy said stubbornly. "You're here and you may as well stay. I don't mind, and neither does Jezebel."

He grimaced. "Yeah, but what about the neighbors? My car's parked out front, y'know."

"Charlie, you're sweet, but my neighbors—with the possible exception of Mrs. Langston—couldn't care less. If it really bothers you, feel free to put your car in the garage, but then I want you to come upstairs and bed down in the guest room. Will you do that, if I promise to wake you up in time for you to be back at the hospital by two?"

He rubbed the back of his neck. "Try and stop me, lady. Believe me, I'm grateful. From the curb to the garage is probably the outside limit on how far I'm competent to drive right now. I suspect you're saving me from a ticket, if not an accident. Or worse."

"You don't have to move your car at all, you know."

"Humor me. My sense of chivalry may be a little rusty, but it hasn't atrophied completely. I'll sleep better."

"Then by all means," she said, tousling his hair, "go and do it."

The gesture was spontaneous, and the unexpected intimacy of the moment caught her by surprise. Taking her hand away, she stepped back and opened a nearby drawer. "Here's the spare opener for the garage door. Just leave it on the counter when you come back in. I'll go up and make sure the room's ready."

"I'll be there in a minute," Charlie promised, rising from his chair. "And Joy..." He smiled wearily. "Thanks."

"It's the least I can do," she said, and headed upstairs, uncomfortably aware of just how eager she was to offer Charlie Comfort a refuge.

FOR SHELLEY, accustomed as she was to lace table-
cloths and turkey with all the trimmings, the shock of
spending Thanksgiving Day at the movies, followed by
a "feast" of Chinese takeout, was profoundly de-
pressing. Rising on Friday morning, she found the
thought of a three-day weekend of solitude almost
unbearable. She was half tempted to walk to the bus
station and catch a Greyhound for home.

But the home she longed for no longer existed; only
an empty mockery of it remained. Without Penny, the
house had become a silent, sullen battlefield where she
and Matthew drove each other farther and farther
apart. Considering the memories it held, she could
only feel worse there, not better.

She couldn't go home . . . but she didn't have to be
alone. And she didn't have to continue the aimless
floating prompted by Matthew's withdrawal. Charlie
had been right; participating in the playground project was one small way to strike back at the careless
universe that had allowed Penny's death.

Retrieving her coat from the back of the sofa, she
dug in the pocket until she found the piece of paper
she had tucked there after lunch on Wednesday, with
its neatly printed address: 3469 Arelyn Drive.

JOY PULLED an armload of clean towels out of the
dryer and buried her face in them, taking comfort
from their fragrant warmth. She had passed the early
morning hours in small household chores—starting a
load of laundry, emptying the dishwasher, setting
fresh food and water in Jezebel's cage—anything to
distract herself from the silence of the second floor,
where Charlie lay sleeping.

Keeping her hands busy did little to occupy her mind, and even while she worked, it was hard to put Charlie's kisses out of her mind. But she knew she would be wise to try. He was recovering from a loss in his life, just as she was—hardly the time to start a healthy relationship. Learning to count on him, to lean on him, would set a dangerous precedent.

In a few months, the playground would be an accomplished fact, and Charlie Comfort would need to move on to the site of his next project. If she wasn't careful, she would be left behind, carrying a torch.

In all good conscience, she wouldn't be able to reproach him. The work he was planning to do, the crusade he was preparing to launch, held the same attraction for her that her father's work always had, the sense of something larger than life, something truly worthwhile.

So you're going to unhitch your wagon from your father's star and try to fasten it to Charlie's? Maybe it's time you lived your own life for a change, instead of being an eternal handmaiden to someone else's dream.

The front doorbell interrupted her mental debate. "Who is it *this* time?" she asked Jezebel rhetorically. "Come on, let's pop you back in your cage before they ring again and wake Charlie." Until recently, it hadn't been unusual for a whole week to pass between one visitor and another. Now, she seemed to have taken up residence in Grand Central Station.

She was panting a little by the time she opened the front door, and the sight of the slender blond woman waiting patiently on her porch robbed her of what breath she had left. "Sheila!"

"Hi. I know we talked about my regular hours starting on Monday, but I had some free time this morning and I thought I'd see if you could use me."

Joy felt as if she were vibrating in rhythm with the pounding of her heart. "Actually, with the holiday and all, I haven't had time to organize any of the material from the Wednesday night meeting yet—"

"Is it the sort of thing I can help with?"

"Well, I wasn't really planning—" A sense of fatalism swept through her. "Oh, what the heck. Sure. Come on in. At the very least, we can talk about it over a cup of coffee."

Once Sheila was inside and the front door was closed behind her, Joy's dilemma increased. Why had she invited Sheila in? Stopping in her father's office just long enough to snatch up the folder that contained the results of the playground meeting, she escorted her guest into the kitchen and filled two clean mugs with coffee.

Every time a floorboard creaked, she came to attention. *Am I worried,* Joy asked herself, *or is there a part of me that's hoping Charlie will wake up and come downstairs?*

"These are the handwritten notes on the new committees we formed on Wednesday night," she explained, spreading the papers on the table. "One of the first things we'll want to do is type up a master list of names and addresses, so that the left hand knows how to find out what the right hand is up to."

Look who's talking about left hands and oblivious right hands! Feeling as self-conscious as an actress in a cheap melodrama, Joy added sugar to her coffee. It was within her power to orchestrate a reunion between brother and sister. All she had to do was excuse herself and go upstairs.... It was the sort of manipulation she would normally have gone to any lengths to avoid, and yet there was an undeniable fascination in the thought.

It appalled her to think that she was sitting across the kitchen table from a woman whose husband had just tried to kill himself...and that Sheila was completely unaware of it.

"Is something wrong?" Sheila asked.

Without making a conscious decision, Joy took refuge in at least a portion of the truth. "I was just worrying about a friend of mine—the man who's designing the playground for me, actually. His brother-in-law's in the hospital and he's pretty worried about him."

"Gee, that's too bad," Sheila said, and took a sip of her coffee. "Say, have you thought about setting up a card file on your volunteers? If we do it with actual index cards, we can color code them by committee. Later on, if we need to, we can handle the whole thing even more flexibly on computer, if you've got some decent data-base software, but a card file would be a good place to start. How does that sound?"

"Fine," Joy said glumly.

"Well then, if you'll trust me with the notes, I'll take them back to my place and get started. I can probably get the card file done over the weekend, and we can get a fresh start next week."

As she stood up, Joy's kitchen timer rang, the timer she had set to remind herself when it was time to rouse Charlie.

"Well," Sheila said with an easy smile, "I can see you're in the middle of things. I won't take up any more of your time. See you Monday."

"All right," Joy said, too deeply shaken by Sheila's cool demeanor to meddle further. "Monday."

The moment for intervention had somehow passed her by. There didn't seem to be any choice but to walk Sheila to the front door and wave goodbye, watching in silence as she walked off down the street. Then, chastened, Joy turned to mount the stairs and awaken Charlie.

CHAPTER TEN

"THEY WANT TO SEND ME away," Matthew said, sounding like a frightened child.

It was late on Sunday morning, the first opportunity Charlie had been given to have a meaningful exchange with Matthew. On Friday afternoon, the doctor had stated that his patient wasn't up to more than a five-minute visit, and had ordered Charlie not to excite him in any way. Saturday morning, Matthew had been sulky and withdrawn again, seeming to resent Charlie's presence in his room, and that afternoon he had grown so emotional when they tried to discuss recent events that the nurse had sedated him.

By then, Charlie had had the benefit of the doctor's diagnosis: clinical depression and alcohol abuse. He didn't know which label surprised him more, and yet, in hindsight, he could see the clues clearly enough to redouble his guilt.

"To a private hospital," Charlie said. "I know. They told me." Sitting at the bedside, he wished he felt more confident about what to say and how to say it. "It would only be for a few weeks, Matthew, while you get your strength back."

"While I dry out and my wrists scar over, you mean."

Charlie shifted uncomfortably. "You need a chance to pull yourself together and sort things out."

"What is there to sort out? Penny's gone. Michelle's gone. And now you're walking away from me, too."

Charlie sighed. The psychiatrist assisting with the case had warned him to expect such statements from Matthew. "He's been testing the limits of his world," Dr. Joffrey had explained. "He's afraid to trust anyone, afraid he'll be left all alone to face what's become of his life."

"Matthew hasn't been acting like a man who's afraid," Charlie had protested. "He's been acting like a tin-plated son of a bitch."

"Exactly." The doctor smiled. "Your brother-in-law hasn't truly come to terms with his daughter's death. Whatever his intellect may *know* about her accident, he *feels* as if she had some choice in the matter, as if she chose to abandon him. And so, perversely, his fear that the other important people in his life will vanish has forced him to do his very best to drive you and your sister away. Only if he put you through the stiffest test he could devise could he dare to trust your presence in his life."

"That's crazy."

Dr. Joffrey smiled. "Well, yes. That's why I'm here. But I'm not saying it's a course of action he decided on consciously. And it isn't as 'crazy' as it might appear. On the whole, it's a healthier and more encouraging sign than if your brother-in-law truly wanted to live out his life alone. Tell me, before his daughter's death, would you have called Matthew an outgoing man? One who responded warmly to other people and found it easy to admit his weaknesses?"

Charlie grimaced. "No. Pretty much the opposite."

"Then why should it surprise you that he expresses his grief and insecurity by drawing into himself even more tightly?"

Under Dr. Joffrey's tolerant gaze, it had all made a certain peculiar sense, but it didn't make dealing with Matthew any easier.

Scooting his chair closer to the hospital bed, Charlie eyed his brother-in-law warily. "As I recall, you were the one pushing me out the door, telling me I wasn't pulling my weight in the partnership."

"I was angry." Tears of weakness and emotion seeped from the corners of Matthew's eyes. Turning his head away, he said unsteadily, "I don't want to lose everything I've worked for. I don't want the office to close. With it gone, there really *won't* be anything left for me."

"So, since beggars can't be choosers, you're prepared to 'let' me step in to salvage things? I'm overwhelmed."

If anyone had asked him, Charlie would have denied harboring a wellspring of resentment toward Matthew, but it was raging through him now like a flood tide. "Speak your feelings honestly," Dr. Joffrey had urged. "Good, bad or indifferent, Matthew needs to know where he stands with you. Empty reassurances can only hurt him." But surely, Charlie thought with a pang of conscience, there would be time to go into all this later, when Matthew was feeling stronger.

It quickly became clear, however, that Matthew wasn't prepared to let the matter drop, even if Charlie had been willing. "I suppose you think I should have applauded while you trivialized your talents," the older man said. "But it seemed such a waste for you to spend your time on swing sets and jungle gyms when you could have been designing office complexes or town houses. Do you know what people had begun to call us, Charles? Do you? Tinkertoy and Comfort."

"Sticks and stones, Matthew. What does it matter what other people think, as long as our clients are satisfied?"

"That's easy for you to say. People always seem to like you. You understand them, you get along with them. But I..." He closed his eyes, breathing raggedly. "I don't. Obviously. Damn it, I'm an outstanding architect. That ought to be enough to satisfy people. But it isn't. It never has been. And it's all I have to offer."

"I don't believe that," Charlie said firmly.

"It's true."

"It is not. Michelle didn't marry you because you were a master architect. She fell in love with something she saw in you."

"Whatever it was, she certainly got over it."

"Maybe she just couldn't stand to stay and watch you giving yourself an emotional lobotomy. And what about Penny? Are you going to tell me that a six-year-old kid loved you because you drew great designs?"

"Children don't have a choice. They have to love their parents."

"Bull. She thought you were slicker than Santa Claus. But okay, we could probably argue about Michelle and Penny all day and not convince each other, so let's tackle a relationship we *can* settle. Yours and mine."

Matthew recoiled. "Don't be sadistic, Charles. I know precisely what you think of me."

"Oh yeah? What?"

"You resent me for displacing you in your sister's affections. You find me humorless and conservative to a fault. You think I carry my work ethic to ridiculous extremes, and you disapprove of me for putting profit margin ahead of more public-spirited considerations. Have I left out anything important?"

It was a damning catechism, and an uncomfortable percentage of it was right on target...and yet, in truth, it was only part of the picture. "Yes," Charlie said firmly, robbed of his anger. "I didn't resent Shelley's being with you, I was relieved. You made her happy. You were great to me while I was in school, like an older brother. I admired your work. God, Matthew, it's what made me decide to be an architect. You know that. And I'm grateful for the years of grunt-level apprenticeship you spared me. I wouldn't have come this far, this fast, if I'd had to start at the bottom." He spread his hands in supplication. "Maybe we haven't always seen eye to eye. Maybe we aren't temperamentally suited to be partners. But you helped me in a lot of very real ways, and I do thank you. I just can't *be* you."

Matthew rolled his head weakly on the pillows. "Right now, being me isn't something I'd wish on my worst enemy, let alone my best friend." His face contorted. "And you are the best friend I have, Charles. Isn't that a pitiful admission?"

"Matthew..."

"Promise me something. If you talk to Michelle, promise me you won't say anything to her about what's happened."

"Not tell her? What do you want from me, Matthew?" Charlie demanded in pained exasperation.

He meant the question rhetorically, but Matthew took it at face value. "I want a second chance," he said with fierce intensity. "I want to keep this out of the papers. I want some hope of pasting things back together with Michelle, with the firm . . . with my life. How can I do that if everyone I know looks at me the way you've been looking at me for the past three days, as if I'm some curiosity in a museum? I want you to keep your mouth shut. Can you? Will you? Or is it already too late for that?"

"No, it's not too late," Charlie said, with a conscience that was almost clean. The only person he'd confided in was Joy, and it would be easy enough to ask her, formally, to keep what she knew to herself. Even if she had gossiped in the meantime—which, with Joy, seemed laughably unlikely—what would it matter? She was a stranger to Matthew's circle of clients and acquaintances. "If you really want me to stay quiet about all this, I will."

"Even to Michelle?"

"If that's what you want."

"What about the office? Will you cover with my clients until I'm back at work?"

It was the last thing Charlie wanted to do. He had already come to terms with the dissolution of Tinker & Comfort. And what about his promises of increased involvement with the playground? Just phasing out his current work at Tinker & Comfort would have kept him busy. If he stayed on and added Matthew's client list to his own, he'd be lucky to find ten minutes a day to devote to Joy's project, let alone to Joy herself.

But Penny's death was an unchangeable fact, and there was no guarantee that Michelle's attitude toward her failing marriage would soften. Given the way Matthew had lived his life, his career might very well be all that he had left.

It was time to make a hard and fast decision; either make a clean break right now and tell Matthew he was on his own, or take on the responsibility for keeping Matthew's world spinning for the weeks or months it might take him to recover.

Charlie knew what he wanted to do. He wanted his freedom. He wanted Joy. But that choice went directly against the grain of his sense of loyalty and family.

In the final analysis, it came down to a question of strength. He was strong enough to be able to wait for what he wanted. Matthew wasn't. It was that simple. And that hard.

"Yeah, sure," Charlie said, trying to sound casual, "I'll cover your clients until you get back. I'll open the office tomorrow morning, business as usual."

"You'll have to replace the carpet in my office," Matthew advised with eerie calm. "And you'll need a cover story to tell Claudia."

Startled, Charlie shrugged. "She's our secretary, not our keeper. I'll think of something."

"Well, be sure it's plausible. She'll have to repeat it every time someone calls for me. In fact, you'd better prepare a memo of explanation that can be mailed to my clients."

"Trust me, Matthew, I'll handle it. Or draft the memo yourself, if you'd rather. I'm open to suggestions."

A nurse appeared in the doorway. "It's time for your lunch tray, Mr. Tinker, and then you should get some rest. Why don't you ask your brother to come back later?''

"Will you?" Matthew asked anxiously.

"Sure." Charlie stood up and stretched. "I'll swing back around four, okay?"

The nurse smiled. "That should be fine."

Schooling his pace, Charlie walked to the door. "Catch you later," he said in farewell, and stepped out into the corridor, grateful to escape the sight of Matthew's bandaged wrists and fever-bright eyes.

Feeling grim, he went in search of a pay phone, to tell Joy he wouldn't be making it back to Sacramento in a week, after all.

DECEMBER BECAME a madhouse. Joy found herself careening through the days, always hounded by the conviction that she was short-changing someone. If she was substitute teaching, she worried about Jezebel, home all day alone. If she was playing with Jezebel, she felt guilty about the notes and phone messages that accumulated daily for the playground. If she joined Sheila in tackling the paperwork for the playground, she fretted about neglecting the galleys of her father's book, which had finally arrived. If she spent time on the galleys, she reproached herself for neglecting her budding friendships with Austin Blade and Sheila, and her established relationships with Eleanor and Lisa. If she made time to call one of them, then her students' uncorrected homework rose like a specter to haunt her.

And through it all, like background music, ran her worry about Charlie. His sporadic phone calls were consistently upbeat, but she could hear the weariness in his voice. She began to suspect that he called her as much to gain moral support as to lend it.

After the candor of his unscheduled visit on the morning after Thanksgiving and his subsequent telephone request that she hold what he had told her about Matthew in the strictest confidence, he had had no more to say about his brother-in-law's condition. Reading his moods, however, Joy assumed that matters weren't going well. It didn't take a master detective to deduce that Matthew Tinker had not returned to work; if he had, Charlie wouldn't be so overrun with responsibilities. By the same token, she assumed that Matthew was still alive. If he had died, Charlie would have said so... and would then have been free to determine his own future. That left her with the assumption that Matthew must be recovering, but more slowly than Charlie might have hoped.

She would gladly have ignored Christmas, but her teaching assignments at the elementary school made that impossible. Spelling tests left by the regular teachers included words like *reindeer* and *chimney*. Art projects called for cotton balls and quantities of red paint. Arithmetic assignments included story problems about four elves, each of whom made six dolls and three toy trains.

By the middle of the month, it seemed to Joy that the whole world had gone Christmas crazy. Even the grocery store was broadcasting carols, and every house on the street except her own was adorned with colored lights. A year ago, she had risked life and limb on an extension ladder to create a similar display of electric cheer, to indulge her father's love of the season. This year, without him, she simply didn't have the heart.

The only red-letter day on her December calendar
was Monday the twenty-third. In a sane world, the
school system would have set its official Christmas
vacation to begin on the previous weekend. Instead,
for arcane reasons beyond her comprehension, they
had designated Monday the twenty-third as the last
day of classes before vacation began. Eleanor had
compensated for the school board's lunacy by setting
the day aside for various class pageants and for Charlie's meetings with the students. For Joy, the chance to
see Charlie was all the holiday she needed.

As the date neared, she inherited a class of fourth
graders and had the pleasure of supervising them as
they conducted a free-spirited debate on the relative
merits of a circus-theme playground, a castle or a
"monkey jungle." To her secret delight, the monkey
jungle won in the class vote, and Joy couldn't help
suspect that Jezebel's cameo appearance in the classroom earlier that week had been an influencing factor.

That was on Friday. On Saturday, Charlie phoned
to reconfirm the plans for his meeting with the children at Dunnett Elementary. On Sunday night, a
storm system moved in, bringing high winds and
drenching rains.

Monday morning the rain was still coming down in
torrents. Driving to work, Joy felt as if she were navigating in a submarine. She passed four accidents on
the road between her home and Dunnett Elementary
School, and breathed a sigh of relief when she reached
the parking lot unscathed.

Predictably, keeping the classroom under control
that morning was a major undertaking. None of the
usual schedules and rules applied, and Joy had little to

do but supervise as the class's room mother conducted a game of Santa bingo, refereed a spelling bee
and handed out paper Christmas trees, to be colored
with crayons and decorated with sequins. After
morning recess, Joy escorted her class to the multipurpose room, where the fourth, fifth and sixth graders were performing Christmas carols for the lower
grades. Giggles and silliness abounded, and she
counted herself lucky when the assembly ended without a major upheaval.

After lunch, a student messenger appeared at the
door of Joy's classroom with a note from the principal's office.

I've arranged for Mrs. Hawkins to merge your
class with hers for the next hour, brave soul that
she is, so why don't you sit in with Mr. Comfort
and the student representatives? It wouldn't seem
complete without you.

Eleanor

The meeting was scheduled to take place in the
conference room near Eleanor's office. By the time
Joy was able to hand her group over to Mrs. Hawkins
and shepherd her fourth-grade representative to the
appointed place, everyone else was there.

Everyone but Charlie.

Joy glanced uneasily at her watch. It was already
one-thirty. Unlike the pre-Thanksgiving meeting,
where Charlie had managed to arrive in the nick of
time, this time he was late. So far, the half-dozen
children in the room were taking the delay pretty well,
but Joy was sure that it was due more to Eleanor's
presence than to their innate patience.

"Here she is," Eleanor said in a cheerful voice as Joy closed the door behind herself. "Ms. Porter, while we wait for Mr. Comfort to get here, why don't we ask the class representatives to tell us their ideas? If you'll write them down on the blackboard, we can cross out any duplicates and be all ready to start when Mr. Comfort arrives."

Taking her cue, Joy walked to the blackboard. "That's a very good idea, Mrs. Anderson. Let's start with our first graders and work up, okay? Who's here from the first grade?"

A diminutive redhead held up her hand.

"Good. Why don't you tell us your name and the idea your grade agreed on?"

"I'm Jan. We want a zoo!"

"Wonderful," Joy said, picking up a piece of chalk. "Zoo. Now, who's from the second grade?"

A little girl with soft brown hair raised her hand shyly.

"What's your name?"

"Andrea."

"And what idea did your grade like best?"

Andrea squirmed self-consciously.

Joy knelt in front of her. "Did your class want a zoo, too?"

Andrea shook her head in fierce negation. "McDonald's."

Startled, Joy asked, "The place where you buy hamburgers?"

Again, Andrea shook her head in denial.

While Joy racked her brain for another possibility, Eleanor said, "With a woof-woof here and a woof-woof there?"

Andrea smiled incandescently.

"Great," Joy said in relief, rising to write on the board. "Now we have a zoo and a farm. Third grade?"

"I'm Katie. We voted for a spaceship!"

Joy dutifully added it to the list. "Fourth grade," she asked, smiling down at the girl she had escorted. "Roxanne?"

"We want a monkey jungle, Ms. Porter, so we can swing and play like Jezebel."

"Fifth grade?"

"I'm Brant. We want a giant castle, with a moat and a drawbridge and—"

"Let's save the details for Mr. Comfort," Eleanor suggested.

"Sixth grade?" Joy prompted.

"I'm Jennifer, and we want—"

The door opened and Charlie appeared, soaked to the skin and grinning. "Hi, Mrs. Anderson. Hi, Ms. Porter. Sorry I'm late." Putting down the small gym bag he carried, he said, "Hi, kids. My name's Charlie. I'm glad you started without me. Whose turn is it?"

Jennifer raised her hand and said, "We thought a haunted house would be neat, with secret doors and ghosts and things."

As Joy turned to write the suggestion down, she heard an odd noise, and realized that Charlie's running shoes were squelching audibly. How had he gotten so thoroughly drenched? Where was his trench coat? He had lost weight in the month since his last visit, and the skin around his eyes looked thin and bruised. But he was spinning a cheery line of patter for the children, coaxing them into speaking their thoughts about each of the playground suggestions, diplomatically ruling out the zoo idea as not being much fun without real animals, since nobody wanted to play in a cage, and suggesting that a haunted house out in broad daylight might not be such scary fun as it was on a moonless night. As a group, they concluded that a spaceship might be too small and cramped for large groups of kids to use all at the same time.

That left the farm, the monkey jungle and the castle. "What would you have on a farm?" Charlie asked.

Emboldened, Andrea said, "Cows and horses and pigs and—"

"But there wouldn't really be any animals there," Jennifer pointed out with lofty sixth-grade superiority. "Just like we wouldn't have elephants and zebras even if we chose the zoo."

"Well, we could have a pretend tractor," Brant volunteered. "And a barn with a hay loft and a ladder to get up to it."

"What about the monkey jungle?" Charlie asked.

"Vines to swing on, like Tarzan," Brant said, changing allegiances, "and caves to hide in, and trees to climb, and maybe a village with huts, and a river with alligators with a rope bridge across it."

Charlie laughed. "Brant, you've got a great imagination. I may have to hire you on as my creative consultant. But let's give somebody else a chance, too. How about the castle?"

"But that was my class's idea!" Brant protested.

"Okay, I admit defeat. Go ahead and tell me what the castle should have."

"Well, a moat and a tower and a drawbridge... but I think the jungle would be better."

"Why?"

"Kids might fight about who got to go into the castle and who had to stay outside. But there could be lots of trees in a jungle, and lots of huts in the village, and lots of vines, and everybody could do everything."

"Smart *and* creative," Charlie said. "Okay, is there anybody who likes one of the other ideas better than a jungle? No? Then a jungle is what we'll make. I'll have Ms. Porter send a note around to all the classes, asking everybody to draw pictures of what they'd like to see in our jungle. When the pictures are done, your teachers will send them to me, and I'll figure out a way to put everything together. Then we'll decide what we'll need to make it and we can start gathering our materials. Will all of you help with that part, too? Good. You've done a great job so far and I'd be happy to work with you again." He looked across at Eleanor. "I think that about wraps things up for today."

"Thank you, Mr. Comfort. I know we'll all be excited to see our jungle take shape. Now, children, line up behind me and I'll walk you all back to your classrooms. Ms. Porter, I'll tell Mrs. Hawkins that you'll be by to pick up your class in ten minutes or so, all right?"

"Of course," Joy said gratefully. "Thank you, Mrs. Anderson."

When the last student had filed out of the room and the door was closed, she turned to face Charlie. "Hello," she said, and offered him a shy smile.

"Hello yourself. Can I greet you properly or would that be frowned on here at school?"

With a shock of pleased surprise, she realized that he was asking her for a kiss. "It probably wouldn't be wise," she said, nodding toward the windowed panel of the door. "But thank you for the offer."

"It's probably just as well. I wouldn't want to send you back to class looking damp around the edges."

"I was going to be discreet and pretend I hadn't noticed, but since you brought it up, how *did* you get so wet?"

"I had a flat tire a few blocks from here. Traffic had already slowed me down, and it didn't seem fair to disappoint the kids, so I walked."

"Walked? In the middle of a rainstorm?"

"It was only a few blocks. I figured walking would take less time than changing the tire, and I could see that I was in for a drenching, either way. No harm done."

"Unless you come down with pneumonia."

"Not a chance. But I am looking forward to a hot shower and a change of clothes. I'll call a cab to take me over to the motel, then I'll come back over and change my flat tire."

"And get soaked again," Joy said disapprovingly.

"Probably," he admitted, "but in all honesty, I don't feel up to tackling it right now."

Without the children to distract her, she was increasingly unsettled by how spent Charlie appeared. "Where are you staying?"

"At the Dollar Days Motor Lodge, over by the freeway."

"That's a million miles from here. By the time you get there and get changed and get back, it'll be too dark to do anything about your car. Are those your other clothes?" she asked, looking over at the small gym bag he had brought in with him.

"Yeah. I didn't figure I'd need much, just for overnight."

"Good," Joy said, and fished in the pocket of her cardigan for her keys. "Here. My car's in the side lot, the white Oldsmobile. You can drive it over to the house, and shower and change there. When you're done, you can deal with your car or call a tow truck or just leave it where it is until morning."

"You're sure?"

"Absolutely. You know how to get there from here?"

"Yeah."

"Fine. Just remember to come back and pick me up at four, out in front, okay?"

She had expected more of an argument from him about her plan, but he simply gave a tired nod and retrieved his bag from the floor. "Four o'clock sharp," he confirmed. "I'll be there."

Duty bound, Joy had little choice but to wave goodbye to him in the hallway and retrieve her class from Mrs. Hawkins. Through the last hour of the day she controlled her students as best she could, feeling impatience and anticipation that almost matched theirs. At last it was time to release them, leaving her to complete the ritual red tape that came with the end of her temporary assignment. The minute hand of the clock crept slowly down and then even more slowly up again, until it reached the top and Joy was free to shrug into her raincoat and join the general exodus of teachers and office staff. Unfurling her umbrella, she stood on the top step, watching for the Oldsmobile's distinctive white snout.

She was still waiting twenty minutes later when Eleanor emerged from the building. "Trouble, Joy?"

"I don't know. Charlie was supposed to pick me up at four." It was the sort of situation she hated, fraught with opportunities for crossed signals and missed rendezvous. "I told him I'd meet him out in front."

"I could try to call him, if you like. Where is he staying?"

Joy felt her cheeks redden. "He was going over to my house to shower and change into some dry clothes. He had a flat tire and his motel is on the far side of town, so I let him take my car and—"

"Would you like me to call him while you wait here?" Eleanor interrupted kindly.

"Could you?"

"Of course. I'll only be a few minutes. If he comes while I'm gone, go ahead and leave, but call my house when you get home. Otherwise, I'll expect to find you here when I get back."

Trust Eleanor to cover all contingencies, Joy thought gratefully, and returned her gaze to the street.

Five minutes later, Eleanor returned. "All I got at your number was the answering machine, Joy. Come along and I'll give you a ride home. I've left word in the office, in case Mr. Comfort inquires."

"I hope we don't miss him while we're on our way," Joy said, but when they arrived at the curb in front of Joy's house, they found the Oldsmobile parked in the driveway.

"Perhaps he lost track of the time," Eleanor said. "No matter. All's well that ends well. Merry Christmas, Joy."

"Merry Christmas," Joy replied as cheerfully as she could, but she was embarrassed to have imposed on

Eleanor's kindness, and deeply disappointed in Charlie. Filled with unaccustomed stirrings of anger and chagrin, she made her way through the rain to the house, intent on finding out why he had stranded her.

CHAPTER ELEVEN

TO HER RELIEF, the front door was unlocked.

"Charlie?" Joy called as she stepped inside.

Although several lights were burning, the only reply was Jezebel's distant chirrup of greeting and a muted, rhythmic beeping that Joy couldn't quite identify. Furling her umbrella and shedding her raincoat, she went down the hallway to investigate.

Reaching the kitchen, she found the source of the noise: the timer on the microwave oven was beeping with steadfast regularity. Joy turned it off.

"Charlie?" she called again.

Nothing.

Going to the counter, she cued the tape on her answering machine, hoping it might hold a clue, but the only message was the one Eleanor had left when she called from the school.

Mystified, Joy walked back toward the front of the house, glancing into each room as she went. Could something serious have happened to him? "Charlie?"

Down the hall, she could hear Jezebel chittering quietly in her cage, waiting to be released.

"Coming," Joy called, and went into her father's office.

She found Charlie there, stretched out on the sofa, sleeping as soundly as Goldilocks in Baby Bear's bed.

When Jezebel cried out impatiently at the sight of Joy, he shifted onto his back and began, quietly, to snore.

In the light from the desk lamp, he looked pale and fragile. His rumpled hair covered his forehead and hung over his eyebrows, as if he had been too busy in the past weeks to have it cut. The lamplight cast sharp black shadows beneath the thrust of his cheekbones and emphasized the dark half circles beneath his closed eyes.

Joy supposed, watching him, that his appearance ought to have moved her to pity or tenderness. Instead, she found herself fighting back the sting of angry tears. Lying there, he was all too keen a reminder of her father's illness and decline.

It awoke a rebellious frustration within her. Charlie was supposed to be the strong one, the one in control of himself and his surroundings. She didn't want to see him looking so beaten, or to find herself cast in the role of nurse to yet another man who had a claim on her heart.

Shaken, she opened the cage and took Jezebel onto her arm. "If he needs sleep so badly, we'll leave him to it," she said, and carried the monkey out of the room, closing the door firmly behind herself.

JOY'S DETERMINED POLICY of noninterference grew harder to sustain as the afternoon wore on. The dinner hour neared, and she debated whether to wake Charlie or, at the very least, cook for two, but in the end she fixed her own meal and ate it in stubborn solitude.

Evening grew into night. At ten o'clock, Joy went back to her father's office long enough to return Jezebel to her cage and spread an afghan over Charlie.

Looking down at him, it was hard to remember why she had felt quite so hostile.

If you were that angry with him, why didn't you wake him up hours ago and tell him to take a cab to his motel? Maybe it isn't really Charlie you're so mad at. Maybe it's Dad.

She shied away from the idea. The thought was nonsense... wasn't it? Her father hadn't been ill out of choice. And she had come home voluntarily to care for him. What possible justification could she have for being angry with him?

Maybe she wasn't angry, she thought, but resentful of the way her life had been co-opted. And maybe a little bit afraid, too. Afraid of being left on her own. Afraid of the things Charlie made her hope for. Afraid of what he made her feel. Maybe getting mad at him felt safer than risking a relationship, she mused. There had to be some good reason for her to have spent the past five hours wrapping herself in layers of resentment. It suddenly occurred to her that she ought to have been worried that Charlie slept right through the beeping of the timer and all of Jezebel's chatter. Sleep like this wasn't normal. For all she knew, he could be sick.

Guilt-stricken, Joy pressed her fingers lightly to the side of his neck, but she found no sign of fever. To her disappointment, Charlie slept on, undisturbed by her touch.

Okay, then, he's probably just exhausted. Count your blessings and go to bed. Tomorrow's another day.

Slowly, reluctantly, she left the room and trailed upstairs to settle herself for what promised to be a long and restless night.

WHEN JOY CAME DOWNSTAIRS at seven the next morning and tiptoed into her father's office, she found the couch empty and the afghan neatly folded. Nearby, Charlie's gym bag sat on the floor, unzipped. "Well, Jezzie, where has our mystery guest gotten to now?" she asked as she opened the cage. "Shall we go find out? Tail, Jezzie."

Jezebel raced around her cage.

"Come on, don't be difficult. Tail." She sighed in exasperation. "How do you always know when I'm in a hurry? Please, Jezzie. I want to go see what Charlie's up to. You're the one who wanted to go along, so either come or don't. Tail!"

As if sensing that Joy's patience was at the breaking point, Jezebel came forward and draped her tail across Joy's palm, allowing herself to be lifted from the cage.

In the kitchen, Joy found fresh coffee in the pot and the morning newspaper folded neatly on the table, but no Charlie. A glance outside revealed that the Oldsmobile was still parked in the driveway. In the downstairs bathroom, she found a safety razor and an unfamiliar toothbrush resting on the edge of the sink, but not the man who must have used them.

Stepping back into the hallway, Joy called his name loudly, but there was no answer.

"This is getting eerie," she complained to Jezebel as she returned to the kitchen. "I suppose we'll just have to treat him like Little Bo Peep's sheep—leave him alone and he'll come home...."

As if on cue, she heard the low growl of a car engine draw near and then stop abruptly. Stepping to the window, she pulled the curtain aside and saw the little red Miata at the foot of the driveway, beyond the

Oldsmobile. A moment later, Charlie climbed out and started toward the house, carrying a square white box tied with string. When he reached the door, he stopped and knocked.

She was glad to see him—not just relieved, but gladdened. The anger that had so unsettled her seemed to have vanished in the night, leaving behind an uncomplicated willingness to be happy in Charlie's company. Smiling, Joy opened the kitchen door for him.

"Mea culpa," he said by way of greeting. "I don't know if you're still speaking to me, after yesterday, and I'll understand if you don't want me to come in, but I brought you an 'I'm sorry' present." He held out the box. "Greeks bearing gifts. I wasn't sure what you'd like, so I got a little bit of everything."

"Good morning," she said, accepting the box. "Come in. It looks like you've already had a busy day. What time did you get up?"

"About four. The *wrong* four, unfortunately. I really am sorry. How did you get home?"

"Eleanor gave me a lift." Joy opened the box and laughed at the profusion of breakfast rolls she found there. "Good grief, you *did* buy a little bit of everything. A croissant, a blueberry muffin, a cinnamon roll, a cherry Danish, a Bismarck, a French cruller—Charlie, who do you think is going to eat all this?"

"Me, actually. I didn't have lunch *or* dinner, yesterday, and I intend to make up for lost time."

"With doughnuts?"

"With anything that doesn't bite me first. Take your pick and then stand back. It may not be a pretty sight."

"Why didn't you fix yourself something to eat when you got up?"

"I didn't want to take a chance on waking you. Besides, it seemed a little too presumptuous, under the circumstances. I knew you liked coffee, so I made a pot before I left, but beyond that I didn't feel right about helping myself."

"Well, there's no need to stand on ceremony now." Joy set the box on the table and poured herself a mug of coffee. "Isn't this a little early for changing flat tires?"

"I needed a jog to work the kinks out, after sleeping so long," Charlie said, claiming a jelly doughnut, "so I killed time shaving and reading the paper until first light and then figured I'd check on the car while I was out. I was afraid it might have been towed, or stripped. But it was fine, so I changed the tire before it could start to rain again. It didn't take long, and I'd passed a doughnut shop on my way, so I drove back and bought 'em out."

"I almost believe you," Joy said, selecting a cruller.

For the next few minutes, they munched in companionable silence. Then, as Charlie finished a muffin and reached for a Danish, he asked, "Do you already have plans or can we spend the day together?"

"Spending the day with you would suit me just fine," Joy said, genuinely pleased. "Is there anything special you'd like to do?"

"Well," he said, "I thought I might help you fix up the house."

Joy stared across the table at him, mystified.

Charlie gestured expansively. "No tree. No lights. No wreath. No garish greeting cards prominently displayed. No mistletoe." He quirked one eyebrow. "I have to admit, I particularly noticed the lack of mistletoe."

"I've been busy," she said lamely.

Charlie looked relieved. "That's all? Just busy? I mean, you aren't philosophically opposed to the holiday? Your mother's maiden name wasn't Scrooge?"

"No, of course not."

"Great! Scotch pine or a Douglas fir?"

"No, Charlie. I don't want a tree."

He looked crestfallen. "Why not?"

"It's too much trouble. What's the point? I'm alone here—"

"No, you aren't. Not today."

"But I will be, after you go home. I don't want to have to wrestle with taking a tree down in a few days."

"Then invite me to spend Christmas with you, and I'll take it down for you before I leave tomorrow. I don't mind."

"You can't be serious," she said, but she could see by the reckless light in his eyes that he was. "It wouldn't be worth all the work."

"It would, to me."

"It's too late."

"No, it isn't. We've got a whole day."

"You're crazy."

"Is that a yes?"

If she didn't speak up, it would be too late to stop him. "No," she said firmly, "it's not a yes. I've given this a lot of thought. I've already fought Eleanor off, and I'll fight you, too, if I have to. I know my limits, and I'm not going to ask for trouble by digging

through boxes in the attic and stirring up a lot of—''
Determined not to cry, she took a deep breath and let
it out slowly. ''—a lot of old memories I'm just not
ready to handle yet.''

''And you think I don't understand that?'' Charlie
asked softly, putting down his half-eaten Danish.
''Forget the boxes in the attic. Forget the memories.
I'm talking about new traditions. Instant holiday. Just
add water and stir. We'll do it all from scratch.''

His words were whimsical, but the fervor in his tone
told her that he longed for this holiday for his own
sake, as well as for hers.

Charlie reached across the table and captured her
hand. ''Make a Christmas with me, Joy. Please.''

She had seen enough of him since October to know
how he could be when his enthusiasm took hold. If she
agreed to his suggestion, the day would become a
whirlwind ride with Charlie at the controls, and who
could say how it might end? By saying no and sending him on his way, she could ensure herself an untroubled, untroubling day. Alone.

Alone? With a jolt, she realized that it wasn't what
she wanted. But it was what she would end up with,
unless she found the nerve to open her mouth and ask
for more.

Terrified and exhilarated, she tightened her fingers
around his. ''All right, Charlie. Let's make a Christmas.''

BECAUSE IT WAS Christmas Eve, the tree lots had
opened early in an attempt to make the most of every
remaining hour. Soon, the trees that remained would
be no more than trash, but for now they were the

proud emblems of the season, their green boughs spread in regal splendor.

Joy walked down fragrant corridors of evergreen, reaching out to brush her fingertips over the cool needles. "Here's a nice one," she called to Charlie, admiring a knee-high spruce. "We could put it on the dining-room table."

"Here's a cute one," he called back, and she turned to find him patting the branches of a fourteen-foot giant. "When we're done with it, we could turn it *into* a dining-room table."

She grinned. "I take it you'd prefer a big tree."

"Absolutely. Maybe not *this* big, but big enough so we don't have to worry about stepping on it. In fact," he said, making a show of measuring her with his eyes, "I think we should look for a tree that's just your size."

The notion amused her. "You mean they have a special row for Christmas trees with size-eight branches and seven-double-*A* roots?"

"Let's try this one," Charlie said, and reached through the branches of a nearby tree to grasp it by the trunk and set it down beside Joy.

"Well?"

"Perfect," Charlie pronounced. "By the time we cut an inch off the trunk so it can soak up some water, we won't be able to tell the two of you apart."

"The tree is green," Joy pointed out.

"So were you, on Halloween."

"Very funny." She cast a critical eye over his choice. "It's got a few bare spots."

"Makes it more fun to decorate. Perfection is boring."

"How will we get it home?"

"Tied to the top of the Miata."

"Will that work?"

"If it doesn't, we'll put it in the front seat and tie *you* to the top of the Miata."

Joy laughed. "You have an answer for everything, don't you?"

"Absolutely."

She raised her hands in surrender. "Then we may as well buy it."

By the time they had dropped it off at the house, the shopping mall was open. "We'll buy presents next," Charlie declared. "Can't have Christmas without presents, can we? I'll go this way, you go that way. Twenty-dollar total limit. Oh, and I'd like to buy something for Jezebel. What do you think she'd like? Video games? The *Encyclopaedia Britannica?*"

"Head for the toy department," Joy advised. "Anything a bright toddler would like is bound to be a hit."

"Okay. Meet me back here in forty minutes or risk being left behind."

Their third stop was the Import Warehouse, where Charlie roamed the aisles, gathering necklaces of scarlet wooden beads, handfuls of origami birds, six batik scarves, four packages of filigreed napkin rings, three rolls of French wrapping paper and a brass candlestick.

Joy trailed along in his wake, watching in amazement.

From there, they drove to an office-supply store, where Charlie selected paper clips, tape, scissors and a bag of small foam packing pieces. At a nearby drugstore, he added a packet of needles, a large spool of white thread and a pair of thimbles.

The grocery store was their final stop. Moving quickly up and down the aisles, Charlie loaded a cart with apple cider, three oranges, a bottle of stick cinnamon and two more of cloves, a tall bayberry candle, a loaf of sourdough bread, a coffee cake, two steaks, a bottle of red wine, two potatoes for baking, half a pound of fresh green beans and a basket of New Zealand strawberries that might as well have been gold-plated, given their price.

By then, hungry and exhausted, Joy was beginning to lag. Looking over his shoulder at her as he guided the cart into a checkout line, Charlie said, "What do you like on your pizza?"

"On my pizza? Pepperoni. Why?"

"Wait here. I'll be back before it's our turn."

Before Joy could protest, he had vanished into the crowd of shoppers. Left alone, she leaned against the cart, wondering wanly why she had agreed to a morning of such lunacy. The holiday smiles on the faces around her were too anonymous to bring her any pleasure, and the clamor of the crowd was aggravating the headache that had begun to pound beneath her left temple.

The woman at the cash register was ringing up the last of their choices by the time Charlie returned at a run. Joy had expected him to be carrying a box of frozen pizza, but he was empty-handed. When he saw her open purse, he waved her off, producing his wallet.

"But you've paid for everything so far. Even the tree."

"Of course. My idea, my treat. You supply the house, I supply the trimmings."

In the parking lot, he ushered Joy into the passenger seat of his little red car and settled the grocery bags around her. "Now that we have the raw materials, we can get started," he announced enthusiastically as he started the car.

Get started? Joy resisted the temptation to groan. If the afternoon was going to be as hectic as the morning, she wasn't sure she was up to it.

Charlie drove with cheerful abandon, zipping through the streets at a rate that made Joy grateful for her seat belt. When they were roughly halfway home, he suddenly triggered his flashers and pulled up to the curb outside a pizza parlor.

"Oh, Charlie, don't bother," Joy said. "It'll take forever. I can fix us something back at the—"

"No problem," he said, opening his door. "Just sit tight."

Two minutes later, he was back, bearing a cardboard pizza carton.

"Dare I ask how you managed that?"

"O ye of little faith," Charlie said smugly, pulling away from the curb. "Don't you believe in Christmas miracles?"

"Charlie..."

"All right, I confess, I called them from the grocery store."

She couldn't help herself; she had to laugh. And whether it was the laughter that did the trick or the enticing scent of hot pizza, by the time they pulled into the driveway, her headache was gone.

"PASS THE BEADS, please," Charlie requested.

"There's only one left."

"Good!"

Joy slid the bowl across the table to him and watched as he fished the final scarlet bead out of it. Five foam packing pieces and then a bead—that had been their pattern. At first the supply of scarlet beads had seemed endless, but the work had quickly become automatic, freeing them to talk about everything under the sun.

For the past twenty minutes, they had been challenging each other's memories in pursuit of the most obscure verses from well-known Christmas carols. Joy had scored the advantage point by singing "Good King Wenceslas" in its entirety, after Charlie failed to get beyond the first verse of "It Came Upon A Midnight Clear."

"There." Charlie threaded the final bead onto the garland, followed it with a piece of packing foam, and tied a knot in the end of the thread. "Grab an end and let's get this sucker strung."

The long loops of the garland weighed almost nothing. With Charlie's help, Joy draped it around and around the tree, then stepped back to study the effect.

In the firelight, the materials of the garland created a pleasing contrast, reminiscent of popcorn and cranberries. "Now the ornaments," Charlie urged, and they undertook the delicate task of attaching origami birds to the tips of the branches. Then, using unbent paper clips for hangers, they suspended the filigreed napkin rings at intervals, and finished off by tying the scarves into bows around the branches, creating startling bursts of color. The wrapped presents beneath the tree completed the picture, a scattering of bright boxes and frothy bows.

"It all looks wonderful!" Joy said in delight.

"Not half-bad, if I do say so myself." Charlie smiled his approval.

"Are you hungry yet? Shall I put the potatoes in to bake?"

"To tell you the truth, I'm still pretty full of pizza."

"Me, too." Joy surveyed the tree again. "It's perfect."

"Almost."

She turned to Charlie. "Why just 'almost'?"

"Because there's something we're still missing," he said, "and I wish we had it."

"What? What did we forget?"

"Mistletoe."

Joy looked away, disconcerted by the sudden intensity in his gaze.

"What about you?" he asked softly, and she heard his footsteps on the rug as he crossed the floor to stand behind her. "Are you sorry we don't have any?" The breath of his words ruffled her hair. "Or are you relieved?"

"Charlie . . ."

He placed his hands on her shoulders and turned her to face him again. "Just tell me what you want, Joy. Please. I need to know."

"I . . ." Her throat felt hot and tight, too narrow for words to push through, but Charlie's hands on her shoulders were strong and supportive. "I wish . . . Oh, Charlie, I wish we had it, too."

"Then we do," he said with quiet assurance, and kissed her.

CHAPTER TWELVE

IT WAS A GOLDEN KISS, a kiss from some perfect dream made real. When it ended, Joy gave no thought to pride or propriety or self-doubt; she simply raised her trembling fingers to cup Charlie's face and drew him gently down until his lips touched hers again. The magic began once more.

All day long, in the crowded stores, along the windy streets, through the laughter and the banter and the tears, they had been traveling toward this moment. She could see that, now. She could admit it freely to herself, reveling in the admission, liberated from her fears by the sweet benediction of Charlie's kiss.

Intoxicated by the nearness of him, she let her fingertips wander from the curve of his cheekbones up into the rich thickness of his hair. Silently proclaiming her need, she kissed him again and again, at first so lightly she scarcely touched her lips to his, then deeply and more deeply. She lost herself willingly, trying to escape her fear of the moment when their embrace would end, when she would have to face Charlie and try to read the look in his eyes.

As if he sensed her panic, his hold on her shoulders tightened and he drew back far enough to smile down on her and say, "If you're the present in my stocking, I must have been a very, very good boy this year."

Joy chanced a smile. "Maybe I'm the female equivalent of coal and switches."

"No way." He kissed her again, briefly, and drew back again. "Let's talk for a minute."

To Joy's way of thinking, it was the worst idea he'd had all day. "Do we have to?"

His smile was equal parts amusement and sympathy. "I think we'd better. Does it sound like such an awful fate?"

"I'd rather just kiss you," Joy said without thinking, and felt a hot blush rise from her chest to the roots of her hair.

"As it happens," Charlie said, pressing cool fingers to her flaming cheeks, "so would I. That's why we need to talk, at least for a minute. Come on. Cuddle on the couch with me and we'll get it over with."

Short of a full retreat, she couldn't see any way around complying. Reluctantly, she let him draw her down onto the couch and settle himself beside her, with his arm wrapped snugly around her shoulders. "Now," he instructed solemnly, "listen carefully while I make a total fool of myself. Ready?"

She nodded, wondering what on earth he was about to say.

"Put at its most genteel, I'm sweet on you, Ms. Porter."

"Pardon?" Joy squeaked.

"Sweet on. Attracted to. Enamored with. Turned on by. Desirous of getting to know more intimately." He dropped his voice to a stage whisper. "If it won't panic you, I'm even willing to use the *L* word."

Joy sat motionless in the circle of his arm, searching for a reply.

The silence dragged on.

"I'd be fairly grateful if you'd say something now," Charlie prompted. "Maybe 'Oh, Charlie, I feel the same way.' Or 'Gee, I had no idea.' Or, if it's the only honest response that comes to mind, 'You're way out line, Mr. Comfort, and I'd thank you to unhand me.'"

But her tongue had turned to lead in her mouth, too thick and heavy to move.

"Joy?" Charlie gave her a reassuring squeeze. "How about it? Do I need to unhand you?"

The answer to that, at least, was clear. "No."

"That's a relief. But you're still uneasy."

"No. Yes. Not the way you think." She shrank in upon herself, not because his touch was unpleasant but because his nearness made it almost impossible for her to think. "I'm . . . interested in you, too, Charlie."

"But . . . ?"

She shook her head helplessly. "No 'but,' except that I'm not very good at this kind of thing and I'm afraid of what will happen if we start mixing business with pleasure and something goes wrong."

"Well, for starters, you can tell me to stop right now, and I'll still do your playground for you. I'm not trying to pressure you into anything."

"I know. I wish you would," Joy said with despairing honesty. "Then I wouldn't have to think or decide or worry or wonder. I know it's a craven thing to wish, but it gets paralyzing, trying to second-guess what's going to happen."

"Then let's be right up front about what we're going to do and not do. And why."

Her skin itched and burned, but Joy sat still, hanging on Charlie's words, with a growing hope that his unrelenting directness would clear a path they could travel together.

"First off," he said, "at the risk of offending you and sounding like a presumptuous egotist, we are—I hope—going to make love tonight. But I don't have any birth control with me, so we're going to have to be a little imaginative. Want to know what I have in mind?"

"Yes," Joy whispered, convinced that this was the most unnerving discussion she'd ever experienced and yet fiercely unwilling to end it. She could hardly believe that Charlie would sit there and say such things, yet his openness cast a liberating light into the murky corners of insecurity and doubt that plagued her. It was fascinating and flattering to hear him talk this way, and she could feel her defenses falling, one by one, under the influence of his voice.

"Well, for starters," he said, "I'd like to pick up where we just left off with that kissing. It was pretty heady stuff, at least from my perspective. And then, when we've brought it to a rolling boil, I'd like to disentangle you from that sweater, and undo the buttons of your blouse, one...by one...by one." His chest rose and fell as he took a deep breath and released it. "After that, I'd enjoy tracking down every button and snap and zipper on you so that I can undo them all and then peel your clothes away, until there's nothing to stop my eyes and hands and lips from learning you. All of you. But first I'd want to get out of my clothes, too, so that I could hold you against me, skin to skin, and you could see exactly what the sight and scent and touch of you does to me. When we were both bare, with nothing to hide us from one another, I'd want to explore you, finding as many ways as I could to turn my pleasure into yours, until we both went up in flames...

"Then I'd start all over again, but this time it would all seem new, because we'd know a little more about each other's bodies and the magic they can make. And when we were finally all loved out, we'd crawl into bed together and I'd hold you against me and drift off to sleep that way, so that even in my dreams I'd know I wasn't alone."

She could find no defense within her heart against such words.

Charlie kissed her hair. "But those are only *my* wishes. If you don't want them, too, they're just so much hot air."

Joy closed her eyes. "Charlie..."

"Hmm?"

"I want those things. I do. Every last one of them. But..." She shivered. "Charlie, I'm a coward. I'm afraid."

"Of what?" His hold on her tightened. "Tell me. They're only words. Tell me all the worst things that could happen."

His reckless candor was infectious. "I'm not very... experienced," she confessed, ruing the understatement.

"So?"

"So I might do something wrong—hurt you, or bore you, or make you angry."

"Not likely. Go on. What else?"

"You might get frustrated and change your mind."

"Nope. Architects are experts at delayed gratification. What else might happen?"

"You might not like the way I look. Without my clothes on, I mean."

"Fat chance. What else? Come on, try harder. Worst-case scenario."

"I might hyperventilate. Or faint. Or end up covered in hives, too itchy to be of any use to either of us."

"Hives don't last indefinitely, and I'll bet you dollars to doughnuts that I could distract you well enough to make them go away. At the very least, I'd have a good time trying. What else?"

Joy shook her head. "Ghosts. Transparent, free-floating angst... I don't *know* what else. I just worry that it would be horrible, whatever it was."

"Are you going to let it stop us?"

"I hope not. Help me, Charlie. Can I tell you, right now, once and for all, that this is what I want and then just... just leave it up to you?" she asked uncertainly. "Is that too unfair?"

He shook with gentle laughter. "Sweetheart, you hand me carte blanche to work my wicked will on you and then wonder if I'm going to object? My shoulders are broad. Consider it done."

"Promise you'll ignore me if I dither or get cold feet," she persisted. "Please, Charlie."

"All right, I'll ignore your maidenly blushes, on one condition—we need a code word. A panic button. If you really do change your mind and you want me to stop whatever it is I'm doing, just call me Charles. Say it and I'll come to a grinding halt, guaranteed. Otherwise, you can dither to your heart's content and I'll promise to turn a deaf ear and forge ahead. Fair enough?"

"More than fair."

"Any other items of business that need our immediate attention?"

"None that I can think of."

"Then I'd like another kiss, please."

Grateful and eager, she turned in his arms to oblige him.

ON CHRISTMAS MORNING, Charlie awoke from a vague, contented dream of hearth and home to find Joy curled against his side.

Smiling at the ceiling, he matched the measure of his breathing to hers, doing his best to ignore the strident requests his body made beneath the warm covers as Joy stirred in her sleep.

What a strange evening it had been, strange and wondrous. At the start, it had been like a flashback to his school days, all sweaty palms and self-doubt. By the end, it had been as sweetly serious as anything he'd ever known.

He moved his head carefully on the pillow until he could gaze down at Joy's sleeping face, serene in the gray light of early morning. The urge he felt to protect her was almost painfully intense, born of her innocence and her honesty, her beauty and her vulnerability. She had brought to their lovemaking an aura of revelation, the sense that everything they did was a first for her, and uniquely theirs.

He felt privileged to have been with her when her eagerness finally outstripped her insecurities, freeing her to give pleasure and to receive it with dizzying abandon. The sight of her face as the first delicious spasms of release had overwhelmed her would live in his memory until the day he died.

But their intimacy hadn't been wholly untroubled. Again and again, in the midst of their explorations, they had stumbled into difficulty. Again and again he had coaxed and teased and reasoned until she could bring herself to admit the nature of the problem and then, with his help, put it behind her. Laughably, the first—and worst—barrier had sprung from Joy's reluctance to reveal that her underwear was of white cotton, practical and unadorned as a schoolgirl's.

"Believe me," he had assured her with heartfelt sincerity, "I'm interested in the gift, not the wrapping. Besides, I've got the opposite problem—I'm afraid I'm going to shock you speechless with what I've got on." And he had stripped down far enough to display the low-slung navy briefs he was wearing.

All in all, it had been a wooing achieved by inches and increments, fraught with side trips and detours that might well have defeated them if Joy herself had been any less determined. He only hoped that now, having fought the battle through, she would be able to cling to the victory and enjoy its spoils with a clear conscience and a happy heart. He didn't know what he would do if, when she awoke, she regretted all the things they'd done together, or felt ashamed to find herself in bed with him, side by side, skin to skin.

It was Christmas morning. It was Christmas morning, and he was in a place, in a room, in a bed that he hadn't known existed two months ago. Two months ago he hadn't even met Joy Porter.

Charlie closed his eyes.

A lot had changed in two months, not all of it for the better. Two months ago, Shelley had still been home, and Matthew had been at work...but that had all been a lie, a flimsy veneer of normalcy over a festering wound.

His mind reeled with questions. What would Matthew's holiday be like, at the clinic? How much longer would he have to stay? What would he be like when he came home? How long would it be before the ropes that tied Charlie to Tinker & Comfort could be loosened, and then cut?

And where was Shelley? During her last call, he had tried again to talk her into coming home, but there was little he could say to compel her, restricted as he was by his promise to Matthew. As a result, she, too, was facing this first difficult Christmas alone. Splintered off, each of them was weaker than they had to be, robbed of their rightful measure of strength and support. How were they ever going to recover?

"Charlie?" It was Joy's soft voice, and her hand shaking his shoulder. "Charlie, wake up!"

He opened his eyes in confusion.

Joy was hovering over him, her face a tender portrait of concern. "You were having a bad dream."

But it hadn't been a dream, and waking up wasn't going to make things any better.

"You're okay now," she said earnestly.

He opened his mouth to answer, but the tips of her breasts brushed against his chest, and the surge of desire that rippled through him made him feel dizzy and disoriented as his body's pleasure fought against the sorrows in his mind.

"You're okay now," she repeated, and lowered her mouth to his in a kiss that overrode everything, short-circuiting thought as it swept Charlie up and swirled him along to a place beyond worry or regret.

IT WAS THE HAPPIEST Christmas morning Joy had experienced in ages. The past four years had been progressively bleak, as her father had grown more and more ill, and the few before that had been largely solitary, with Christmas celebrated in a sedate, adult fashion with her acquaintances in Boston. Born and raised in California, Joy had found snow at Christmas disconcerting, a fairy-tale trick not quite to be trusted, too much of a stereotype for comfort. But this Christmas morning was like the Christmases of her childhood, a day when she rose from her bed tingling with expectation and was not for a moment disappointed.

They woke early but rose late, to Jezebel's loud displeasure. To Joy's delight, Charlie insisted on sharing a morning shower with her, showing no signs of regret or resentment after the intimacy they had shared. Once they were dressed, she in a scarlet-and-black sweater, Charlie in one of forest green, they went downstairs and, with Jezebel in attendance, settled themselves on the floor at the foot of the Christmas tree to delve into the packages there.

"The youngest always goes first," Charlie stated, as if quoting a law of the universe.

"Well, then, I may as well start with my present to Jezebel," Joy said. "It's nothing very impressive, just things she'll have fun with." Opening the package, she set it down in front of Jezebel, who upended the box, spilling out an assortment of small toys: Ping-Pong balls, a small plush teddy bear, a rattle and a long plastic pull toy in the shape of a centipede.

"Well, the more the merrier, I guess." Charlie pulled out the biggest box and set it down in front of Jezebel. "Here you go, Jez. Enjoy."

Eager to see what he had chosen, Joy removed the ribbon and wrapping paper, then opened the box within. "What on earth . . . ?"

Looking pleased with himself, Charlie explained, "It's a busy board for the bathtub—or, in Jezzie's case, the kitchen sink. There's a water wheel, a squeaker and a little sailboat that'll rock back and forth when she pushes it. I thought it might make a change from the rubber duck.''

''It's wonderful,'' Joy assured him, touched by the aptness of the gift. ''Thank you! I'm sure Jezzie will have a great time with it.''

''Yeah, well, like you said, she's a typical toddler,'' he added, and laughed as Jezebel squeezed into the empty box, ignoring the gift entirely. ''I never yet met a kid who didn't like the box better than the toy.''

Before her courage could desert her, Joy lifted the small package she had wrapped for Charlie and handed it to him. ''Here. I hope you like it . . . but the man in the shop promised you could exchange it if you don't.'' She watched anxiously as he peeled back the paper and lifted the lid, folding back layers of tissue paper until he had revealed a slender brass tube, the size of a small cigar. ''Look through it,'' she prompted.

Charlie lifted it to his eyes. ''A kaleidoscope!'' he exclaimed, and Joy felt a wave of relief at the enthusiasm in his voice. ''Incredible. I've never seen one this small. And such intense colors!'' He smiled with boyish glee. ''If I carried it with me into a meeting, people would think it was a fountain pen. Can you imagine the look on their faces if I held it up to my eye? Thank you. I love it.''

He leaned forward to kiss her, but Jezebel exploded out of the box where she'd been playing, shrieking a warning as she climbed possessively onto Joy's arm.

''Stop it, Jezzie,'' Joy scolded.

Jezebel hunched her shoulders and glowered, baring her teeth at Charlie.

"I'm sorry," Joy said, abashed. "I've never seen her act quite like this. I'll put her back in her cage."

"Oh, you can't. Not yet. It's Christmas. If Jezebel objects to public displays of affection, I can bide my time. Don't punish her on my account. I'm sort of flattered, actually. And I'm not altogether opposed to you having your own personal watch-monkey."

"But I don't need to be protected from you!"

"Good. I'm glad you feel that way. But it was still a pretty brave thing for her to do, if you stop and think about it. Leave her where she is."

Joy sighed. "All right. If you're sure."

"Absolutely. She isn't going to do anything to me, as long as I keep my hands to myself." He wadded up a handful of wrapping paper and tossed it onto the floor. "Right, Jezzie?"

Jezebel pounced on the crinkled paper.

"See? We're still pals." He lifted the last package and handed it to Joy. "Now it's your turn."

The box was wide and deep, and it rattled and rustled in an intriguing way as she removed its wrapping paper. Opening the lid, she found herself confronted by half a dozen smaller presents, each wrapped and beribboned. "No fair," she cried. "You said *one* gift."

"I said no such thing. I said a spending limit of twenty dollars. If I chose to divvy up my twenty dollars, it was a perfectly legitimate thing to do. Remember, I made up this game. Go ahead. Open them."

It was hard to say, afterward, what she had supposed the packages might contain—safe, pedestrian things, perhaps, like scented soap or an address book. Charlie's presents, however, proved to be an eclectic assortment whose only common thread was their giver.

A candy cane. A single silk rose. A card of colorful heart stickers, bearing messages like Yours Alone and Forever True. And, in the final box, a tiny lapel pin in the shape of a key.

"The key to my heart," Charlie said softly, "if you'll forgive an old cliché."

"Wait right here," Joy said abruptly, and scooped up Jezebel and a handful of her new toys. It took only a minute to return the little monkey and her toys to the cage. "I'll be back for you in just a little while," she promised breathlessly. "You're a good girl, but you couldn't have picked a worse morning to get territorial."

She took a moment to be sure that Jezebel was settling down happily to play, and another moment to smooth her own tousled hair. Then, light-footed, she hurried back to the living room to offer Charlie the kind of thank-you that her heart demanded.

IN THE SPIRIT of the day, Michelle Comfort Tinker packed a tin of home-baked Christmas cookies and walked the ten blocks that separated her apartment from Joy Porter's house. With luck, perhaps they could share a pot of tea, or even go out for a holiday brunch....

Rounding the final corner, she stopped dead at the sight of the red Miata parked in Joy's driveway. For five painful minutes, she stared at its candy-apple curves while her heart thundered in confusion. Then, slowly, she turned on her heel and started the long walk home.

CHAPTER THIRTEEN

December 26

To my Joy:
Leaving you yesterday afternoon was a lot harder than I'd expected it to be. I wanted to hide with you under the covers, while the world hunted and howled for us in vain. Instead, I'm sitting at this desk, doing a job that no longer means much to me, fulfilling a promise I probably never should have made, to a man who may or may not ever be in a position to benefit from it.

As you can tell, the post-holiday blues have struck with a vengeance, but I have the perfect antidote: my memory of how you looked when you fell asleep in my arms.

I'll be back in Sacramento to present the finished playground plans to the committee on February 14, if not before. And if you think that date is going to give me ideas, you're absolutely right.

Missing you more than I know how to say,

Charlie

December 28

Dear Charlie:
Thank you for your letter. Thank you for Christmas. Thank you for making me feel this way

about myself.

P.S. Jezzie sends her love—surly but sincere. The bath toy is a definite hit.

P.P.S. Forty-nine days until Valentine's Day. That's forty-eight too many. Will you at least take care of yourself?

Joy

January 1

Joyful:
I love you.

I wanted those to be the first words I wrote, to start this New Year. Can you stand the shock of seeing the *L* word right there in black and white, for God and the whole world to read?

I spent most of yesterday working on the preliminary sketches for our monkey jungle. At the risk of jinxing it, I think it will turn out to be the best playground I've done. Maybe it's because I have Jezebel to act as inspiration. Then again, maybe it has something to do with my burning desire to please a certain soft-spoken brunette I know. What do you think?

The latest word on Matthew is guarded but encouraging. His doctors say he may be well enough to come back to work soon. He still doesn't want me to visit him at the rehab center, but they say that isn't unusual. "Soon" and "may" are better than I expected to hear when this whole mess started, so I try to count my blessings.

Shelley's another matter. She called me the day after Christmas, but she didn't sound good. For

Matthew's sake, I've kept my mouth shut about what's been happening to him, but what difference will it really make whether Michelle files for a divorce because he tried to kill himself or files for a divorce because she still thinks he doesn't give a damn about where she is and why she left?

I'm sorry. It isn't fair to cry on your shoulder. Things will get better—that's what we have to remember. A time will come, before too long, when we're free again to choose how we want to live our lives. Had any interesting new thoughts about that, lately? I certainly have.

Don't disappear. I need to know you're there.

Charlie

"I WON'T BE AROUND on Friday," Sheila Taylor said.

Disappointed but not surprised, Joy looked up from the computer, searching for an adequate reply.

During the long, wet weeks of December and January, and on through the first week of February, Sheila Taylor had appeared on the doorstep by nine on any weekday morning when Joy wasn't out teaching. Monday through Thursday they worked together until noon, typing letters, making phone calls and, from time to time, stealing five or ten minutes to play with Jezebel, then finishing off the work session by eating lunch together in the kitchen. On Fridays they met at Joy's front door, then drove together in the Oldsmobile to take the week's financial information to Austin Blade at Good Sports.

After all those weeks, Joy felt that she knew Sheila little better than she had at their very first meeting. Her hope that Sheila might confide in her had faded, and Charlie's Christmas visit left Joy feeling less and less justified in her decision to keep the secret to herself. It was cold comfort to think that, given Sheila's callous reaction to Matthew's hospitalization, Joy's continued silence wasn't such an unkindness to Charlie as she had first supposed. Facing his sister's indifference was almost certain to bring him more heartache, rather than less. For the most part, Joy tried not to dwell on it...but Charlie's concern had been mounting lately, and there were times when Sheila's own behavior seemed to offer a deliberate challenge.

"So," she had said to Joy one morning in mid-December, "did the designer ever get his brother straightened out?" Joy had replied guardedly that the brother was better but not yet well. And Sheila, seemingly satisfied, had let the matter drop.

Her next strange comment had come a few days after Christmas, while Joy was still half-distracted by memories of Charlie's visit. "Working pretty closely with the architect, are you?" she had asked, apropos of nothing. Startled, Joy had denied having any particular input into the design of the playground, and Sheila had returned to her work without further comment.

This time, however, Joy was inclined to press the issue. It was easy to understand Sheila's cautious wish to stay away on a day when Charlie was bound to be in town, but it might be informative to hear what excuse she had dreamed up to explain her absence.

"You still won't take any pay for working here, so I know I don't have any right to insist," Joy said with an apologetic smile, "but could you possibly rearrange your plans? With the big meeting on Friday night, I'll have a million last-minute things to do. Even if you can't come to the meeting, couldn't you at least stop by on Friday morning? I could really use the help."

Sheila shook her head in flat denial. "I can come for a full day on Thursday if you want, but I won't be here on Friday."

"Not even for an hour or two?"

"Not at all."

Afraid your brother might see you?

The question tingled on the tip of Joy's tongue, but asking it so suddenly seemed too cruel. Instead, she stored the document she'd been creating and turned off the computer. "I hear a cup of coffee calling my name. Want to drive over to Java City with me?"

Sheila's relief was visible. "Sure," she said, reaching for her jacket. "If the boss can play hooky, so can the unhired help."

They'd drive to a neutral site, Joy thought as she dug the car keys out of her purse, and order a cup of coffee. There were changes in the air that Shelley needed to know about. And maybe, if the time seemed right, they'd have something more important to discuss.

"MR. COMFORT?"

Charlie looked up from his desk to find his secretary standing in the doorway. "Hi, Claudia. Problem?"

"No, sir. I just . . ." She looked down at the carpet, clearly uncomfortable, and Charlie's mood darkened from weary to grim. In the face of Matthew's continued absence, he was just barely managing to hold things together, with Claudia's help. She knew the clients and subcontractors, and she had a good head for details. Moreover, she knew enough to judge the importance of most phone calls herself, and that enabled her to save up all but the most urgent so that Charlie could work for blocks of time without interruption.

He had come to rely on her more than he'd realized, but he realized it now, with a sick foreboding in the pit of his stomach. If, as he suspected, she had come to his office to hand in her notice, he didn't know how he was going to carry on.

You should have given her a raise, he berated himself. *Matthew is no kin of hers. What made you think she'd be content to do twice the work for the same old pay?*

Before he could decide how to forestall her, Claudia hugged her elbows and said, "I know how busy you are, but could I talk to you for a minute?"

"Of course," Charlie said morosely. "Pull up a chair."

"No, this won't take long. I just wanted to apologize."

"What?"

"It's partly my fault," she said in a sudden rush, her face a portrait of guilty misery.

"*What* is?"

"What happened to Mr. Tinker. I knew he'd been drinking. But I didn't do anything about it."

"Are you talking about Thanksgiving?" Charlie asked uneasily.

She nodded. "He called me at home and asked me to come in for a few hours. But it had been going on for a long time before that, the drinking had. For months, really. I didn't say anything about it to anybody, but now I know I should have."

"Did you actually see him drinking?" Charlie asked, perplexed.

"No. I didn't need to." Now that she had begun, Claudia spoke more quickly, as if eager to clear her conscience. "He started coming in later and later every day. He'd stay on after you and I had gone home, writing out the letters he wanted to send. In the morning I'd find a big stack of drafts on my desk, and I'd type them up and leave them for him to sign. Only something was wrong with them."

"What do you mean?"

"Well, the top ones would be okay, but the ones he'd done later on were harder to read, with the handwriting all loopy and wild, and...well, some of them couldn't go out the way he'd written them."

"Didn't they make sense?"

"They made too much sense. He'd start out writing a letter to some subcontractor we'd had a problem with, and pretty soon the language would get rough, swear words everywhere and threats about what he'd do if they made a mistake again, and..." She shrugged unhappily. "I couldn't send out letters like that."

"What *did* you do with them?"

"I'd just put those drafts back on his desk."

"What did he have to say for himself, when he saw them?"

"Nothing. He'd just redo them when he came in the next day." She shifted uncomfortably from one foot to the other. "But then it started getting worse. A couple of times I found empty liquor bottles on his desk or in his wastebasket...and then, about a week before Thanksgiving, I came in early one morning and found him passed out on the couch in his office, with

a glass in his hand and nothing on but his underwear.'' She shook her head. ''I didn't say anything
because I didn't want him to get mad and fire me. I
thought it would be okay. I didn't know he'd try to
hurt himself.''

''Neither did I, Claudia. Neither did I.''

After a tense little silence, she said, ''I should have
told somebody. You can fire me if you want to. I'll
understand.''

''Fire you?'' Charlie rubbed his forehead. ''No. Just
the opposite. You deserve combat pay. How does an
extra fifty dollars a week sound, effective a month
ago?''

''Like more than I deserve,'' she said, with a shy
smile of gratitude. ''But I'll take it. Thank you.''

And she went back to her desk, leaving Charlie to
acknowledge that good fortune hadn't deserted him
completely.

FOLLOWING JOY to their table, Sheila thought, *She's
excited about something.*

The possibility wasn't a pleasing one. Excitement
usually meant change, and change invariably spelled
trouble. She'd had her fill of trouble. However bad the
present seemed, it always held the potential for something worse.

''After the first of the month,'' Joy said as soon as
they were settled with their coffee and muffins, ''we're
going to have to rearrange our work schedule.''

Sheila eyed her warily. ''Oh? How so?'' she asked,
and took a first cautious sip from her mug of French
Roast. It was painfully hot and painfully good; the
robust flavor scoured her tongue, demanding at least

her momentary attention. Closing her eyes, she savored a second mouthful.

"I had a call from my friend Lisa, the one who's having a baby."

"The teacher," Sheila said, to prove she remembered.

"That's right. It seems she went to see her doctor last week, and he's recommending that she take things easier until the baby comes." Joy took a quick swallow of coffee. "A lot easier. And so, after the first of the month, she'll be staying home...and I'll be teaching her first graders for the rest of the school year."

Change. Trouble. "Congratulations," Sheila said glumly.

If Joy noticed the tepid response, she gave no sign. "So what we have to figure out," she continued, "is how we're going to keep up with the workload. I've got a suggestion, if you'd like to hear it."

"Sure. Shoot."

Joy reached into the pocket of her blazer and produced a key, which she laid on the tabletop between them.

"What's that?"

"A key to the house. I want you to start working full time for the playground project, with pay. You can still go to Austin's on Fridays, and you and I can coordinate by phone or notes. Maybe you could even come early or stay late one day a week, so that you and I can put our heads together on anything that needs both of us. We've still got three or four months before the playground is finished, and I haven't come up with any better way to have my cake and eat it, too. You can think about it, if you need to. And you may as well take the key, in the meantime. You'll need it soon, even if you're just coming in the mornings."

It was one thing to masquerade under a false name, keeping to herself in everything but the work she devoted, in Penny's memory, to the playground project. It felt like quite another, somehow, to accept this tangible evidence of Joy's trust. "I don't think the key's such a good idea," Sheila said lamely.

"Why not? You'll need access to the computer and the typewriter, and it wouldn't be fair for you to have put all the project's calls on your phone bill—"

"I don't have a phone," she admitted, although she knew it was an invitation to further questions.

"All the more reason for you to take the key."

"Hasn't it occurred to you that there are a lot of things you don't know about me?" she asked in despair. "Too many for you to be handing me the key to your front door. Don't be so trusting."

"You're not a danger to me," Joy said with maddening conviction. "Face it, Shelley, the main harm you've been doing is to your own peace of mind."

Shelley. The sound of her name was like a blow. Stricken, she stared across the table. "How long have you known?"

Joy's mouth looked pinched, and her eyes narrowed in concern. "From the first day."

"How?"

"Charlie had shown me a picture of you and your family."

"Does he know I'm here?"

"No." Her voice trembled with quiet intensity. "You don't have to be afraid of me, Shelley. I only want to help. I'm your friend."

"And what about Charlie? Is he your friend, too?"

"Yes."

"You must know that he's been looking for me. How do you decide which friend to help?"

"The one who needs it more."

Coming from Joy, it was an answer Shelley felt she could believe. Here was a friend she could trust. A listening ear, finally, in whom she could confide fully.

Shaken, she pressed a napkin to her lips, fighting for control. After so many months alone, it was hard to let go of her secrecy, and harder still to unbend without crumbling entirely. Blinking back tears, she said, "You know, then, about... Penny?"

"And about Matthew."

"Tell me," Shelley said, feeling like a beggar. "Charlie hasn't said a thing about him. Not a thing. What happened? I know you said he was doing better, but why was he in the hospital in the first place?"

"You really should talk to Charlie about this," Joy began, looking uncomfortable.

"No. Tell me. Please."

With her gaze fixed on her coffee, Joy said, "He tried to kill himself."

She had imagined a dozen explanations—anything from an ulcer to a nervous breakdown—but not that. Never that.

"Matthew's on the mend." Joy delved in her purse. "Here, see for yourself. Charlie wrote this on New Year's Day."

Shelley took the letter from Joy's hand and unfolded it.

The first thing that struck her was the familiar sight of Charlie's handwriting. The next was the astonishing opening line: *I love you.* But even that wasn't enough to deter her as she scanned the letter for Matthew's name and read what Charlie had written about his prognosis...and then the paragraph that followed, about herself.

"Are you going to call your husband?" Joy asked.

Shelley folded the letter and handed it back to her. "I can't."

"Why not?"

"He won't want to talk to me. Don't you see? I left. I drove him to this. If I'd stayed, he never would have—"

"You can't know that," Joy said stubbornly. "Talk to him, Shelley. Tell him how worried you've been."

"I don't have the right. Not anymore."

Joy sighed. "I think you're wrong...but I'm not going to sit here and argue with you about it. If there are things you want to know, you can ask me, and I'll ask Charlie."

"You'd do that for me?" She held out the letter. "I should think Charlie would be your first consideration, if what he wrote here is any indication of how things are between you."

"I'd rather be honest with him, yes. But it seems to me, right now, that the best thing I can do for Charlie is to help the people he loves."

"I hope he'll see it that way, if all this ever comes out."

"I hope so, too. Now, will you take the key?"

"Yes. Thank you."

Joy raised her coffee mug. "To friendship."

"To friendship," Shelley echoed, touching her cup to Joy's. "And to love."

CHAPTER FOURTEEN

"WE'LL KEEP THE EXISTING trees for the sake of the shade they provide," Charlie explained, "but the 'climbing trees' of our monkey jungle will be man-made. That way we can scale them to a usable size and ensure that they're safe climbing structures, with sturdy 'branches' and enough cushioning underneath."

It was February and once again the rows of chairs in the school's multipurpose room were filled with enthusiastic volunteers. As he talked, Charlie was aware of Joy sitting at his side, absolutely still, her expression rapt. Maybe she was absorbing his presentation. Or maybe, like him, she was having trouble keeping her mind on the matter at hand. Maybe, like him, she was remembering a magical December night, and speculating on how to better it.

"In a few weeks," he said, dragging his eyes away from her, "a professional landscaping crew will be coming in to do some selective grading, now that we can map out the exact shape that our monkey jungle is going to take. If any of you want to take 'Before' shots, or remind yourselves of what the site looked like originally, now's the time, because soon you'll be able to see the first tangible results of all your hard work."

The crowd indulged in a spontaneous round of cheers and applause. Charlie nodded and smiled, but he was finding it increasingly difficult to concentrate on the words he had prepared. All he really wanted was to find some unused classroom where he and Joy could be alone to savor their reunion.

Using the projector Eleanor had commandeered from the audio visual department, he displayed a new slide to illustrate the next segment of the playground plan.

"Here, near the back of the property, we'll build a circular slide that wraps around the biggest of our artificial 'trees,' and a horizontal ladder that connects two of the smaller ones, with rope 'vines' on either side. And on the knoll—" He pressed the button to display the next illustration. "—we'll have a maze for our jungle adventurers to explore."

The presentation went on, picture by picture, until he had given them a feel for the entire playground. He finished with an overview, demonstrating how the playground elements would integrate with each other and with the natural features of the site.

"When the lights come up, we'll be taking a ten-minute break. Grab some refreshments and then feel free to examine the scale model I brought," he invited. "At eight, we'll regroup to go over the preliminary supply list and building schedule. Actual construction will take place over the long Memorial Day weekend, and tonight we'll start breaking that down into shifts and specific assignments. The end of May sounds like it's a long way off, but it'll be here before we know it. There's enough work to keep everybody busy, from the littlest toddlers right up to our latest group of volunteers from the Birchwood Retirement Home. I can't promise it'll be the most restful Memorial Day weekend you've ever spent, but I guarantee it will be one of the most rewarding."

At his signal, the lights came on and people started to step forward, with eager, admiring smiles, to inspect the mock-up he'd brought of the playground. Mounted on interlocking sections of plywood, the model was large enough to cover the card table on which it sat. Charlie could still feel the satisfying ache in his fingers and the back of his neck that had come from fashioning the tiny, articulated pieces of the trees, the maze, the swings and vines and slides.

He had constructed such a model for his very first playground, not so much as a visual aid to the volunteers as to reassure himself that he had balanced space with function. After that first project, the assembly of a model had become standard procedure, and one of his favorite parts of the job. At one time, nearly every flat surface in his office had been dominated by models of playgrounds, and he had sometimes strolled from one to another for the sheer pleasure of it, touching the elements gently, kneeling to examine them at eye level, remembering people and places and projects successfully completed.

After Penny's death, he had packed them away and put them into storage. *But I'll display them again, one of these days,* he told himself. *When I have my own business. When playgrounds are all I'm doing.* He could only hope that that day wouldn't be too far distant.

"Why so pensive?" Austin Blade asked, bringing his motorized wheelchair to a halt in front of Charlie. "I thought it went real well." He gestured toward the crowd at the playground model with his chin. "Nice touch. Seeing it in miniature will make it seem like it already exists. All they have to do now is build it."

"What do you mean, 'they'? Don't tell me you're quitting!"

"No... but I figure my main contribution is being made now, in the preliminary stages." His gaze flickered down to rest on his motionless body. "Swinging a hammer isn't really my forte."

"You think the brain work ends when construction begins?" Charlie scoffed. "Somebody has to man the registration table. Somebody has to supervise tool distribution. Somebody has to act as communications central. Somebody has to—"

"Okay, okay," Austin said, laughing, "I get the picture. No rest for the wicked. Don't worry, your loyal troops will march until we drop, General."

"See that you do," Charlie said grandly. "Now, if you'll excuse me, I need to find Lieutenant Porter."

"That's an easy one, General. When last sighted, she was headed for the mess tent."

"That'll be all, then, Sergeant. Dismissed."

Austin turned his chair adroitly and moved off, leaving Charlie free to make his way toward the refreshment table to join Joy.

At first he didn't see her, and the reason soon became clear: she was in the center of a milling, chatting crowd. More than a dozen people were vying for her attention, talking and laughing, and Joy was doing her best to respond to each of them, her face animated, her manner relaxed.

"A far cry from the first meeting, when facing this crowd made her feel faint," Eleanor observed approvingly, joining him.

"My thought exactly," Charlie replied, choosing not to reveal his other thought—that Joy had never looked more beautiful to him, or more appealing.

Eleanor smiled. "She's made a number of good friends in the course of this project. We all have. I noticed you talking to Austin Blade a few moments ago. A remarkable young man. Joy tells me he's been accepted as a candidate at Monkeys Do. Despite the formidable waiting list, one of these days he may be given access to a monkey like Jezebel. Until this playground project began, he hadn't even heard about Monkeys Do, although their headquarters are right here in town. Isn't life strange, with patterns forming within patterns, and good leading to good?"

"I'd certainly like to think so," Charlie said, heartened. "Could you excuse me for a minute, Eleanor? I need to have a quick word with Joy before we start up again."

Even then it took him another five minutes to win a private moment with her. "When this wraps up," he said, escorting her firmly away from the refreshment table, "is there someplace we could go? Out for coffee and dessert, or dancing, or something? Please?"

She tilted her head, as if the question required serious thought. "That depends. Where are you staying tonight?"

"At the Bluebell Motor Lodge."

She made a face. "Really? I know a much better place than that. Good rates, good food, friendly staff."

"Sounds appealing," he said, hoping that he was correctly interpreting the shimmer of mischief in her eyes. "Where is it?"

"Over near the college." Joy looked up at him, sweet and shy in her eagerness. "On Arelyn Drive."

At the front of the room, Eleanor had mounted the speaker's platform, and people were starting to drift back to their seats. Charlie closed his hand around Joy's. "Do you suppose there's still a vacancy?"

"Guaranteed," she said, doubling his pulse with her smile. "The management's expecting you."

HOWEVER SLOWLY time might seem to move, Joy decided, eventually patience was rewarded and long-awaited moments came to pass. At Christmas, it had seemed to her as if Valentine's Day would never arrive. But it had. Rising this morning, it had seemed to her as if the day would never pass and allow the evening—and Charlie—to arrive. But it had. Once the meeting had begun, it had seemed to her as if it would never end and free her to drive home, with Charlie's little Miata following in the Oldsmobile's wake. Now that was exactly what was happening.

Oddly, she felt closer to him now, with each of them encased in their separate cars, than she had during the meeting when she sat at his elbow but had no shred of his personal attention. In the parking lot, leaving the meeting, his hand had sought her waist and she had shivered with pleasure.

That one touch had ended the sense of waiting, and time had begun again to flow. The coming hours belonged to her and to Charlie. Out of a lifetime of self-doubt and insecurity, she believed this much: that she had earned whatever pleasure she and Charlie could find together on this night.

She wore the pledge of that belief beneath her sedate skirt and blouse tonight: a brassiere of gossamer blue, with matching bikini briefs. Buying the ensemble had prompted a sweeping bout of hives, but she was expecting a different kind of heat to overtake her when she revealed her unaccustomed finery to Charlie.

On Christmas Eve they had shared a hundred intimacies. She knew the shape and line of his body, the feel of his skin and hair, the pattern his breathing followed as passion overtook him. She had given him pleasure and taken pleasure from him. But they had not yet shared the final intimacy, the merging of their bodies into one. It was a union she had known only once before in Boston, before she had to return to California to care for her father.

It was a union she looked forward to exploring with Charlie.

Turning onto Arelyn Drive, she noted that the porch light still burned at Mrs. Langston's house. *Prying eyes,* she thought with resignation, but it didn't deter her as she pushed the button on the garage door opener and turned in at the driveway.

A moment later, Charlie's Miata sped on by.

Joy hit the brakes, craning her neck to watch in disbelief as the red gleam of his taillights grew smaller still. Schooling her breathing and refusing to jump to unfair conclusions, she told herself to remain calm.

At the meeting there had been nothing but pleasure in Charlie's eyes when she had summoned the courage to invite him to come home with her. And his actions as he walked her to her car had told her, more clearly than words, that he was as eager as she to pick up where they had left off in December. Nor could she convince herself that he had panicked in the course of the short drive from the school. *She* might do such a thing, but Charlie never would.

Then why were his taillights vanishing at the end of the block?

The answer came to her as she pulled into the garage and triggered the door to clank slowly shut: Mrs. Langston. Sweet, silly, chivalrous Charlie had driven off to protect her reputation, determined not to leave his red Miata in her driveway for the Mrs. Langstons of the world to see.

Charmed, Joy laughed, letting the soft, indulgent sound of her amusement ripple through the car. Now that it had occurred to her, she was as sure of the explanation as if Charlie had whispered it into her ear. He had simply gone in search of a more discreet parking place, and he would be back as soon as his mission was accomplished.

Calmly, she let herself into the house, turned on the lights in the hallway and turned off the light on the porch. She realized that she was humming an expectant little tune. Where had it come from, this unaccustomed trust, this strange and radiant ease? When had her heart learned such an expectation of happiness? What had become of the shabby gray cloak of worry she'd worn for so long?

She didn't miss it.

In another time or place, she might have made a pot of coffee, or put a record on the stereo in the living room. But tonight, borne along on a surreal cloud of confidence, she climbed the stairs, switched on the lamp in her room, closed the curtains and turned down the coverlet on her bed. Then, satisfied that the room looked private and welcoming, she went downstairs again.

Still no Charlie. Smiling to herself, she refilled Jezebel's water bottle and cuddled the monkey, talking nonsense to her until the doorbell rang.

"Wish me luck," she whispered against soft, warm fur, then said clearly, "Cage, Jezzie."

Obediently, Jezebel climbed into her cage and pulled the door shut behind herself.

"Good girl. Thank you." Joy's pulse had quickened, but with anticipation, not panic. Like a well-rehearsed actress, she moved smoothly to the darkened entryway, removed the security chain and began to open the front door.

A tightly furled red rose appeared in the gap.

Startled, Joy accepted it.

Another rose appeared. And then another. And another. And another. And another.

By the time it was over, Joy held thirty-six flawless roses in her arms, their thornless stems hard and cool against her skin, their scent rising to envelop her in the evening's first embrace.

She felt a deep elation rising within her, not because of the extravagance of the gift, but because its unusual execution was so typical of the giver. By the time the final rose was released to her, she knew that this night with Charlie was hers for the taking, and that take it she would, with tenderness and gratitude and love. When it became clear that the flood of roses had ceased, she swung the door wide.

Charlie came inside, smiling a heavy-lidded greeting that elicited a quiver of response deep within her. "I'm a little late," he said, raising a hand to the zipper of his jacket. "Did you hold my reservation?"

Dry mouthed, Joy nodded.

With an economy of motion, he removed the jacket and hung it on the coat rack near the door. Then his gaze traveled from the dark living room to the gently lit landing and, from there, up the stairs. "Do you suppose you could show me to my room?"

"It would be my pleasure," Joy said softly.

Charlie made a courtly gesture, inviting her to precede him.

Acutely aware that she was being watched, she turned and started slowly up the stairs. She heard him moving behind her, then gave a gasp of surprise as his hands came to rest lightly on her hips, not impeding her progress but absorbing the rhythm and sway of it.

Instead of making her feel awkward and self-conscious, Charlie's touch transformed her, lifting her out of thought and context into a heady realm of the senses. Memories of their Christmas tryst returned to tantalize her, promising unparalleled delights. Charlie had already proven that he found her desirable, worthy of his admiration. He had seen her naked, he had slept in her bed and now he had returned to her. There was little room in the present moment for doubt, and none at all for fear.

The roses were still in her arms. When they reached the top of the stairs, she turned to Charlie and lifted her beautiful burden slightly, with a bemused smile. "These are too beautiful to neglect. I should put them in water..."

His answering smile was an assured one. Taking the roses from her, he vanished into the bathroom with them. She heard the sound of running water, and then he was back, with a single long-stemmed bloom still in his grasp. Slipping his free hand into hers, he came to a halt, allowing her to resume the lead.

Without hesitation, Joy led him into her room, welcoming him to the chamber that had always been hers alone.

When she released his hand, Charlie walked to the bedside and positioned the ruby rose diagonally across the nearest pillow. "I have something to show you, if you'll bear with me for a minute."

Joy smiled and nodded.

Charlie unbuckled his belt.

The action disconcerted her, but she kept silent, reserving judgment.

He unbuttoned his cuffs and then the long line of buttons down the front of his shirt.

It didn't appear to be any sort of macho display or veiled demand for submission. There was nothing particularly provocative in his manner as he removed his shirt and kicked off his shoes. She didn't understand the purpose behind this measured disrobing. Knowing Charlie, however, she trusted that there *was* a purpose.

He bent to remove his socks, then straightened, watching her watching him as he raised his hands to the waistband of his slacks. One quick movement lowered the zipper. Then his pants fell to the floor and he grinned at her as he stepped free of them, wearing nothing but a very conservative pair of white jockey shorts.

Joy felt her own smile growing wider, threatening to blossom into laughter. She restrained herself for a moment, afraid of wounding Charlie's ego, then surrendered to the gaiety of the moment, confident that he had orchestrated events in pursuit of winning just such a reaction from her.

"Very reassuring," she said when the little bubble of laughter had spent itself, leaving her warm and unstrung. "But I have something to show you, too."

Charlie stood politely at attention.

Filled with a rich sense of the pleasure yet to come, Joy stepped out of her own shoes and unbuttoned her blouse. Taking her cue from Charlie, she resisted the urge to do it coyly, trying instead to undress as she would have if she had been alone in the room.

When her skirt and blouse were gone, she removed her panty hose, then gripped the sleek material of her white slip and drew it off over her head. When she emerged a moment later, free of it, revealed in her frivolous pale blue lingerie, she raised her gaze to meet Charlie's.

The sight of him put an end to her attempts at composure. His face was suffused with color, and she could see the rapid rise and fall of his chest as the breath jolted through him. His hands hung at his sides as they had before, but his fingers were splayed and trembling, as if they yearned for the touch of her. And his shorts, however conservatively cut, left her in no possible doubt as to the hunger she had unleashed in him.

She crossed the floor to stand before him. "Aren't you going to unwrap your present?" she asked. Taking his right hand in both of hers, she guided it to the little clasp between her breasts that secured the lacy cups of her brassiere.

It opened at his touch. "It's just what I've always wanted," he said as he slid the tips of his fingers beneath the edges, dislodging the lace, replacing it with his own warm flesh, cupping her breasts with gentle strength, cradling the weight of them in his palms. "I hope you like your present half as well."

"Shall I open it now?" she asked, teasing him for the sheer pleasure of prolonging her anticipation.

"That's up to you," Charlie said huskily. "I'm a little busy at the moment." He kissed her left temple, briefly caressing the pulse that throbbed there with the tip of his tongue, then trailed a string of kisses along her cheekbone before concentrating on her lips.

Joy closed her eyes as their kiss deepened. Delighting in the subtle play of muscle beneath skin, she slid her fingers from his shoulders down to the broad waistband of his undershorts.

The small of his back was damp from the fever heat that possessed him. As she reached beneath the soft knit cotton and tensed her fingertips against the slight curve of his buttocks, he mouthed a wordless syllable, the vibration of it passing from his throat to hers. She arched her fingers, pricking his sensitive flesh slightly with her nails.

He arched against her with a groan.

Intoxicated by his reaction, Joy shifted, moving her hips slowly from side to side, feeling the iron length of his erection trapped uncompromisingly between them

Charlie broke from their kiss, gasping for air like a drowning man as Joy sent her questing fingers deeper, feeling the throb and shift of his body as control slipped further from him.

Under the goad of her caresses, Charlie's answering movements took on a cadence that grew strong and insistent. With a guttural cry, he tried to step back, but Joy refused to let him go. Pulling him closer still, she wooed him with pressure and motion, inciting him with her touch until he crushed her to him in a bruising embrace and thrust against her rapidly in avid spasms of release.

When it was over, Charlie wavered on shaky legs. As his hold slackened, Joy guided him onto the bed, keeping him close, kissing his neck, his ear, his cheek, gentling him against her.

When his breathing had steadied, he rose on one elbow to eye her with a pleased but shamefaced smile and scolded, "You don't play fair, Ms. Porter. And you give a whole new meaning to 'generous to a fault.' Are you prepared to suffer the consequences?"

"That depends. What are they?"

"That I'll have to find some pastime to occupy me while I recover from being debauched. And that you are predestined to be the pastime I choose. I just hope this wasn't your exquisitely polite way of letting me know that you'd prefer our physical relationship to remain unconsummated."

"Look in the drawer," she said, and nodded toward the bedside table.

Slowly, Charlie sat up and opened the drawer. "My, my," he said in tones of delight, flopping down beside her again. "You *have* been a busy little bee. Decadent lingerie, and now condoms. To be honest, I'm having a hard time imagining the scenario. Did you bribe Lisa to buy them for you, or would that have been even harder on your nerves?"

"I bought them myself." She reached for him, swamped by a wave of embarrassment. "It became a point of honor," she said against his neck as he enfolded her. "If making love to you was what I wanted, then I had to be adult enough to handle everything else that went with that decision." She kissed his ear. "So I did. Because I do."

"Say no more, fair maiden. Your wish is mine. But first..." Rising from the bed, he stripped off his shorts, mopping at himself briefly with a rueful grimace. "Messy creatures, men. It's a good thing you love us in spite of our faults." Returning, naked, to kneel on the bed, he eased her down onto the cool sheets.

Joy closed her eyes, abandoning herself to Charlie's whims.

At first he contented himself with running his hands over her skin in long, sweeping strokes, as if reacquainting himself with the curves of her body. From time to time his fingers flirted with the lace trim that edged her panties, or glided tantalizingly over the satiny triangle that covered the dark curls clustered there, but he made no move to insinuate his hands beneath the fabric. Not yet. Instead, he rested the heel of his palm on the elastic of her bikini briefs and with the full length of his agile fingers kneaded the soft flesh below, awakening a riot of sensation within her with each delicate new assault.

Joy fought against the urge to move greedily beneath the courtship of his touch—fought, and lost. Her hips began to undulate, and the slide of satin against skin changed as moisture seeped from her, called forth by the sweet torment of Charlie's attentions.

The mattress creaked and shifted, and Joy felt something move lightly over her breasts, teasing her nipples into sharper arousal and tickling gently across her skin. Opening her eyes again, she saw that Charlie was caressing her with the rose, using it to trace her navel, the curve of her ribs, the rise of her breasts, the circular outline of each tightly gathered areola. Smiling indolently, he dusted the crimson blossom across her forehead and down the line of her nose, over her parted lips and down the column of her throat before laying the stem between her breasts, with the tips of the petals just brushing the underside of her chin.

"Don't let it fall," he murmured, and moved down to kneel between her feet. Reaching forward, he gripped the top edge of the dainty panties and coaxed them down her thighs, over her knees, along her calves and over her left foot, leaving them gathered wantonly around her right ankle.

"So beautiful," he said softly, and Joy colored as his eyes swept her body. His palms were warm and smooth and strong as he slid them up her legs, pressing outward with gentle insistence, widening the space between. "So soft." At the apex, he stroked her with a single finger, releasing a convulsive shudder of pleasure that nearly dislodged the rose. "So welcoming." Again, a stroke; again, a shudder, stronger than the first. "I am welcome, aren't I, sweet Joy?" His finger dipped deep, then slid high to dizzy her with a flurry of deft caresses that left her whimpering. "Welcome to come inside and warm myself?"

"Yes," she whispered, closing her eyes. "Welcome. Yes . . ."

Phantom like, he was everywhere and nowhere: a kiss, a caress, a heated breath, a murmured word, feeding the fires within her to a pitch that frightened her, until the moment came when he said softly, "Don't you want to see the magic we're about to make?"

When she opened her eyes, he filled her vision, poised above her, his face vivid with renewed desire.

Unable to stop herself, she encircled him with her arms, begging mutely for him to lower himself into her, but still he held back, his eyes bright and searching, as if some final assurance were needed to set him free.

Slipping one hand between their heated bodies, she closed her fingers lovingly around his rigid shaft and guided him between her legs. Lifting her hips, she captured him within her.

She had expected her boldness to unleash a torrent of frenzied action, but Charlie sank into her by heart-stopping degrees, giving her body every chance to accommodate itself to his invasion. When he finally rested fully against her, his chest pressed solidly to her breasts, his thighs lodged between hers, filling her with a completeness that might well have been painful but for his care, she felt the tremors that shook him, evidence of the price of his control. "Are you all right?" he asked in a voice shredded by effort.

Joy kissed his chin, then traced the cords of his throat with her tongue before answering. "I will be," she said at last, "as soon as you put us both out of our misery. Not that misery was ever this sweet . . ."

He began to move then, slowly, rhythmically, surging within her at a dreamy pace, reaching down from time to time to titillate her, nudging her closer and closer to the moment when the pulsing bud of arousal would explode into completion. She flung her head from side to side on the pillow, forced beyond herself, eyes wide but blind, breath whistling in her dry throat, knowing only that it was almost . . . almost . . .

Charlie's control broke first. With a hoarse animal roar, he drove forward with a sudden lunge that ig-

nited them both. Crying Charlie's name, Joy was
overcome by the pulsing waves of her own climax.
Lost in sensation, she clung to him with manic
strength as her body bucked and shook.

Then, as the spasms faded, she pulled away from
Charlie and began to weep—not daintily, but in deep,
shuddering sobs that were as far outside her control as
her orgasm had been.

She cried from happiness and from loss, from
pleasure and tension and an odd, elusive melancholy.
She cried for the loss of her father. She cried for the
gift of Charlie's presence and for the sorrow of his
impending departure. She cried until Charlie's mur-
murs of sympathy turned to kindly protests of concern.

When the tears finally stopped, she sat up and accepted the box of tissues that he had retrieved from the
bureau. When she'd wiped her eyes and blown her
nose and felt relatively certain of herself, she looked
at him with a watery smile and said, "I hope you
didn't take that personally."

"Not at all." A belated expression of alarm crossed
his face. "Should I have? I didn't hurt you, did I?"

"No. You were wonderful."

"Good. Then we're still on speaking terms?"

"Definitely."

"Would you like me to leave you alone for a few
minutes? I could go grab a shower. Or I can go on
home, if you want me to."

"Absolutely not."

"Are you hungry?"

"No."

"Thirsty?"

"No." She took his hand. "I'm fine, Charlie. Truly. Good as new."

"In that case," he asked, his eyes wide in the lamp-light, "would you consider marrying me?"

CHAPTER FIFTEEN

AS CHARLIE'S WORDS sank in, Joy's astonishment brightened into elation...then transmuted, without warning, into terrified denial.

She forced herself to take a breath and think.

Marriage to Charlie? She had daydreamed about the possibility more than once, longed for it and all it could mean. Why, then, was her stomach clenching in doubt and despair?

Because the timing's all wrong, a frantic voice warned her. *Because Charlie's just romantic enough to think he has to make an "honest woman" of me, now that we've made love. Because his life is in turmoil, and so is mine. Because I'm still in the process of figuring out what I want to do with myself. Because, out of the four months we've known each other, we've spent less than a week together. And because there's a part of me that wants to say yes just so that I can drop all my problems and doubts into Charlie's lap and have him resolve them for me.*

She intended to express all of that to Charlie, calmly and kindly, but the words that came out of her mouth instead were, "Marry you? Why?"

A horrible silence fell.

"Because I love you," Charlie said at last, looking daunted but determined. "Because I thought you loved me."

"I do," she said without hesitation.

"Then marry me. I'm lonely, and so are you, but we don't have to be. Not if we love each other. I'd like to think that something wonderful can come out of all the heartache we've been through, this past year. And it *would* be wonderful, Joy."

"How can you be so sure? You hardly know me. If you think you do, then you must just be projecting, imagining I'm what you need me to be, or what you think I ought to be."

"So," Charlie said with droll gravity, "if I think you're wonderful, I'm wrong. And if I love you, I must be crazy. Is that about it? I suppose next you'll ask me to believe that tonight was nothing but a casual, physical thing for you. A case of hopping hormones."

"No, of course not. You know it wasn't. But it's a far cry from this—" she gestured awkwardly at the rumpled sheets "—to marriage. I'm not saying no. I'm saying not now, not yet."

"But later?"

"I don't know," she said, turning away from the hope in his eyes. "There are too *many* things I don't know. I can live with being lonely, if I have to. But I couldn't live with ruining your life, and that's what I'm afraid would happen if I made a hasty decision."

"And what if you ruin both our lives by refusing to make a decision?"

"I don't know. I just know that it doesn't feel right to make such a big commitment right now, Charlie. Even if marrying you turns out to be the right choice, this is the wrong time. What harm can there be in waiting?"

"How long? For what?"

"For a while. Until some of the craziness settles out of our lives. Until the playground is built, and you know what's going to happen to your brother-in-law, and I've had a chance to finish out the school year and see if teaching is still what I want to be doing. Until I've had a little more time to get used to being on my own." She touched the smooth skin of his shoulder. "Until I've had a little more time to think about the possibility of the two of us, together, forever."

"Is it such a tough thought to get used to?" Charlie asked, sounding forlorn.

Joy smiled. "Not tough. But radical. Until you came along, I'd pretty much stopped thinking about ever being someone's wife. Too many other responsibilities came along, and I got older, and..."

"Withering on the vine," Charlie teased softly, reaching to stroke the swell of her breast.

Joy's pulse leaped, and she leaned into his touch before she could stop herself. "Charlie," she murmured, and her heart melted as he bent to close his lips around her nipple with gentle force. "Oh, Charlie...."

Nothing had been resolved, but that seemed less important than reassuring him of her love. Welcoming him into her arms, Joy let the sweet delirium of his caresses brush the web of worry from her mind, grateful for the temporary reprieve.

CHARLIE WOKE a few minutes after five, and smiled to feel the soft warmth of Joy's body beside him beneath the covers.

Then memory roused itself and his smile faded.

What a fool he had been, asking Joy to marry him when she was already reeling from an evening of

lovemaking and high emotion. What on earth had
made him think she would say anything *but* no, under
those circumstances? In hindsight, it was painfully
obvious that the situation had called for tact and patience, and yet he had bulldozed ahead, so swept away
by his own feelings that it never occurred to him that
silence might be his best ally.

Her arguments for postponing their decision made
more sense to him than he was comfortable admitting. The final weeks of the playground project would
be lively, and the rest of his workload wasn't going to
let up. Matthew was a definite wild card, as was Shelley. In addition, Joy had commitments that she needed
to honor, through to the end of the school year.... It
was a wonder she hadn't dumped him out of bed on
his head.

He turned over carefully, so as not to disturb her,
and closed his eyes, letting his thoughts and worries
drift away on a drowsy wave. After all, there was still
hope. She hadn't actually said no.

February 16

Dear Joy:
Where do I even start? We shared something
special on Friday night, and I will always be glad
for that. Maybe it was just as well that I had to
leave on Saturday morning, since you say you
need more time to think. I don't. I know exactly
what I want... but it can only work if you want
it, too. I tell myself that anything this precious is
bound to work out, eventually. But waiting is
hard.

Matthew's rehab counselor called this morning, to ask if Matthew can move in with me when he's released next week. Since my top choice for a roommate turned me down flat, I didn't see any good reason to tell them no. I really don't know what to expect, but I guess time will tell.

I guess time will tell about a lot of things.

Love,
Charlie

February 20

Dear Charlie:

I was glad to hear that Matthew is doing so much better. With luck, maybe your workload will lighten up, once he's had a chance to adjust to being back. Letting him share your apartment is one more proof of what a good man you are—but then, I already knew that.

Thank you for being patient. Thank you for introducing me to a side of myself I never knew was there. I'm thinking about everything you said, I promise you.

More soon,
Joy

"ONE DAY CLOSER to my deliverance," Lisa Stone announced as she entered the teacher's lounge. "If you'll pardon the pun."

Joy groaned. "Bad, Lisa. Really bad." She eyed her friend's increased girth with sympathy. "Here—sit down and take a load off those poor ankles of yours."

"Are they still attached? That's encouraging. I don't see them much these days." With difficulty, she lowered herself into the chair beside Joy. "So, are you ready to take over my little darlings next week?"

"As ready as I'm apt to get."

"Good." She looked up at the big clock on the wall. "I'm waiting to meet with Eleanor for my exit interview, but what's *your* excuse for being here? You were free to head home twenty minutes ago."

"I know."

"Then do Jezebel a favor and get going. You can call me on Monday night and tell me how your first day went, okay?"

"Will do," Joy promised, and rose to collect her coat.

THE DOORBELL RANG.

Matthew, Charlie thought, and his stomach tightened.

What would it be like to have Matthew in residence, having to hear that cool voice call him "Charles" before he'd even had his first cup of coffee in the morning?

On the telephone that morning, Matthew had declined his offer of a ride, stating mildly that he preferred to make his own way from the rehab center to Charlie's apartment. Charlie had been grateful for the postponement.

Now it was the zero hour.

Deep breath, Charlie advised himself as he walked toward the door. *Casual smile, relaxed manner, no big deal.*

But it was a big deal, and the thought of the responsibility he was undertaking chilled him. What if it didn't work out? What if there hadn't been any lasting improvement? Throughout Matthew's lengthy stay at the center, he had declined Charlie's offers to visit. Had the past months changed him at all?

There was only one way to find out.

Taking another deep breath for good measure, he opened the door.

"Hi," Matthew said, standing in the hallway, suitcase in hand.

He had lost weight; his expensive raincoat hung on him like a hand-me-down. His hair had grown out of its traditional near-military cut, and the extra length added to the gray that showed at each temple. His glasses were the same, but the eyes behind them were shadowed with weariness and sorrow. His posture was still ramrod straight and he held his chin high, but the effect was more proud than pugnacious.

"Welcome back," Charlie said, and felt an unexpected stirring of sympathy as Matthew crossed his threshold. "You can put your shaving kit on the shelf in the bathroom." He closed the door, anxious to get them past the awkward opening moments of Matthew's return. "I'm sticking you with the sofa bed, but I cleared out a couple of dresser drawers for you, and some closet space. I'll need to do a grocery run tomorrow, so take a look around the kitchen. If there's anything you want that you don't find, feel free to add it to the list on the refrigerator door."

"What I'm really going to need," Matthew said, taking off his raincoat, "are some new clothes. Or at least some suspenders."

He was making a joke of sorts. Charlie's spirits rose. Maybe this was going to work, after all. "We could take a run over to the mall after dinner," he suggested, "if you aren't too tired."

"After dinner would be fine. Better yet, let's have dinner out. My treat. We have a lot of catching up to do." With his coat draped over his arm, Matthew came closer. "And I have some apologies to make."

"Not to me. It isn't necessary."

Matthew waved his words away. "But it is. It's all part of the process—facing up to the things I've done and the people I've hurt. I'd take it as a personal favor if you'd pull up a chair and let me say what's on my mind...Charlie."

He'd never heard the name "Charlie" pass Matthew's lips. Astonished and gratified, he nodded in mute acquiescence and sat down.

WHEN JOY REACHED HOME, she found Jezebel scrambling around restlessly in her cage to the accompaniment of the ringing telephone. "First things first," she said, opening the cage door. "Come here, sweetheart. Tail. We'll just let the answering machine get it, okay? Whoever it is, I can call them back later." *And if it's Charlie,* she thought guiltily, *I'd rather have a little advance warning.*

More than a week had gone by since she had mailed her last letter, and no reply had arrived. She hated the self-conscious quality that had crept into her communication with him, but she was at a loss to know how to avoid it. It didn't seem right to stick strictly to business, talking and writing only about the playground project. Yet what purpose would it serve to be more personal, when she wasn't prepared to say the one thing she knew he was hoping to hear?

The voice that spoke when the answering machine finished its speech was female. "Hello, Joy," it said, "this is Dr. Westrup at Monkeys Do. Please give me a call as soon—"

Joy snatched the receiver from its hook and turned off the answering machine. "Dr. Westrup? This is Joy. I just walked in. What can I do for you?"

"I was wondering how Jezebel's doing these days."

It didn't sound like an idle inquiry. Joy stroked the monkey anxiously, wondering if some anomaly had shown up on Jezebel's latest card. Over the past few months her weight had stabilized, but Joy had assumed it was simply a sign that Jezebel had finished her adolescent growth spurt. Had there been some more dangerous explanation for her failure to gain? "Jezzie's fine," she said defensively. "Just fine."

"Good. Glad to hear it. I'm calling today because we've just had some exciting news. Monkeys Do has been selected for a new grant, one that will cover the salary of an additional staff member."

"That's wonderful!" Joy said with genuine enthusiasm. She knew what a constant struggle funding had been for the organization. Despite their best efforts, the demand for trained capuchins exceeded the supply by a factor of nearly ten to one, leaving people like Austin Blade to wait anxiously for the fulfillment of their dreams.

"We're reviewing applications now and we expect to hire someone in the next few weeks. As soon as we do, we'll be able to increase the number of monkeys called in for training and placement."

Belatedly, Joy saw where the conversation was headed.

"I just wanted to let you know," Dr. Westrup was saying, "since Jezebel is shaping up so well. You've done a marvelous job with her, Joy. Needless to say, we won't call her in until we have a trainer available and a candidate in mind. We like to make as quick a transition as we can between homes. It's easier on the monkeys that way."

Joy hugged Jezebel to her chest. *And what about the people?* she thought desperately. *What makes it easier for them?* But there was no answer for that. She had known, when she and her father signed on to raise Jezebel for the Monkeys Do project, that this day would come. She just hadn't anticipated how much it would hurt.

"The timing will depend on who we hire and when they can start. If we're lucky, it could be a few weeks, or it might drag on for months. We wanted to start alerting people now, so that everything can go smoothly once we have our new personnel in place. I'll call you as soon as I know something more specific, okay, Joy?"

"Of course." Despite her efforts at control, her voice had begun to thicken with emotion. "Thank you, Dr. Westrup. Goodbye."

As Joy reached out to replace the receiver, Jezebel wriggled free and bounded away to skitter around the room.

Joy knew the monkey was only venting the pent-up energy that came from a day spent closed in her cage, but it still felt like an abandonment. "Toughen up," she ordered herself aloud, but the words wobbled. This wasn't some nebulous black mood. The problem was real, and so was the pain.

Nevertheless, she groped instinctively for a way to thwart the downward spiral of her emotions. As Dr. Westrup had said, it might be weeks or months before Jezebel was recalled for training—time during which Lisa's first graders would need to be taught and the final stages of the playground would have to be planned and executed. Joy couldn't afford to spend that time immersed in the kind of impotent frustration that had settled over her during her conversation with Dr. Westrup.

Call Charlie.

She rejected the thought as quickly as it formed. Call him and tell him how empty the house would seem when Jezebel was gone? It didn't take a mental giant to predict what his response would be.

But calling *someone* wasn't a bad idea. The only question was who.

Eleanor would have been her first choice, but she would still be at school, wrapping up Lisa's exit interview.

Austin? He certainly had the ability to distract her from her troubles and brighten her spirits . . . but it seemed insensitive to ask him to sympathize with her sorrow when its cause would be a source of excitement for him—the expansion of the program at Monkeys Do and the increased rate at which it would be able to supply trained capuchins.

Then who? Who would help her fight the tidal pull of depression?

Shelley.

It was a good solution, but it wouldn't be an easy one to implement. Shelley was always the one who came to her. In all the time they had worked together, Shelley had never accepted so much as a ride home. Where, in a city the size of Sacramento, could Joy even begin to look?

Again, Austin Blade came to mind—Austin and his computer, which was chock-full of information about the playground-project volunteers.

Hoping for the best, she dialed his number.

"Good Sports," a lilting voice answered. "How can I help you?"

Over the past months, Austin and Garrett had recruited more than half of the Good Sports staff to work on the playground, and Joy had no trouble recognizing the voice of the receptionist who had greeted her on her very first visit, and who now doubled as assistant chairman of the publicity committee. "Alison? It's Joy. Is Austin around?"

"Sure thing. Just a second and I'll put you through." Her voice fell silent, supplanted by the soothing strains of a soft-rock radio station.

Joy waited unhappily through two songs and a public service announcement before Austin came on the line, sounding winded as his voice projected from his speakerphone. "Sorry for the delay, Fearless Leader. Garrett and I were just finishing my daily workout—I supply the body, he supplies the muscle. What can I do for you?"

"I need to talk to Sheila and I don't know how to get in touch with her. Could you check the computer?"

Austin laughed. "I thought you two were living in each other's pockets."

"Practically, but I need her right away and she isn't due here again until Monday morning. Could you look up her background information?"

"I'm loading the personnel data base. Hang on.... Yeah, there we go. Now let me do a search." He fell silent again, and Joy knew it was from necessity; he used a mouth stick for typing on the computer, with a speed and accuracy that had stunned her when she first witnessed his keyboard technique. "Bingo," he said a minute later. "Well, half a bingo. No phone number listed, but there's an address. Do you have something to write on?" He recited the address, spelling out the street name. "Anything else you need while I've got the program loaded?"

"No. Thanks anyway."

Without altering his casual tone, he asked, "Want to tell me what's wrong?"

Joy froze. "Who says anything's wrong?"

Austin made a rude noise. "Look, if you don't want to tell me, that's your business. Just don't bullshit me, okay?"

"Okay," she agreed soberly. "Sorry."

"Forget it."

"And thanks for the info."

"Forget that, too. This project has been more fun than—you should pardon the expression—a barrel of monkeys."

Joy closed her lips against a sob.

When the silence had dragged on for an uncomfortable interval, Austin said, "All right, I get the message. 'Don't ask.' And I won't, if that's what you really want. But you know where to find me if you need me."

"Mmm," Joy mouthed in assent, not trusting herself to speak.

Austin sighed. "Go talk to Sheila," he suggested, not unkindly, and broke the connection.

But that was going to be easier said than done. Hanging up, Joy looked again at the unfamiliar street name and went in search of a city map.

IN THE ROUTINE of her newly adopted life, Shelley habitually spent Friday afternoons down the block at Super Suds, shepherding her week's meager laundry from washing machine to dryer. Winter had begun to soften into spring, in the accelerated manner of the Sacramento Valley. Hedges of flowering quince were displaying their salmon-pink blossoms everywhere she turned. Before the weekend was over, it would be March. The whole world was being reborn before her eyes, but she was in suspended animation—not the voluntary coma of emotions she had sought when she fled San Francisco in October, but a restless, smothering confinement.

She didn't know what she wanted. She only knew that she needed more than the half life that was currently hers.

For now, working for the playground committee brought a measure of relief from the grief of Penny's death and the pain of Matthew's defection. But in another three months, the structuring influence of the playground project would be gone from her life. Where, then, would she find her purpose?

The dryer cycle ended, prodding her out of her melancholy introspection. There was a certain pleasure to be found in the simple act of pulling the warm clothes out of the dryer's maw, item by item, until the tumbling chaos that had shown through the little round window had been reduced to well-ordered stacks of clean, folded clothes. From there, she placed them in the little wheeled cart that did double duty when she went to buy her groceries, and started back to her rented room.

Half a block from home, she spotted a car parked at the hydrant in front of the building. A big white car that she knew.

Shelley's hands shook as she fumbled in the pocket of her jacket for her key. Joy Porter, here? From pride and fear, she didn't want it to be true—pride because the run-down room where she lived was nothing she wanted Joy to see, and fear because she knew that Joy would not have searched her out unless it was an emergency. What horrible thing had happened to Charlie? Or was it Matthew?

She unlocked the outer door of the house and dragged her cart into the foyer. As she'd expected, Joy was there, just past the mailboxes, huddled on the bottom step in a tight knot of misery. She looked up at the sound of the door, and her stricken gaze locked with Shelley's.

As horrible as the truth might prove to be, not knowing was worse. Abandoning her cart, Shelley ran to Joy and knelt in front of her, gripping her icy hands. "Tell me," she entreated. "Just take a deep breath and tell me."

Joy tried, but it took three attempts before she was able to say hoarsely, "They called. They're going to take her."

"Who called?" Shelley fought the urge to shake the information out of her. "Take who?"

"Jezebel."

It took a moment for Shelley to absorb Joy's words. When she did, her first impulse was to shriek, *A monkey? You scared me half to death over a monkey?* But reason prevailed, with compassion on its heels, and she said instead, "Who's going to take

Jezebel? I don't understand. Did somebody complain to the health department? The SPCA?"

Joy shook her head. "Monkeys Do is taking her. They own her."

"I thought *you* owned her."

"No. I raised her, but she belongs to them. There's nothing I can do about it. They have every right. I've known from the start that she'd have to go back to them eventually. I just thought...I'd hoped...I didn't realize how attached..." She took a gulping breath. There were no tears in her eyes, but her hands trembled in Shelley's. "I shouldn't be reacting like this, I know. Most of this isn't even about Jezebel. It's just...everything."

"What kind of 'everything?' "

"Losing Dad. And now Charlie..."

"What about Charlie?" Shelley asked sharply.

Joy ducked her chin, avoiding Shelley's eyes.

"Damn it, Joy, talk! What happened to Charlie? Is he hurt?"

"No. He's fine. It's just..."

"Just *what?*"

"He asked me to marry him."

"Charlie? My brother Charlie?" She realized her incredulity must sound insulting, but it was the only honest response she could manage. "Are you serious?" she asked in the face of Joy's continued silence, then shook her head wryly. "Of course you're serious. Just look at you." She stood up and tugged at Joy's hand. "Come on upstairs. I want to hear you explain why a marriage proposal from my brother qualifies as a tragedy in your life."

"It doesn't! It's just—"

"Nope. Not here. Upstairs. I made brownies last night. We're going to brew coffee and stuff our faces while you tell me all about it."

"But I—"

She pulled Joy to her feet and gave her a quick, sympathetic hug. "I know it isn't easy, but you wouldn't have come all the way down here if you didn't want to talk to me about it. Right?"

"Right," Joy admitted.

"So lend a hand and help me drag this laundry upstairs," Shelley ordered, gripping the handle of the cart. "After all, this is the closest I've ever come to having a sister-in-law, so don't think you're getting out of here until you've spilled your guts, kid, chapter and verse. This is one story I have *got* to hear."

CHAPTER SIXTEEN

March 16th

Dear Charlie:

It still feels laughably premature to me, but we're busy confirming the food donations and eating supplies for construction weekend. You should see the look on the merchants' faces when I tell them to count on more than five hundred volunteers on Memorial Day alone!

And yes, when I say we've started to line up donations, I do mean that "we" literally. Sheila Taylor drafted me as her partner to canvass some of the local restaurants and grocery stores. It would have made your day to hear me thank the manager at the Fish Palace sweetly for donating clam chowder and then turn around and muscle him for cups to serve it in. Unbelievable. Who is this pushy woman?

Things are hectic, now that I've taken over Lisa's class, but I've got a good team of people on the project to pick up my slack and we're managing to keep our noses above water. At this point, I think it would be almost impossible to stop the playground from happening—it's developed a momentum all its own. There was an update article in last Tuesday's paper, and a group of our volunteers will man the telephones next week during the local public television station's spring auction. They'll be wearing our "Monkey Jungle" T-shirts, with a logo drawn by a fifth grader from Dunnett Elementary (Jezebel posed), and we're starting to incorporate that same logo into our fliers.

I'll keep you posted on all the latest.

Joy

P.S. This is a horrible letter—busy and surfacy and arm's length—but I'm afraid to write you a better one. I do miss you. I am thinking about what you said. I just don't have any answers yet, for you or for myself. Be well.

"HAVE YOU HEARD anything more about Jezebel?" Shelley asked when Joy came home from school that afternoon, looking windswept and damp.

"No. Not yet."

"Have you told Charlie about it?"

"No." She set her load of books and papers on the corner of the desk and unbuttoned her raincoat. "I haven't told anybody but you, and I'm not going to. What good would it do?"

Exasperated, Shelley looked up from the document she'd been typing. "What good? Just the chance for some sympathy. A little support and understanding. Nothing much, really. Friends are strange creatures— they actually like to feel as if they're a part of what's going on in your life. Believe me, I wish I hadn't thumbed my nose at so many of *mine*, when things were at their worst. But if you're having more fun being a martyr..."

"I have to learn to stand on my own two feet."

"That's the kind of thinking that breeds ulcers."

"I can't keep expecting other people to prop me up and give me a purpose," Joy said forlornly. "In a few months, the school year will be over, the playground will be finished, Dad's book will be out and Jezzie will be...gone. And I don't have the first idea what I'm going to do with myself then. But I intend to figure it out."

"Don't you suppose Charlie might like to offer some input on that decision? Would it hurt just to talk to him about it?"

"I can't. Not yet. If I agree to marry Charlie, it has to be because it's the best answer for both of us, not because it's the only answer I can come up with. The pursuit of happiness may be a constitutional right, but nobody ever guaranteed we'll find it. People don't get everything they want in life, but they go on anyway and make the best of it. You know that better than I do."

The oblique reference to Penny's death stung, but Shelley hardened her heart to the pain. "You're right," she said sternly, "I *do* know that better than you do. I also know that, if you want things to get better, sometimes you have to reach out and *make* them better."

Joy crossed her arms defensively. "Is that why you left home?"

Is she trying to pick a fight? Shelley wondered, outraged and astonished. She wasn't used to this kind of tenacity from Joy. "What is this," she asked, "interrogate Shelley week? Yes, if you really want to know, I left home because I hoped it would make my life better. I still don't know if it was the right deci-

sion. I may never know. But at the time it felt like the
only positive choice I could make. Anything else
would have been just surrendering to misery, so I left.
Still, times change and so do people, and I've been
thinking about going back before long, to make sure
this is the way it has to be. I'm not particularly keen
on being alone if I don't have to. What about you?
Does being all on your own give you a thrill?''

''No.''

''Do you love Charlie?''

''I miss him. I admire him. I have fun with him.''

''Do you love him?''

Joy shrugged helplessly. ''I know you want me to
say yes, but it depends on what you mean by love.''

''Well, turn it around. What ways *don't* you love
him?''

''That's hard to answer.''

''Too bad. Try.''

''Well, for starters, I don't love him enough to say
yes just because I know he wants me to.''

''Good.''

''And I don't love him enough to walk out on my
responsibilities.''

''If I know Charlie, he isn't asking you to. What
else?''

''I guess I don't trust him enough to believe he can
really mean it when he tells me how much he loves
me.''

Why wasn't life ever simple? ''All right, if those are
your reasons, then you're probably right to put off
giving him an answer,'' Shelley admitted. ''But you're
the one who isn't seeing straight, not Charlie. And
don't kid yourself that you can keep things floating in
limbo until every last question and insecurity has been

settled. Charlie's a pretty patient guy, but he's no saint. You may have to settle for making up your mind on a strong hunch instead of a dead certainty. A majority vote instead of a landslide. The time's gonna come when you have to take a chance, Joy—or else risk losing the right to choose at all. Refusing to decide eventually becomes a decision, y'know.'' She stood up. "So. End of lecture."

Joy took a shuddering breath. "I'm sorry, Shelley."

"For what, saying what was on your mind? Friends disagree. Friends argue. It doesn't mean they stop being friends. Okay?"

"Okay."

"Good. See you tomorrow."

"It's still raining a little. Let me give you a lift."

"No thanks, not today. I've got my umbrella. Besides, I need the exercise."

The walk home seemed long, but not because of the rain. It was all well and good to set herself up as some sort of authority where suffering and hard decisions were concerned, Shelley decided, but in her own heart of hearts she felt like a charlatan. For weeks—maybe months—she had wanted to see Charlie, face him, sit down with him to talk, but she had passed up several easy opportunities to do so. Even her phone calls to him had become less frequent, as if the gradual increase in her own sense of well-being was sufficient excuse for letting the contact lapse.

It wasn't. If she'd harbored any doubts about that, Joy's candor had dispelled them. Charlie had to be hurting over Joy's guarded response to his proposal, and now he had Matthew on his hands as well.

Matthew. What was she going to do about Matthew? What did she *want* to do about Matthew? How was she going to handle all the anger she still felt toward him, all the anguish his withdrawal had cost her, all the guilt she felt over the attempt he'd made on his own life? What possible hope was there for a relationship like theirs that had been tested and twisted and finally smashed?

She couldn't deal with him yet. *But I can deal with Charlie,* she thought, *and it's high time I did.* Her kid brother was no kid, and the least she owed him was the peace of mind of a call.

So decided, she crossed the street and changed direction slightly, walking until she reached the pay phone she had begun to think of as her own. It was tucked in the back corner of a small coffee shop a few blocks from her apartment.

As usual, the girl behind the counter was agreeable about trading her a tall stack of quarters for a ten-dollar bill. Armed with the coins, Shelley ordered a mug of coffee and a piece of cherry pie. "Communications surcharge," she joked, and carried them to the table next to the pay phone.

It was early evening, not quite dinnertime, but nearly. After a short internal debate, she decided to try Charlie's apartment first, in the distant hope that he would be home. His answering machine was set to kick in on the fourth ring; she could hang up before that if he wasn't there, and it wouldn't cost her anything.

She fed a quarter into the telephone, dialed Charlie's number and waited while an automated voice told her how much additional money to feed into the pay phone for the first three minutes. More quarters, more waiting, and then Charlie's phone began to ring.

Almost at once, she heard the crackling noise that indicated a connection had been made. "Hi, it's me," she said quickly, to commit herself to the call. "I know I should have called sooner and I'm sorry, so can we just get past all that and talk?"

"Michelle?"

Oh, God. It was Matthew. *Stupid, stupid, stupid,* her brain chanted, immobilizing her.

"Micky?"

It was the nickname he had coined for her on their honeymoon. No one else had ever called her that. Even Matthew hadn't used it in years.

Years.

"Charlie isn't here," he said quietly. "Do you want me to tell him you called?"

He sounded... younger. Warmer. Not like someone to be afraid of. Not like someone who could sear her soul with a look, or a word, or a word withheld.

"He should be home by seven, if you want to try him again then. Or I could have him call you back, if you give me your number. Or you could stay on the line," he suggested in the same gentle, uninsistent voice, "and we could talk until he gets here. If you want to. If you can. I— I have a lot of things to say to you."

"You do?" she said, more belligerently than she had intended. "Like what?"

"I love you. I miss you. I'm sorry. I'm changing."

Four short sentences, but they startled her out of her defensiveness. "You are?"

"There's more I need to tell you. A lot more. Do you think you could listen, for just a little while?"

It wasn't a dream; her dreams had never been this bold. "Yes. I'll listen. I want to hear it all."

Before Matthew could reply, the automated voice cut in. "Please deposit seventy-five cents for the next—"

"Give me your number and I'll call you back," Matthew suggested.

She could deposit the additional money. She could give the number to Matthew. Or she could simply hang up.

If you want things to get better, she had told Joy, *sometimes you have to reach out and make them better.*

Take a chance. Take a chance. Wasn't it worth taking a chance, one last time?

"Matthew? Do you have something to write with? It's area code 916 . . ."

FOR CHARLIE, April and May took on a surreal quality, as if the rest of the world was moving at a subtly different speed than he was. Food didn't taste quite right, business dealings didn't go quite right, sleep didn't come easily or bring much sense of ease. . . . He was at odds with life, too busy, too tense, held at a distance from Joy and his own best self.

The only really bright spot was Matthew's astounding admission that he and Shelley were now talking together on the phone several times a week, and that she had told him about the Sacramento playground project Charlie had described to her. His relief, on both counts, was intense.

On the down side, Matthew stubbornly refused to give Charlie Shelley's telephone number or tell him where her calls were coming from, for fear that any new pressure might put an end to the tenuous contact he had established.

"She has to come around in her own time, in her own way," Matthew had insisted quietly. "Everybody's got their own emotional timetable. When she's ready, she'll know."

By contrast, Joy was frequently in touch, but his contact with her brought him little satisfaction. He had last seen her at the end of March, when he drove to Sacramento for coordination day, which was nine hours of nonstop meetings with the various committee chairmen. Joy had been present throughout the long day, asking questions and taking notes, but there had been no chance to see her privately, and at that time he'd still been too worried about leaving Matthew on his own to linger at the end of the day. Not that Joy had given him any particular encouragement to stay. . . .

It shouldn't have come as any great surprise to him. He knew how all-consuming the final weeks of a playground project inevitably were for the project coordinator, but the coordinator's preoccupation had never before had such a direct personal impact on him. He wanted Joy to be talking to him, dreaming of him, thinking about him and about his marriage proposal. Instead, she could barely squeeze him in.

It was laughable.

It was breaking his heart.

But his hopes reawakened as he blocked out the five days necessary for the Monkey Jungle's construction on his May calendar. He and Joy would be together, at least, though there would be no peace and absolutely no privacy for either of them, and little room for the luxury of personal feelings. Nevertheless, his heart knew that there would be an inescapable subtext to each moment he spent in her presence.

In his pocket was a box. In the box was a ring—a ring he had bought for Joy because the hope in his heart demanded some outward expression. The ring was there, in its box, in the zippered pocket of his windbreaker. And that was where it would have to stay, until the Monkey Jungle was complete.

His alarm rang before dawn on the Thursday the project was to begin. As quietly as he could, he showered and shaved, dressed himself in a pair of jeans and a comfortable rugby shirt, and picked up the small suitcase he had packed the night before. Then he made his way toward the door of his apartment, hoping not to disturb Matthew, who still spent each night on the sofa bed rather than return to the memory-laden rooms of his own house.

As Charlie reached for the security chain, the sudden sound of Matthew's voice made him jump.

''Charlie? Wait up. I'm going with you.''

CHAPTER SEVENTEEN

DUMBFOUNDED, Charlie turned on the light.

Matthew, fully dressed, was standing near the door with an overnight bag in his hand.

"I really don't think that would be such a good idea," Charlie said. "I hate having to turn you down, but I'm going to be spread pretty thin. It's going to be a hectic couple of days with a lot of hard work to be done. Besides, the place is going to be alive with kids. That wouldn't be easy for you to face. And you'd have to take orders, like everybody else. You might end up on a crew that's raking pea gravel all day, or scrubbing tires."

"Charlie?"

"What?"

"Michelle's going to be there."

"Shelley? In Sacramento?"

Matthew nodded.

"At the playground site?"

"Yes."

"My God, is that where she's been all along?"

"The story is hers to tell, not mine. The point is, she'll be there today, unless her nerve fails her. And I intend to be there, too. Will you take me with you?"

There were a thousand good reasons to talk Matthew out of it—and not one of them mattered a damn.

"Of course I will," Charlie assured him, pushing his own mixed emotions aside. "Welcome aboard."

AT SEVEN IN THE MORNING on a near-perfect day, Joy met up with Austin and Garrett Blade at the playground site.

For the duration, the Blades had put their health club, Good Sports, at the disposal of the project. Everything from rest rooms and shower facilities to the electrical outlets was being commandeered. "You're sure your regular clients don't mind?" Joy asked as she accepted the cup of coffee Garrett offered.

Austin laughed. "With that big We Support the Monkey Jungle poster hanging in the lobby? They wouldn't dare. We offered a five-day membership credit to anybody who wanted to file a formal complaint, but most of them are already volunteers for some part of the build, and the rest are too ashamed to speak up. The wonders of peer pressure, y'know?"

It gave Joy an uneasy feeling to know she was finally poised on the brink of such a huge undertaking...or maybe the uneasy feeling came from knowing that Charlie would soon arrive.

She had missed him cruelly in the past eight weeks—missed his company, his energy and the warm glow that seemed to surround her whenever she was with him. For every scribbled letter or hurried phone call she had allowed herself, there had been a dozen conversations with him in her head. In bed at night, she relived the memory of their glorious lovemaking, remembering the physical thrill and the incredible sense of wholeness that had been hers when she was in his arms.

When she saw Charlie today, she would find out if the warmth was still there in his eyes, or whether his love for her had been worn as thin as his patience.

The possibility made her throat ache.

"Heads up," Austin said, nudging her with his wheelchair. "It's about to get crazier. Here come our fellow henchmen."

The remaining committee chairmen were walking onto the site in threes and fours. Shelley was in their midst, looking excited as she joked with Barry White, the local hardware store owner who was chairman of the tools committee.

"Hey, Sheila," Austin called out, "is that big lug giving you trouble? Want me to beat him up?"

"No need. Barry was crazy enough to think the tools committee had more to do with getting this playground built than the food committee. But I set him straight—people will work without sandpaper but not without sandwiches."

"Sounds reasonable to me," said Garrett, who had taken on the role of site manager. "Come on, everybody. Grab a cup of coffee and we'll review today's schedule."

Joy swallowed against an inconvenient lump of emotion in her throat as she listened to their friendly banter. Some of the people around her, like Nathaniel Stone, were old acquaintances. Others, like Shelley and the Blade brothers, had come into her life only a few months before, when the playground project was barely a dream. Now she counted all of them as her friends. Even after the Monkey Jungle was complete, she was bound to come across them from time to time—in a supermarket checkout line, at a gas station, at the bank or library. She knew they would nod to her in recognition, and smile in acknowledgment of the special time they had all shared on behalf of the playground.

Unless you move away.

She shook her head as if the intrusive thought was a bothersome fly. She would have more than enough to handle in the coming hours without borrowing any additional worries. The intricacies of her involvement with Charlie would just have to—

An announcement from Nathaniel broke her train of thought. "Here comes the man of the hour," he said.

Turning, Joy saw Charlie coming toward them, with a stranger at his side.

No. Not a stranger.

Matthew Tinker.

Fearing disaster, Joy dove into the crowd in search of Shelley.

"SHE'S HERE SOMEWHERE," Matthew said, his tone of voice more optimistic than the look in his eyes. "She would have told me if she'd changed her mind."

Charlie hoped, for all their sakes, that his brother-in-law was right. He hated to think what the disappointment would do to Matthew if she failed to appear.

It was impossible to walk three feet through the gathering crowd without being stopped and greeted and conferred with on some detail of the coming project, but he searched the faces around him with ceaseless intensity, in hope of seeing his sister.

Charlie looked toward the refreshment tent, and caught his breath as he spotted Joy hurrying through the crowd. He was about to call out to her in greeting, in love, but before the words could leave his lips, she called out instead, not to him but to someone else.

Following the direction of her gaze, he saw Shelley serving coffee to a line of volunteers. At the sound of Joy's voice, she turned to greet her, with the look of one friend welcoming another.

"There she is!" Matthew said.

Charlie didn't respond, absorbed in the sight of the two women as they met and spoke. Then Joy rose on tiptoe, scanning the crowd. Across the intervening space, her gaze sought . . . sought . . . and locked suddenly with his own. She gestured broadly for him to hurry to her side, and turned in the next instant to speak again in Shelley's ear, pointing in his direction.

Matthew hurried forward, but Charlie, jolted by what he had just seen, slowed and then stopped, trying to reason it through.

Joy already knew Shelley; that much was clear. It was also clear that Shelley, to judge by the T-shirt she wore, was more than a chance acquaintance; she was a project volunteer.

Most damning of all, the little pantomime he had just witnessed made him almost certain that Joy knew the identity of the woman beside her. Why else hurry to Shelley and point him out?

For weeks he had wrestled with his own resentment over Shelley's decision to confide her location to Matthew, and Matthew's quiet refusal to pass the information on. The discovery, just hours earlier, that Shelley and Matthew had arranged to rendezvous at the site and had left him in ignorance of it had been a further blow. Still, he'd tried to be adult about it. Marriage was a law unto itself. It wasn't unreasonable for Shelley and Matthew to shut him out of their plans and confidences, despite the extremes to which he'd gone to aid each of them.

Joy, however, was another matter.

His thoughts churned, yet he was aware that a reunion of major proportions was taking place with a subtlety that rendered it almost invisible in the bustling crowd. Matthew slowed as he neared Shelley, holding out his hand, then stopped before he actually made contact.

Shelley in turn took a hesitant step forward and reached out to touch his hand with the tips of her fingers.

Matthew stood before her with the same ramrod posture he had shown on his arrival at Charlie's apartment, but his lips were moving in speech.

Shelley took another step and lifted her hand to touch the backs of her fingers to his cheek.

Matthew tilted his head and leaned into her touch. She spoke and, amazingly, Matthew laughed. They turned and walked together toward the huge coffee urns.

Neither of them spared a glance at Charlie.

"Isn't it wonderful?"

The words were Joy's. Turning his head with a jerk, Charlie found her standing a few feet away, her face luminous with pleasure and...what? Pride? Smug satisfaction at having been the instrument of Shelley and Matthew's reconciliation?

He eyed her warily. "How long, Joy?"

"What do you mean?"

"Charlie?" Garrett Blade strode over to join them. "Could you come and take a look at—"

"In a minute." *How long has she worked with you?* he wanted to demand. *How long have you left me twisting in the wind, wondering what had become of my sister, when you could have put me out of my misery with a word?* He pinned Joy with a look. "How long have you known about her?"

Even then, with months of accumulated worry and weariness conspiring to spin him out of control, he hoped that Joy would be able to explain it all away and put things right again. But he read the guilt in her eyes and watched as it stained her cheeks. "Almost from the beginning," she said. "But, Charlie—"

"No." He held up his hand, refusing her words. "Don't even start. We've got too much to do in the next few days to go into this now. Let's put the whole...topic on hold until the playground's done. All right?" Without giving her a chance to respond, he swung the focus of his attention to Garrett. "Now, I'm at your disposal. Sorry to have kept you waiting. What was it you wanted to show me?"

IT SHOULD HAVE BEEN a day of miracles. Instead, Charlie operated in a corrosive cloud of confusion, resentment and self-doubt. When he saw that Garrett Blade's low-key style of leadership was setting an effective example, infecting those around him with quiet confidence, Charlie gratefully deferred to him whenever he could.

Under Garrett's supervision, the stake-out team marked the layout of the playground elements, while a crew at the far end of the site began cutting poles. It was the first real manual labor of the build, and it brought with it the ear-itching accompaniment of whining chain saws.

As a rule, the noise was music to Charlie's ears. Today it sounded worse than fingernails on a blackboard. He braced himself against the annoyance, well aware that he would hear it almost constantly during the next few days.

The utility company arrived with boom augers to drill the post holes, and, to Charlie's relief, a cadre of weight lifting enthusiasts from Good Sports showed up a few minutes later to set the first assortment of cut poles and offer pointers to the other helpers on the form and technique of handling deadweight. The trickle of early morning volunteers became a steady stream.

When Charlie boosted himself up into the moving van that doubled as the project's supply shed, he found an impressive collection of tools assembled there—long lines of saws, drills, rakes, wrenches, screwdrivers, shovels, paint brushes and dozens of other implements that would help to turn the mountains of raw lumber and tubs of nails and screws into a captivating Monkey Jungle.

From the back of the van, he surveyed the site. Over by the trees he spotted Matthew, who was part of a crew busily sorting tires. Shelley and Joy were nowhere in sight.

"If you're looking for Joy—" Barry White began.

"I'm not looking for anybody."

"Well, if you need her later on, I think she was headed for the child-care tent." Setting out paint brushes and cans of sealant, Barry grinned. "Life would be simpler if our committee heads didn't have so many kids...but then I guess they wouldn't be half so interested in getting this playground built, eh?"

"You've got it," Charlie agreed, climbing down from the van. "Kids are the name of this game."

He meant it simply, an honest answer to Barry's observation. But it woke the memory of Penny in his mind, and he was forced to walk away quickly through the bustling crowd, manufacturing the look of a man on a distinct and urgent errand to discourage anyone from stopping him before he had himself under control again.

IN THE COURSE of a morning more hectic than any she could remember experiencing, Joy still found it impossible to put Charlie out of her mind. They had talked for less than two minutes, but that had been long enough for her to be scoured by the bitter accusation of his tone and to read the look of wounded betrayal in his eyes. She had suspected, when she first made the decision to keep Shelley's secret, that she was playing with fire. She hadn't known then that her own heart would be consumed by that blaze.

Eventually, Charlie would probably calm down enough to listen to her explanation. In the meantime, however, the demands of the first day of the build held them both captive, allowing the anger and hurt to sink more deeply into Charlie's mind, while she struggled against despair.

At the end of the weekend, when the playground was complete, they would have time to sit down calmly and talk . . . assuming that, by then, Charlie was still willing to talk to her at all.

WHEN LUNCH WAS ANNOUNCED, Charlie checked his watch in disbelief. As accustomed as he was to the flow of such a project, it still seemed to him that the morning had evaporated. When the chain saws shut down for the break, he became aware of birdsong and laughter and a vast emptiness within himself that he chose to believe was hunger.

As Charlie approached the lunch line, Matthew joined him. Even with sawdust in his hair and a small bandage wrapped around one finger, he looked happier than Charlie had seen him since Penny's death. "Micky's been trying to catch up with you," he said in greeting.

Charlie shrugged. "Hectic morning."

"She's on the food committee, so she'll be tied up until the noon break is over, but she really wants to see you as soon as you can break free for five minutes."

Why the sudden rush? he wondered cynically. *She could have seen me any time she wanted to, these past six months.* "Look, I'll tell you what I told Joy—what we've got going here is eighteen-wheeler madness and it doesn't leave me time for untangling anything else. I'll see Shelley after the build. I don't think a cozy threesome was what you had in mind for this weekend anyway, was it?"

"Well no, but that doesn't mean—"

"Are you staying at the motel tonight or at Shelley's?"

Looking chagrined, Matthew said, "It's just so we can talk. She and I still have a lot to work through."

"Fine. I'm happy for you. Truly."

"But we don't want you to be—"

"Just worry about yourselves, okay? If anybody ever deserved a second chance, it's you." He meant it; he did, and yet he couldn't shake the feeling of having been treated badly by those he had tried hardest to protect. Unwilling to stay and sour Matthew's happiness, he said abruptly, "I've got a few more things to wrap up before I break for lunch. I'll be back in a lit-tle while.''

He walked away from the lunch line, away from the playground site, putting physical distance between himself and the source of his distress. All too soon he'd have to return, but he could at least give himself five or ten minutes of solitude before the chaos of the afternoon's activities began.

He was happy for Matthew, but he would also have welcomed the chance to take both his sister and brother-in-law out and kick them around the block. What kind of game had they been playing? Damn it, he had tried to be there for both of them throughout their travail. He'd turned his life inside out for them. But their actions made it seem as if he'd been some kind of threat, somebody who had to be tricked and drawn off the scent.

Maybe he was being petty, but it hurt.

HE CAUGHT SEVERAL glimpses of Shelley and Joy be-fore the day was over, but mostly at a distance and al-ways in a crowd. Shelley looked energized and happy.

Joy didn't.

Watching her, Charlie took note of the dark smudges beneath her eyes and the strain in her man-ner as she fielded people's questions. She smiled at everyone, patiently, blindly, her voice as soft and kind as ever, but there was an underlying tension in her stance.

Not my problem, he tried to tell himself. *Not my fault.*

Dinner was eaten informally at the site, as lunch had been, and then the task of cleanup from the day's work had to be undertaken. Slowly, wearily, the workers tidied up the site and returned their tools to the equipment van. While the majority headed for home, Charlie met with the committee chairmen, the crew foremen and anyone else who still had the energy and interest to listen.

The Day One postmortem he delivered was generally favorable, but it was nearly ten o'clock before he had finished handing out the next day's work assignments. "We'd better hope we got all the major kinks worked out of our system today, because we're going to have more of everything tomorrow—more jobs to coordinate, more untrained volunteers to supervise and feed and more classes from the elementary school coming by for tours. Probably more media, too, so don't forget to wear clean T-shirts." As he had intended, they laughed; his own Monkey Jungle T-shirt bore smears of dirt and oil. "I'll look for all of you back here by seven a.m.," he said in summation, and nodded sympathetically at their good-natured groans of protest. "Go home now, all of you, and get some sleep."

It was good advice. He just wished he had a little faith in his own ability to take it.

CHAPTER EIGHTEEN

WHEN JOY REACHED HOME, she closed the door, locked it and leaned against it with a sigh of relief.

She had gotten through the day. She had fulfilled her duties. And she hadn't broken into tears at the sight of the cool contempt in Charlie's eyes.

In the past three months, she'd discovered strengths within herself that she'd never suspected she possessed, but she hadn't foreseen that she might need those strengths to withstand this kind of emotional assault. It had cost her dearly to work near him and maintain her composure, but she had done it, for the sake of the project. It was a bittersweet victory, but a victory nonetheless. And she had learned to count her victories.

Since February, living day to day had become a way of life, a shelter against the knowledge that Jezebel would soon be taken away. Looking back, Joy was grateful for the million details of the playground project because they had forced her to focus on something besides her impending loss, but the frequent phone calls of the other volunteers wore on her nerves, making her wonder each time whether this might be the call she was dreading. Through March and April and most of May, she had basked gratefully in the knowledge that the playground project would eventually bring Charlie back to Sacramento. But now his return had become one more burden to be borne, one more loss to contemplate.

To everything there is a season, she told herself as she cradled Jezebel, trying to believe the words. *And a time to every purpose under Heaven....*

But it was hard.

JOY FOUND THAT THE SECOND day of construction was far busier than the first, and the third brought a kind of controlled madness as each level of organization was challenged by another influx of volunteers. On Thursday they had served lunch to a hundred people. By Saturday that number had doubled. Progress moved beyond the back-breaking preliminaries and became more and more visible. Board by nail, tire by bolt, Charlie's model was becoming a full-scale reality.

To locate Shelley at any given moment, Joy had only to look for Matthew; they were inseparable. Locating Charlie, on the other hand, required a ladder, a pair of binoculars, a bullhorn and a rabbit's foot. He was constantly in demand—the walking answer to every question, the arbiter of every dispute, the one man who had seen the picture on the lid of the life-size jigsaw puzzle they were so busily constructing. If Charlie Comfort didn't know how everything was supposed to come together, no one did.

Under such pressure, it would have been amazing if he had managed to remain merely civil. Instead, he was unfailingly patient with the volunteers, despite the lines of stress and weariness that Joy saw creasing the skin around his eyes.

It hurt to watch him. It hurt to hear the ease with which he spoke to others turn to tightness and tension when he spoke to her. Soon, knowing her own limitations, she took to sending others to ask questions of him for her.

Each morning's work began at seven. Each day's activities took place in a torrent of simultaneous effort that paused only at the half-hour meal breaks. Each night's wrap-up session dragged on until ten or later. It was all-consuming, exhausting beyond anything Joy had ever experienced, yet she found herself lying awake until long after midnight, bedeviled by thoughts and fears and regrets.

The rigors of the build were revealing Charlie's truest nature—the essential man—and what she saw drew her irresistibly. How could she condemn herself for hero worship if the object of her love truly was a hero? What possible failure of will could it be to want to ally herself with Charlie and devote her energies to the service of his dream? She loved his cause passionately, and she loved the man even more.

She had simply come to that realization too late.

By Sunday, new sections of the Monkey Jungle were springing up like mushrooms. If Joy was forced to leave the site on an errand—picking up lunch donations from a local fast-food restaurant or making a hasty run to Barry White's hardware store in pursuit of three more metal tape measures—she would return to find that the maze had doubled in length, or that the massive circular slide was finally in place.

At fifteen-minute intervals throughout the day, Austin Blade's amplified voice could be heard delivering the orientation lecture to the latest flood of volunteers. Within hours, newcomers became old-timers, advising the most recent arrivals. A carnival atmosphere prevailed despite the necessary but sobering reality of the liability waivers everyone was required to sign before taking part in the build. Productivity was high, accidents were low, and they ended the fourth day modestly ahead of schedule. In another twenty-four hours, the Monkey Jungle would be an accomplished fact.

And not a moment too soon, Joy thought, disheartened by the unrelenting tension. *For Jezebel's sake. For Charlie's. And for mine.*

MEMORIAL DAY DAWNED, so bright, so clear, so beautiful that Charlie was tempted to pull the covers over his head.

He felt capable of sleeping for a week. Instead, he needed to rise, shower, shave, dress and drive himself to the playground site. "Come on, Comfort. You have to get up," he chided himself.

Why? his body demanded. The mattress, which had felt like a sack of potatoes beneath him when he went to bed, now seemed a haven of ease.

"Last day," he said, trying to pump energy into his voice. "Big push. Grand finale. Everybody's counting on you. Let's *hit* it!"

Don't hand me that pep-talk crap. I've heard it all before. There isn't a thing you can say that would make me budge.

"Oh yeah?"

Yeah.

"Care to bet?"

You're on. Give it your best shot. I'm waiting.

"Joy will be there," he said.

Without hesitation, he pushed back the covers and got up.

In the shower, he tried to sort one feeling from another. Why did the thought of Joy's presence pull him so inexorably forward into the day?

He knew himself well enough to know that pride played no small part in it. As long as she continued to uphold her responsibilities at the build, he could do no less. But another part of his motivation was less tainted. He wanted to see her. To be where she was. To hear her voice, even if she was speaking to someone else.

It grew harder, each morning, to cling to his anger. Anger was an abstract concept, distant and unfulfilling when it was counterbalanced by his longing for Joy.

When had he ever known her to act from any impulse but kindness? What had made him assume there could be any malice in her actions? What was he so afraid he might hear, if he let her explain?

You got your feelings hurt. Don't get me wrong, a lot of it was legitimate. You had a right. But Joy wasn't the only guilty party. Do you hate her?

No. He loved her.

Bingo. You couldn't have reached this blazing pinnacle of insight yesterday, when there was still some hope of a quiet minute?

Maybe he could track her down at lunchtime.

Get real. From now until sunset, it's strictly fasten-your-seat-belt time. Nobody's allowed to have a personal life until the build wraps up, and that's true in spades for you, so don't get any cute ideas. Besides, don't you suppose this deserves your undivided attention? You told the lady you'd talk to her when the project was over, and that's exactly what you're going to have to do.

It was going to be a long, long day.

BY LATE MORNING the temperature was approaching eighty. Joy was on her way to the food tent to check on the lemonade supply when she heard someone behind her say, "Ms. Porter?"

No one connected with the build called her that. Joy stopped and looked back in confusion.

An elderly man in a conservative gray suit walked toward her, looking ludicrous in the midst of the hundreds of T-shirt-clad workers. He extended his hand. "Ms. Porter?" he repeated. "I'm Ian Patterson."

The name left her no wiser. "Hello, Mr. Patterson," she said politely, accepting his handshake. "How can we help you?"

"I'm here from Cross & Day," he elaborated, looking mildly amused.

Even then, it took a moment for the name of her father's publishers to sink in, and another for her to recall the extremely prominent position Mr. Patterson's name occupied on their letterhead. "I wasn't expecting anyone until this afternoon," she said, flustered. "I thought Donna Emery was coming. She's been Dad's editor for—"

"A very long time. Yes, indeed. She's here as well, of course. I went one way in search of you while Donna went the other, and I was fortunate enough to find you first. I had to be in San Francisco this past week for a meeting, and so I decided to invite myself along for today's festivities. I hope you don't mind."

"Not at all."

"Good. Donna and I have brought copies of your father's book and we'd be pleased to say a few words about it, at the appropriate time."

Once the television crews have arrived, you mean, Joy thought with wry amusement, blessing the efforts of the publicity committee. "We'd be honored, Mr. Patterson."

"Excellent. By the way, Donna and I are hoping that you will be our guest for dinner tonight. May we count on you?"

"Actually, we'll be serving dinner here on the playground site for all our volunteers."

"Afterward, then, for a drink or a cup of coffee. I have to fly back in the morning, and I really would like to have a chance to talk with you privately before I go."

Sorry, Jezzie, she thought with a pang as she smiled and said, "Of course. I'd like that very much."

"And bring the architect along, as well."

"I don't know whether he'll be available." *I don't know whether he'll agree to sit at the same table with me.*

"Track him down and see if he can join us, won't you?"

"If you like," Joy conceded.

"Good. Well, then, I'll let you get on with your work. I can see this is a busy time. There's just one more thing..." His smile grew boyish. "Do you suppose I might impose on you for one of those Monkey Jungle T-shirts? I was a fairly competent carpenter in my day, and this looks as though it might be good fun."

AT LUNCHTIME, Charlie made his way over to the food line, accompanied by Garrett and a cluster of work-crew foremen. "It's crunch time," he told them. "People are going to want to start letting down. It's only natural, but we'll never finish on deadline if we let it happen. Grab a good meal and a cold drink, and then let's crank things up for this afternoon, okay?"

"Sure thing, Charlie," they assured him. "You've got it." But he knew he would have to redouble his own efforts as well, keeping a finger on the pulse of each work crew's pace, channeling the flow of last-minute volunteers to the areas where they were needed most. This was one project that wasn't going to be allowed to run over, not even by a minute. As soon as he'd eaten, he would—

"Charlie?"

It was Shelley; she was weaving her way through the men and women around him to take her place at his side. "Excuse me," she murmured again and again until she was finally close enough to stand at Charlie's side. "Two minutes," she said urgently. "I've got somebody covering for me. Can you give me two minutes? Please?"

It was such a close echo of what he had wanted to say to Joy that he almost laughed. "Sure," he said gently. "Just give me a second to wrap this up." He turned back to his companions. "Garrett, what about the sign? We're getting down to the wire, you know. Has the carver shown up yet? He said he'd have it here two days ago and I still haven't seen it. We're supposed to mount it today as part of the opening ceremony. If it isn't here, we need to track it down."

"I'll take care of it personally," Garrett assured him.

Satisfied, Charlie allowed Shelley to extricate him from the line. As soon as they were apart from the others, she stood on tiptoe to kiss him on the cheek.

"There. I should have done that days ago, but I was too scared and you were too busy and—"

"Wait. Scared? Of me?"

She hung her head. "I feel like the prodigal sister, making such a muck of things." She threw her arms around him. "God, Charlie, I'm sorry," she said against his shirt. "I've been a crazy woman this past year. It's no excuse, but..."

"At least you're safe."

"Better than just safe. Oh, Charlie, Matthew and I have so much we need to talk to you about! Could you come back to my place with us, after the playground's officially done?" When he hesitated, she said, "Look, I know you're bushed—we all are—but this is important and I don't think it should wait. Will you come?"

Charlie sighed, feeling beleaguered. "All right."

"Promise?"

"I promise." He tousled her hair. "Does this mean you're finally coming home?"

"That's one of the things we need to talk to you about tonight." Her gaze slid away from his and he felt her jump.

Looking around to see what had startled her, Charlie saw Joy standing nearby, waiting in patient silence.

"Hi, there," he said helplessly.

I love you, his mind elaborated. *Run away with me. We'll find a hidden place far from all this commotion, a place where we can make love until we fall asleep, exhausted by our passion, and then wake up in each other's arms and make love again.*

But all his stupid tongue could say was, "The project's looking good. We've still got a lot of work to do, though."

It was obvious that his friendly tone disconcerted her. Looking from Shelley to Charlie, she said, "I'm sorry, I didn't mean to interrupt."

"It's okay. What can I do for you?"

"A representative from Dad's publisher is here. He'd like to take us out for coffee or drinks after things wrap up tonight, if..."

Beside him, Shelley stiffened.

Charlie knew what he should do, but his heart rebelled. He wanted to be with Joy. He hadn't dreamed, when he'd agreed to Shelley's request, that this would be the price. She and Matthew could meet with him tomorrow, couldn't they? Why did it have to be tonight?

He looked down at Shelley uncertainly.

"You've got other plans," Joy said. "That's okay."

"He was just coming over to my place," Shelley said gamely. "We can put it off until—"

"No need," Joy assured her. "I can introduce you both to Mr. Patterson at the opening ceremony. Don't worry about tonight, Charlie. He's just taking me out as a favor to Dad." She turned her smile on Shelley. "Is everything okay?"

"I think it will be," Shelley replied. "Don't worry, Boss, I won't disappear without filling you in."

"You'd better not, or I won't give you that letter of reference I've been drafting." Still smiling, she turned to walk away without meeting Charlie's eyes.

It was intolerable.

"Tomorrow morning," he called out.

Joy looked back at him, clearly startled. "What, Charlie?"

"Could I come by and see you tomorrow morning? The crew foremen and committee chairmen are going to meet with us back here at noon tomorrow, to be sure the last of the loose ends are tied up. Could I come by your place beforehand, say ten o'clock or so?"

"If you like. I wasn't sure how long the meeting would run, so I arranged to take the whole day off."

It was something, at least. And it was all he was apt to have time to arrange, given the size of the group of workers standing behind Shelley, waiting with diminishing patience to demand his attention. For that matter, a group nearly as large was massing near Joy, eager to claim her. Trying to be content, Charlie said, "With luck, we'll be ready for the opening ceremony by five-thirty. Let's meet at the circular slide at five, to be sure we have all our ducks in a row."

"I'll be there."

And with that, he had to let her go and get on with the business at hand, to keep that five-thirty target for completion from becoming an impossible goal.

"*HI.* Are you Joy Porter?"

If she'd thought she had a prayer of denying it successfully, Joy would have been tempted. For someone who had never craved notoriety, she'd certainly had her fill of it since the build began, and the last few hours had been the worst. As the workers drew closer and closer to finishing the Monkey Jungle, the number of well-wishers, reporters and television crews on the site had swelled, each seemingly determined to claim a chunk of Joy's time—time she couldn't spare.

The young woman addressing her now was a tiny, bright-eyed brunette whose Monkey Jungle T-shirt and name tag marked her as a volunteer, although her name—Lita James—struck no spark of recognition in Joy's mind. It was likely that she was one of the hundreds of last-minute helpers taking part in the build.

"Yes, I'm Joy Porter. Was there something you needed?" Joy asked, beyond caring whether she sounded less than gracious.

"I wanted to introduce myself. I just started working at Monkeys Do last week, and when I saw your name in the paper this morning, I remembered it from a report I'd been reading. Small world, eh?"

"Small world," Joy agreed, feeling sick.

Maybe it was nothing. Monkeys Do, like many of the organizations in town, had supplied the project with a number of volunteers. But this woman said she was new there.

She might be something innocent—a secretary, perhaps.

Or she might be the trainer Joy had been told of back in February. The trainer whose presence would enable Jezebel's schooling to begin.

Joy couldn't ask. Bad news would come when it willed; no question of hers would forestall it. If this energetic little woman was going to be the instrument of Jezebel's departure, Joy didn't want to know it in advance.

And if that was cowardice, then so be it.

"WE'RE GOING TO KEEP this brief," Charlie said, his amplified voice booming out over the crowd. "Speeches aren't what any of us came here for, least of all the kids. But some very big thanks are due, and

I threw my weight around and insisted on being the one to make them, so please bear with me for just a few minutes.''

He looked out over the sea of sunburned faces, gathering their attention, choosing his words.

''If you haven't taken a minute to look at the list of corporate sponsors that's posted over by the food tent, be sure to check it out at dinner tonight. Make a point of giving these companies your thanks and your business,'' he urged. ''They help make this city a good place to live. Cynics may say they got involved for the sake of PR, but the fact is that nobody's keeping a list of 'bad' companies that *didn't* help out. It's always easier to do nothing. So let these good ones know that you noticed they cared enough to make the effort.''

The crowd applauded. As the noise began to taper off, Charlie consulted the scrap of paper in his hand and made an invisible check mark in the air with his finger. ''So much for item one. Next in line are this weekend's volunteers.'' He pointed out at his audience. ''That's you. That's every person here who sanded a board or drove a nail or entertained a toddler in the child-care tent or pushed a wheelbarrow of sand from point *A* to point *B*. A job like this has a million small parts—small but essential. If even five percent of you had decided to stay home and watch the ball game on television, we'd be working overtime right now instead of sitting on our... laurels.''

An appreciative chuckle swept through the group.

''Now we're down to item three—the organizers and committee members. You think you're tired? These folks have stuck with the project for months. They've run fund-raisers, they've sent out press releases, they've telephoned, they've mailed letters, they've gone door to door in the rain, asking for donations of money and time and supplies, and all with one goal in mind: to get this playground built. And now, whether they quite realize it yet or not, they've done it. We've got ourselves a Monkey Jungle!''

Cheers and applause.

''But every project like this starts somewhere,'' he said quietly, when the uproar had died down. ''And this one started in the heart of Dr. Jacob Porter.''

It couldn't truly be said that a hush fell over the crowd—that wasn't possible with over a hundred restless children present—but a ripple of stillness came and went, like a cloud passing in front of the sun.

''He wanted to leave a very special present for the children of this city, and so he chose someone very special to see the project through. He chose his daughter, Joy Porter.''

He had planned this speech, these words. What he hadn't planned was the swell of pride and longing that roughened his voice. He wished he could see her face, read her eyes, but she was beside him, her gaze directed downward at her clasped hands.

Charlie took a gulping breath and pressed on.

''Most of you have seen her around this weekend, here on the site. Many of you have had the pleasure of working with her over the past weeks and months. A few of you have known her a lot longer than that. After all, she grew up in this town. But I'm the one she came to, back in October—the one she invited to design her father's dream. I want to go on record here, thanking her for her trust and her patience and her courage. It was a dream that got off to a rocky start, but she wouldn't let it die. And for that, and for her many kindnesses to me and my family, I'm more grateful than I can say. Ladies and gentlemen, Joy Porter.''

In November, he had presented her to a crowd a fifth this size, and the stress of the moment had brought her to the brink of collapse. Today, despite the crowd and the cameras and the high emotion of the day, he had every confidence in her ability to cope. While people shouted and whistled and clapped, he turned and offered her the microphone.

She accepted it with a wry little smile that chastised him for praising her in public, but seemed to thank him, all the same, for his words. Standing up, she lost her composure for a moment when the crowd redoubled its tribute, but then she stuck her tongue out at Charlie and pushed him down onto his chair, and the resultant laughter broke up the applause.

''Thank you,'' she said, as soon as she had a hope of making herself heard. ''He does that to me all the time, you know—works everybody up and then leaves me to deal with the aftermath. You can tell who gets paid and who's the volunteer.''

Their laughter, this time, was indulgent.

''Seriously, Charlie Comfort has delivered on every promise he ever made to this project, and you can see for yourselves the inventive calibre of his work. What you can't see is the level of thought and care that went into making this design as safe as it is fun. In some ways, it's like an iceberg—nine-tenths of what makes this playground special is invisible to the naked eye. But it's there, and you can count on it.'' She grasped the microphone with both hands. ''There's a reason for that. A very special reason.''

A shiver of apprehension shook Charlie. Scanning the crowd, he spotted Shelley and Matthew near

Eleanor Anderson's kindly bulk, their expressions intent, their eyes fixed on Joy.

"Last year, because of a playground that *wasn't* designed with safety in mind, Charlie Comfort's six-year-old niece died. Her name was Penny, and this project owes at least as much to her memory as it does to my father. Thanks to her parents, I have the honor of announcing the official name of our new playground—Penny Tinker Park. Garrett...?"

Garrett removed a canvas tarp from the redwood sign that would stand at the entrance: The Monkey Jungle—Penny Tinker Park.

It certainly cleared up the mystery of the overdue sign, Charlie realized, shooting Garrett a dark look. He'd been had. And he was crying, damn it. Joy and Shelley were dry-eyed and in control, while he and Matthew were the ones fumbling awkwardly for their respective handkerchiefs.

That should have been the end of it, but Ian Patterson was rising from his seat at Joy's right and claiming the microphone.

"There are just two more matters to be attended to," he said. "The first is the future. As Jacob Porter's publisher, Cross & Day applauds what all of you have accomplished, and we'd like to insure that your efforts will last for many years to come. To that end, we are donating five thousand dollars in Jacob Porter's name, to aid the city in the upkeep of this fine facility."

Gratified, Charlie joined in the applause that greeted Ian Patterson's announcement. Praise was all well and good, but sometimes cold cash could be even better. Garrett Blade had already volunteered to head up a Friends of the Monkey Jungle committee that would see to the ongoing maintenance of the playground, but the committee's hands would be tied without enough operating capital. The annual interest on five thousand dollars would go a long way toward financing repairs.

"And last but not least," Patterson continued, "I would like to present Ms. Porter with the first official copy of her father's book, *The Playground Connection*, and I take particular pleasure in reading its dedication aloud to all of you." He opened the handsome volume.

"To my collaborator and muse, my severest critic and most indispensable assistant—in short, to my daughter, Joy, whose bright mind and warm heart have been all that any father could hope for, and more than this father deserved."

Turning, he closed the book and laid it in Joy's hands.

Anticipating the tears that were bound to fall, Charlie stood up and reclaimed the microphone from Ian Patterson. "Okay, group," he called energetically, to divert the crowd's attention from Joy, "the moment is at hand. Don't stampede over anybody else, but I want you all to get ready to inaugurate our Monkey Jungle. Ready? Set?" He raised his arm with a flourish. "Go!"

In the ensuing confusion, it was possible to kneel beside Joy in something that almost passed for privacy. "Are you okay?" he asked tenderly, touching his fingertips to the sun-reddened curve of her cheek.

"I'll be fine," she promised. Her eyes were brimming with unshed tears but her smile was serene. "Don't worry, Charlie. I'm going to be just fine."

CHAPTER NINETEEN

DON'T WORRY, CHARLIE. I'm going to be just fine.

Driving through the dark streets to meet with Shelley and Matthew, Charlie couldn't get Joy's words out of his head. She'd said them. She'd meant them. He believed them.

But where did that leave him? Almost, almost, he wished she had not grown so self-reliant. *Need me,* he wanted to plead. *Not a lot. Just . . . enough.*

The address Shelley had given him wasn't all that far from Joy's house, as the crow flew, but the neighborhood was markedly shabbier. He parked as close to a streetlight as he could manage and locked the Miata with care, hoping for the best as he walked back to midblock in search of Shelley's flat.

It was a nice enough building, given the area. Camellia bushes flanked the front steps of the two-story house, and a weathered porch swing hung in the growing shadows.

Charlie climbed the steps.

A pair of flimsy mailboxes were mounted beside the door. There was just enough daylight left to allow him to make out the white letters on the little plastic strip affixed to the bottom mailbox: S. Taylor.

He rang the doorbell and waited, shifting nervously from one foot to the other, wishing he had some sense of what Shelley wanted to say to him.

From inside, he heard the quick rhythm of feet on a staircase. Then the front door opened and Matthew was revealed, still wearing his Monkey Jungle T-shirt, looking a little nervous as he smiled in welcome. "Come on up," he invited. "Micky just made some fresh lemonade."

I didn't come here for refreshments, Charlie thought rebelliously, but he shook the hand that Matthew offered and followed him up a narrow flight of stairs and through a doorway, into the upstairs apartment.

Shelley was perched on the edge of an elderly sofa, pouring lemonade from a plastic pitcher into a trio of glasses. "Hi. Have a seat. Quench your thirst." She handed Charlie a glass, then a napkin. "Matthew, why don't you pull that other chair over here?" While he did so, she turned back to Charlie. "Are you hungry? I've got some cookies in the kitchen if—"

Charlie put down his glass. "Hey, Shelley, calm down. It's just me, Charlie. Whatever you need to say, you can say it."

She smiled and nodded, and began to cry.

"Aw, Shell, no..." Charlie said unhappily.

But it was Matthew—Matthew, who had never had any patience with messy emotion—who went to her and held her close, stroking her hair and kissing her nape while he murmured endearments and reassurances. Watching him solidified Charlie's growing sense that something fundamental in his brother-in-law's nature had changed, something that could be counted on, now and in the future. The self-censoring straitjacket that had bound Matthew so tightly for so long seemed to have eased its stranglehold, freeing the man within.

In the end, it was Matthew who said, "I'm not coming back to San Francisco, Charlie."

"Tomorrow, you mean?"

"Ever."

"But—"

"I'm sorry. I know it isn't fair. I put the burden on you of keeping Tinker & Comfort afloat while I was in the hospital and the rehab center, and now I'm walking away from it. But the cost is just too high. I know what's important, now. My wife. My life. And *then* my work." His hold on Shelley tightened. "We both agree that trying to start over on old ground would be more than we could handle. Too many old habits and patterns. Too many memories."

"What about the house?"

"We'll sell it," Matthew said firmly. "I'll send movers in to pack up our things and put them in storage until we're ready to settle down somewhere else."

"Shelley?" Charlie said uneasily.

Red-eyed, she turned to look at him when he spoke her name.

"Matthew's talking about a pretty major change. You're comfortable with all this?" he asked. "Really?"

She graced him with a watery smile. "It was my idea."

"But where will you go?"

"Right here."

Charlie glanced around the room. "You mean *here* here? Or just someplace in Sacramento?"

Matthew chuckled. "Someplace in Sacramento."

"I've made a lot of good friends here. And it's a big enough place that Matthew won't have any trouble finding work."

"Which brings us to the next item on the agenda," Matthew said smoothly. "I know we're springing a lot on you, all at once, but give some thought to what you'd like to do about Tinker & Comfort. Either you can buy me out or we can close the office and split what's left over. Obviously, I haven't done my fair share for months now, so we'll have to take that into account—"

"If we split things, we'll do it fifty-fifty," Charlie said firmly. "But what are your plans? Are you going to set up shop on your own?"

"No. Not for a while, anyway. Right now, being my own boss doesn't sound all that attractive. I'm going to look for a position with some architectural firm that's already established. Someplace where I won't have to involve myself with anything but the projects on my drafting table. No personnel decisions. No office decor. No payroll management. Just some straightforward work and the assurance that I can go home at five o'clock with a clean conscience."

"You aren't *both* going to drop out of sight, right?"

"Right. You'll know where to find us. You'll know where to come to visit us. And we'll visit you, too. Just not right away. Give us a while to get strong first, okay?"

"Okay," he agreed softly.

"So, what about you?" Shelley asked.

"I don't know what you mean."

"I think you do. I'm just sorry that I've messed things up for you two. Believe me, if Joy had told you where I was and you'd tried to come and get me, I'd have blown out of town like a tornado. She was never anything but a friend to me, at a time when a friend made all the difference. Don't punish her for that, Charlie."

He shook his head. "I don't want to punish anybody, least of all Joy."

"Good. She'll be needing you more than ever, now."

Charlie blinked, disconcerted. "Why? Because the playground's finished?"

"That and Jezebel."

"What about Jezebel?"

"She didn't tell you?" Shelley shook her head. "Stubborn. The girl is stubborn."

"Shelley!"

She sighed. "Jezebel's being recalled to Monkeys Do for training."

"When?"

"Soon. Before the summer's out, I'd guess. Joy's known for months, and it's killing her."

"It would," Charlie acknowledged sadly. "What a shame. Couldn't she talk to them? Explain the circumstances? Maybe they'd let her buy Jezzie for herself."

"Maybe. I don't know. Joy certainly doesn't talk like it's a possibility. I suppose you could ask."

He left soon after that, more worried than ever about Joy, but guardedly optimistic about Shelley and Matthew's future. The path they were choosing might not be right for everyone; however, their decision showed every sign of being made from hope and determination, not despair, and he wished them well with all his heart.

"Call me," he said as they walked him to the door.

Shelley laughed. "Where have I heard that before? Don't worry, little brother. I will."

Full darkness had fallen. Down the street from Shelley's house, he found the Miata parked where he had left it, unmolested. More relieved than he wanted to admit, he climbed in and started the engine.

The thought of returning to his empty motel room was singularly unappealing. Stepping on the accelerator, Charlie cruised along the hot, drowsy streets, as if he could outdistance the bleak presentiment of loss tugging at his heart. He was happy for Shelley and Matthew...but their decision was going to cause a further upheaval in his own life. It was all too fresh, too raw. He needed time to think.

While one part of his brain grappled with the uncertainties of his future, another part operated with impressive precision. Within ten minutes, without having made any conscious decision to do so, he found himself turning onto Arelyn Drive. Maybe Joy would be back from her outing with the publishers. Maybe she, too, was feeling wakeful and restless. She had agreed to see him in the morning, at ten, but maybe he could talk with her now, as well. Just talk...unless she, too, was anxious for something more....

The windows of her house were dark. Even the porch light had been extinguished.

Whatever he might want, it would have to wait.

Buck up, he told himself as he drove away. *You're just going through postproject letdown. You do it every time. Every single time.*

It was true, to an extent...but this time there was more to it than that. This time, the heart of his depression had a name.

And that name, ironically, was Joy.

MAYBE IT WAS honest exhaustion from five days of
effort at the build. Maybe it was the three glasses of
wine she had consumed in the course of listening to
Ian Patterson and Donna Emery share their memories of working with her father. Maybe it was her
troubled mind's effort to escape. Whatever the cause,
Joy slept dreamlessly until her alarm went off at eight
on Tuesday morning.

Charlie's coming, she thought as soon as she woke.
She wished she knew what to expect from his visit.
Time or circumstance seemed to have tempered the
anger he had projected on Thursday, but she felt in-
capable of predicting what mood would be upon him
when he arrived.

Soberly, she pushed back the sheets and headed for
the shower.

Washing and drying her hair took time. Deciding
what to wear took longer. And when she found herself circling back for a second application of lipstick
before she'd even gone downstairs to eat her breakfast, Joy was so exasperated with herself that she had
to laugh. "What has gotten into you?" she demanded of her reflection. "This is *Charlie* who's
coming. He's seen you painted green. He's seen you
with a wet monkey wrapped around your neck. Do
you honestly think one dab of lipstick more or less is
going to affect what he says to you this morning?
Would you want him, if it did?"

But how could she not want Charlie, ever? Regardless of his foibles or hers, she longed beyond reason or
caution or propriety to make him her own. It was
useless to deny it.

For breakfast, she raided the fruit bowl on the
kitchen table. "Want a grape, Jezzie? Here."

Jezebel inspected the gift fastidiously.

"Don't worry, they're seedless. Nothing but the best for my girl."

The monkey's brow furrowed with an air of apparent suspicion.

"You don't trust me? Watch." Joy popped a handful of grapes into her mouth.

The telephone rang.

Chewing quickly, Joy pushed back her chair and crossed the room.

Another ring.

Was Charlie calling to confirm their date? Or to cancel?

A third ring. One more and the answering machine would intervene.

Hastily, Joy swallowed. "H'llo?"

"Joy Porter?" a woman's voice inquired.

"Yes, this is she."

"Good morning. This is Lita James. We met yesterday, at the playground project. Remember me?"

For a moment, Joy's mind balked at the name. Then the memory came clear. Of course. The dynamic brunette.

From Monkeys Do.

At the table, Jezebel was helping herself to another grape.

"Yes," Joy said softly. "I remember."

The kitchen was cold.

"Well," Lita said, with a note of deference in her voice, "I just got my new assignment list . . . and I'm going to be working with Jezebel."

"When?"

"This morning, if you can manage it."

Where the cabinets met the wall, an edge of wallpaper had begun to curl, probably with Jezzie's encouragement. "She'll be there."

"All right. Thank you. And...Joy?"

"What?"

"I didn't know about this when I talked to you yesterday. I'm sorry. The timing stinks. I wish we could—"

"Don't," Joy said, on the edge of a sob. "I mean...I appreciate what you're trying to say, but just..." She took a desperate breath. "Just don't."

"All right," Lita said quietly. "We'll see you in a little while."

"Right." She cleared her throat. "Bye."

The telephone receiver didn't want to fit properly onto the handset. Joy jammed it roughly into place and walked away, out of the kitchen, down the hallway, into her father's office where her copy of *The Playground Connection* sat, centered, on his desk.

Beyond the desk, Jezebel's cage caught the early morning light.

Again she fled, this time onto the front porch, where she could take long breaths of the cool morning air.

Across the street, Mrs. Langston was retrieving her newspaper from the driveway. She raised a hand in greeting and took a tentative step in Joy's direction.

Joy waved and retreated into the house again.

Foolish to look for a way out. There was no way out. And waiting was only going to prolong the pain.

Charlie was coming, she remembered with dismay. She should leave a note, in case he came before she got back....

But she made no move to do so. The thought of writing out an account of what was happening was too daunting. And it wasn't apt to be necessary. How long could it take to drive to Monkeys Do and back?

Joy took her purse down from the hook in the hall closet and unearthed Jezebel's harness from the shelf. "Jezzie? Come here."

Quickly, too quickly, Jezebel scampered down the hallway to her.

Joy knelt. "Tickles," she invited, and passed the bellyband of the harness around Jezebel's slender middle. She secured the band and bestowed the promised teasing caress. Then, with Jezebel balanced on her arm and the end of the leash held firmly in hand, she walked to the garage, pausing in the kitchen just long enough to pluck a small cluster of grapes from the basket.

In the garage's dim interior, she found Jezebel's carrying cage on the cement floor, dusty from disuse. When she had opened the little door, she showed Jezebel the grapes, then popped them into the cage. "Treats? Or have you had enough?"

Jezebel had no great love of her carrying cage. Usually, when asked to enter it, she balked, or at least made a game of skirting its perimeter a time or two before she complied. But this time she seemed to have no taste for mischief.

"So," Joy asked, "are you demonstrating your keen sensitivity to my moods, or were the grapes that enticing? Never mind. We're going."

The carrying cage fit neatly on the floor of the car, in front of the passenger seat. The garage door opened smoothly. The Oldsmobile's engine came to life on the first try, and the gas gauge showed the tank to be

nearly full. There was no valid excuse for delaying—
no excuse but her tear-blurred vision.

Rolling her window down, Joy backed the car down
the driveway.

"Good morning," called Mrs. Langston.

Joy waved vaguely in her direction, shifted out of
Reverse and drove away.

She had every intention of driving directly to Monkeys Do. . . but there were several routes that would
take her there, and one of them would take her past
the Monkey Jungle. "I want to prove to myself that
the playground hasn't vanished overnight," she told
Jezebel as she signaled a left turn. "I want to see how
things look without two or three hundred people
swarming around. I want. . .I just want to see it again,
that's all. I won't stop. We'll just drive by."

It was Tuesday, a school day. Any children on the
playground would be little, with their mothers in attendance. There might not be anyone there at all, for
that matter. It was still early.

"If nobody's there, maybe we'll stop for just a
minute. If I left your harness and leash on you, I could
even let you climb around a little. After all, you were
the model for the T-shirts. It's only fair."

Nothing was fair.

When she drove up, the playground looked deserted. Sunshine gleamed on the newly mounted sign: The
Monkey Jungle—Penny Tinker Park. Joy pulled over
to the curb and turned off the engine. "Just for a second," she said, and leaned down to open Jezebel's
carrying cage.

When she climbed out of the car, she was struck by
how quiet the playground had become, but the scent
of fresh-cut wood still hung in the air. Slowly, disci-

plining herself to think of nothing but the moment, she walked past the sign, onto the grounds of the Monkey Jungle itself.

Faced with so much open space, Jezebel burrowed into the crook of Joy's arm and hid her face.

"Hi there!"

Joy whirled around guiltily, searching for the source of the greeting.

"Come on in, the water's fine," the voice continued cheerfully. "I'm pretending I'm the Elephant's Child."

It was Austin Blade. Joy knew, in theory, that the thick-layered wood fiber that carpeted the Monkey Jungle had been chosen not only for its ability to soften the impact of a fall but also because it rendered the grounds accessible to the handicapped. Still, she was startled to see Austin there alone on the playground, with his electric wheelchair parked in the center of the rocking platform that bridged the imaginary Crocodile River.

"If I shift back and forth quickly enough, I can swing a little," he said as she ventured closer, along the sun-dappled path. "But it's hard on the motor. Come give me a shove, okay?"

"Who says grown-ups get to play here?" Joy challenged facetiously.

Austin laughed. "Who says they don't? I figure if I helped build this place, I can play here. Besides, the crew inspection doesn't start until noon, so I knew I wouldn't be in anybody's way. What's the point of having a great playground like this practically next door if I can't put it to use on such a gorgeous morning?"

As Joy joined him on the rocking platform, Jezebel poked her head up and looked around.

"You brought Jezebel with you!" Austin's eyes widened in astonished delight. "Hi there, funny face. Come give me a kiss!"

Joy lengthened her hold on the leash. Gibbering happily, Jezebel climbed down and settled to the self-appointed task of grooming Austin's close-cropped golden beard, while he continued to murmur outrageous flatteries and blandishments.

Watching them, Joy felt a small kernel of stillness form in the center of her distress. This was Jezebel's future: to form a one-to-one bond with a quadriplegic like Austin and enrich his world. There would be no more long days spent locked in the solitude of her cage, as there had been while Joy was teaching. The past four years had been the monkey equivalent of infancy and childhood for Jezebel. Now, in the last stages of her adolescence, she would train for her life's work.

She would learn. She would be useful. And she would be loved. To Joy, Jezebel had been a pet, a source of amusement and exasperation to be disciplined or indulged. To her new companion, she would be a working partner, to be respected as well as loved.

At the beginning, Joy had bottle-fed the little capuchin and diapered her like a human baby until she was finally cage trained. In those earliest months, Jezebel had spent most of every day clinging to Joy, and any loud noise or sudden move had been an excuse to bite. But slowly, Jezzie had grown from dependency to curiosity to confidence. And now, under new tutelage, that confidence would be transformed into maturity and mastery. Purpose. Service.

How could she protest?

"We'd better be moving on," she said gently to Austin, and extended her arm. "Sit, Jezzie. Sit."

Jezebel gave Austin's beard a last pat and climbed onto Joy's forearm.

"Good girl."

"Love 'em and leave 'em," Austin said with a teasing grin. "You dames are all alike. Will I see you at noon, or don't project coordinators take part in mundane things like final inspections?"

"For all mundane undertakings, you can bet the project coordinator will be there."

"Good. Where are you off to now?"

"I'll tell you when I see you at noon," she promised, and stepped off of the rocking platform. "Do you still want that push?"

"Yes, please."

"All right. Sit tight."

"My specialty," he quipped, and smiled with boyish pleasure as Joy put her foot against the edge of the platform and pushed, setting him in motion.

IT WAS ONLY A ten-minute drive from the playground to the building that housed Monkeys Do. As soon as Joy had parked the car, she released Jezebel from the carrying cage. "Right now, you're still mine," she said softly, stroking the sleek fur that covered Jezebel's head and neck. "In a minute, you'll be theirs. And then you'll become someone else's, and after a while you won't even remember me. But that's okay. I'll remember you. Always."

She made sure that her hold on the leash was firm. Then she opened the car door and climbed out, with Jezebel riding for one last time on her arm.

Inside, Lita was waiting.

"Hi, Joy. Hi, Jezebel. Boy, aren't *you* beautiful. We're going to have a good time together."

Joy held out the leash.

Lita accepted it and crooked her arm. "Sit?" she invited, moving closer. "Sit?"

Jezebel went to her.

"She's gregarious," Lita said approvingly as the capuchin reached out to finger the shiny buttons on her blouse. "Not timid at all. That'll make everything easier."

Bereft, Joy stepped back. "Sometimes I call her Jezebel."

Lita's smile was warm. "I'll make a note. For that matter, I'd like to learn everything I can about her. Food preferences, games, anything that occurs to you. If you want to give me a call in a day or two, or jot things down as you remember them . . . ?"

Joy nodded.

"Thanks. We'll pass everything along when she's placed." She looked at Joy's empty hands. "Is there anything special you think she'd like to keep with her? A favorite blanket? A stuffed animal?"

"No. Nothing like that. Just—"

Lita waited, stroking Jezebel gently.

"She has a bath toy—a present from...a friend. It's a sort of activity board that hooks over the side of the sink. Would she be allowed to keep something like that?"

"Sure. Just drop it off the next time you've got an errand in this part of town. I'll make sure she gets it."

Will I be able to visit her? Joy ached to ask, but she knew in her heart that it would only do harm to confuse Jezebel's loyalties. For six or eight months, the training would take place, and then she would be gone, shipped off to some stranger who could have only the vaguest notion of what to expect.

"*Good* girl," Joy said in final judgment, and walked away.

FIFTEEN MINUTES EARLY despite his best efforts at self-discipline, Charlie pulled the Miata to a stop in front of Joy's house.

Several upstairs windows were open, but the curtains were drawn.

Wasn't she up yet?

Common sense told him to wait in his car, at least until ten, but he was tired of being sensible. He was tired of being patient. And more than anything else, he was tired of being alone.

The little jeweler's box was in his pocket, but it wouldn't be for long.

Firm in his resolve, he climbed out of the Miata and strode up Joy's front walk.

A discreet knock brought no results. After waiting for a decent interval, he knocked more loudly.

Still nothing.

He tried the doorbell next, but there was still no answer. Maybe the damn thing wasn't working. Pushing it again, he pressed his ear to the door, listening.

Faintly, he heard the chimes.

So much for that theory.

Itching with impatience, he walked around to the side of the house and repeated his performance of knocks and rings on the kitchen door.

Nothing.

Maybe she was in the shower. His watch reported that it was still a few minutes short of ten o'clock. If Joy had overslept, she might still be getting dressed.

I'll give her until ten, he resolved.

But ten o'clock arrived, and Joy's door still went unanswered.

It was crazy. She knew he was coming. She wasn't the sort to stand him up.

Unless she just can't face telling you what she knows she'll have to say.

Shaken, Charlie stepped back to survey the house again. Yesterday at the playground Joy had handled herself with grace and control. But that was yesterday, and in public. Maybe the thought of meeting with him in private still worried her, in the wake of his harsh words at the beginning of the build.

It ought to. He wasn't going to take no for an answer unless she could offer some much better arguments than she had the last time.

The house still looked as it had when he drove up: upstairs windows open, drapes closed.

Upstairs windows open.

Feeling self-conscious, he looked up and down the street. No cars. No pedestrians. Not even a dog in sight.

"Joy?"

His voice split the morning quiet, startling a pair of scrub jays out of the eucalyptus tree that grew beside the house.

"Joy, it's Charlie."

Upstairs, a curtain stirred. Was it just a breeze, or was Joy there, out of sight, peering down at him?

"Please, Joy, come down and open the door. We need to talk."

Feeling challenged by the silent house, Charlie gathered a handful of pebbles from the flower bed and lobbed them at the window he knew to be Joy's.

"Go away. She isn't there."

Charlie turned around. A gray-haired woman was standing in the open doorway of the house across the street.

Of course. The busybody. The one he and Joy had joked about, that night when they stood kissing on the front porch.

"Rock throwing is vandalism," the woman screeched. "If you don't leave, I'm calling the police."

Charlie discovered that he had weathered as much interference and delay over the past twenty-four hours as he was prepared to tolerate. "Then call out a SWAT team," he shouted back. "I'm not leaving until I've talked to Joy."

"Are you deaf or just crazy? I told you, she isn't home."

Charlie looked back at the house, then faced his accuser again. "I say she is, and I intend to stand right here and speak my piece. If you don't want to hear it, I suggest you go back inside and shut your windows."

Looking scandalized, the woman retreated, closing the door with a resounding bang. Her windows, however, remained open.

Fine, Charlie thought pugnaciously. *Let the whole world listen.*

"All right, Joy—if you won't come down, I'll talk to you from here, so you may as well pull up a chair and get comfortable. This may take awhile. I'll start by stating, for the benefit of God, your neighbors and

anybody else who may be interested, that I love you
and I want to marry you.''

He waited a moment, but his announcement
brought no palpable reaction from either of his lis-
teners. Undeterred, he took another breath, marshaling his thoughts as he settled in for the long haul.

''You already know that I went to see Shelley last
night, but you don't know what she had to say, and
you need to, because it's going to affect you, too.
When I got there, she and Matthew . . .''

JOY DROVE SLOWLY along the residential streets, using the breeze through the car window to keep the tears
at bay.

Partings were brutal; that would never change. But
she was learning, through hard experience, that she
could be deeply saddened without being crushed. The
fact that life went on was a hopeful sign, not a callous
one. And memories, however bittersweet, were a precious legacy to be treasured, not shunned.

Tomorrow morning she would be back in the classroom. And soon, in a few days or weeks, there would
be the miracle of Lisa and Nathaniel's new baby to
celebrate. She would stay busy and involved, and the
worst of the pain would pass.

Turning the corner onto Arelyn Drive, she saw Mrs.
Langston standing at the curb, shaking her fist as she
scolded some poor miscreant. Had the Bingham's little boy been playing in the shrubbery again?

Then she saw the red Miata.

''Charlie,'' she said aloud, and pulled over.

He was standing on her front lawn with his back to
Mrs. Langston, and he, too, appeared to be shouting.
Bewildered, Joy turned off the engine.

"—job here and sell their house. That means I'm going to be free to do whatever I want, and what I want is to build playgrounds. But I can't do it alone. At least, I don't want to. I want you with me, organizing people, helping them get their projects off the ground. And when I fly out to the sites, I want you to come along. I figure you could still teach, if you're willing to substitute instead of trying for a class of your own. I can move here, if that would help. Or we can work it out some other way. But to do that, we have to talk."

"Then you'd better talk fast," Mrs. Langston threatened, "because that squad car's going to be here any minute!"

He ignored her. "But that isn't all we talked about. Shelley told me a little about what you did for her, and why, and what a difference it made. She said I wasn't being fair, cutting you off like I did on Thursday. I'm sorry. It just made me see red, thinking that I'd been shut out after all I'd tried to do for Shell. But sometimes it takes more than effort and good intentions. Sometimes it takes the right person, in the right place at the right time... with the right sort of kindness in her heart. You were that person for Shelley, and I'm glad and grateful."

He reached into his pocket and extended his hand toward the house.

"Do you see this? There's a ring inside. A ring I bought for you. A ring I want to put on your finger, if you'll let me get close enough to do it, you exasperating woman!"

She'd heard enough. This wasn't pity, or duty, or any of the other things she had feared from Charlie.

Anything this foolish and endearing had to be love, and deserved to be answered in kind.

"I don't need a ring," she called out.

Mrs. Langston turned to stare.

So did Charlie.

"I don't need a ring," Joy repeated loudly. "What I need is you in my life, forever. Is that what you want, too?"

"Absolutely!" Charlie shouted at the top of his lungs.

"Then you'd better be ready to take me upstairs and make mad, passionate love to me until sundown, to seal the bargain."

"I *told* you she wasn't home!" Mrs. Langston shouted huffily, and turned on her heel, abandoning the scene.

"Stay right there," Charlie ordered, as if Joy were some apparition that might vanish. "Don't move! Not an inch!"

And so she stood and waited, laughing through her tears, as her future ran to her with open arms.

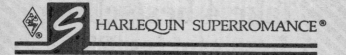

COMING NEXT MONTH

#538 HALFWAY HOME • Marie Beaumont
Mickey Mulvaney and Cameron Scott were locked in battle over
possession of a house. On his side, Cameron had money,
influence and the good will of all the neighbors. On her side,
Mickey had only her determination . . . and her hidden
vulnerability. But against that, Cameron didn't stand a chance.

#539 REMEMBER WHEN • Anne Laurence
Nate Fields had returned to the Missouri town where he'd been
raised to avenge himself on Amber Reinhart, daughter of the
area's wealthiest family. When he purchased her failing family
business, he expected to feel triumphant. But how could he,
when Amber was so warm and kind, and when she'd adopted a
young girl, who, he'd just learned, was his own daughter. . . .

#540 FOR THE LOVE OF IVY • Barbara Kaye
Ivy Loving had come to Texas at her grandmother's request.
But nothing in her background had prepared her for the fast-
paced life-style of Fort Worth. Ivy was an island woman and
was looking forward to returning to her Indonesian home.
However, she had underestimated her Texas grandmother's
determination to keep her in Texas—and the tall dark stranger
who featured strongly in her grandmother's plan.

#541 CRADLE OF DREAMS • Janice Kaiser
Women Who Dare, Book 3
Caroline Charles knew she had a lot of nerve. Tyler Bradshaw
had no reason to love her. No reason to even want to
see her. And certainly no reason to agree to make her
pregnant . . . again.

AVAILABLE NOW:

#534 UNCOMMON STOCK
Terri Lynn

#535 DREAM BUILDER
Julie Meyers

**#536 REFLECTIONS OF
BECCA**
Lynda Trent

#537 WINGS OF TIME
Carol Duncan Perry

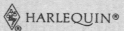

HARLEQUIN®

my Valentine 1993

The most romantic day of the year is here! Escape into the exquisite
world of love with MY VALENTINE 1993. What better way to celebrate
Valentine's Day than with this very romantic, sensuous collection of four
original short stories, written by some of Harlequin's most popular
authors.

ANNE STUART
JUDITH ARNOLD
ANNE McALLISTER
LINDA RANDALL WISDOM

THIS VALENTINE'S DAY, DISCOVER ROMANCE
WITH MY VALENTINE 1993

Available in February wherever Harlequin Books are sold.   VAL93

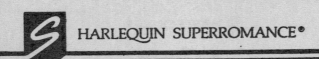

HARLEQUIN SUPERROMANCE®